POISON, POKER AND PISTOLS

POISON POKER AND PISTOLS

BY ELISABET M. STONE

M Evans
Lanham • New York • Boulder • Toronto • Plymouth, UK

M. Evans
An imprint of The Rowman & Littlefield Publishing Group, Inc.
4501 Forbes Boulevard, Suite 200, Lanham, Maryland 20706
http://www.rlpgtrade.com

10 Thornbury Road, Plymouth PL6 7PP, United Kingdom

Distributed by National Book Network

Library of Congress Cataloging-in-Publication Data Available

ISBN 13: 978-1-59077-464-9 (pbk: alk. paper)

♾️™ The paper used in this publication meets the minimum requirements of American National Standard for Information Sciences—Permanence of Paper for Printed Library Materials, ANSI/NISO Z39.48-1992.

Printed in the United States of America

Contents

This book is dedicated to Jim Kelly, Newspaperman. The "Kelly" I loved— and who loved me enough to nag me into applying the seat of the pants to the seat of the chair so that this book would be written and printed. My thanks to that "Kelly."

ELISABET M. STONE

POISON, POKER AND PISTOLS

1. A Doctor Dies

THE old Seth Thomas on the wall of the city room gave the time as 9:00 A.M. Two hours to go before deadline of the City edition and all phones on both city and copy desks were busy—save one. That one was bawling a loud and insistent summons.

Red-haired, burly-backed Dennis McCarthy, city editor, glared balefully at it, took time to finish shouting instructions to a newborn cub reporter, then yanked it viciously from its cradle—the phone, not the cub—shouting: "City desk! McCarthy speaking."

There followed a series of grunts, dotted with an occasional "Yeah? Izzatso?" And finally, "Okay, kid. Thanks. G'by."

Then to me: "Maggie—"

I typed busily, suddenly grown hard of hearing. Damn that nickname!

On a louder note: "Oh, Maggie!"

I went right on typing.

At last: "Maggie! ! ! Dammit! Are you deaf?"

The city desk is just three feet from mine, but that bellow could have been heard three floors below in classified. I decided maybe I'd better answer.

"Were you calling me?" I asked sweetly.

Stifled chuckles sounded around the rim and in the slot of the copy desk where my battles with Dennis had made history of a sort. At the risk of being fired I delighted in advising Dennis to stop reading *Front Page*.

My expression was deadpan while I waited for the explosion. But though Dennis's face matched his hair, his voice came out as soft as a baby's gurgle.

"Why, yes, I was calling you. If you still work here I need you to cover a story. I realize you're very busy and I hate to disturb you, but I'm going to have to send you out on it. Morgan's home sick, and much as I hate to trouble you, you'll have to go."

His sarcasm was wasted. I'd been listening to it for upwards of seven years.

"It's not a bit nice of you." I yawned widely. "Especially since you admit knowing I'm busy. Well, what is it? Someone burning their own trash in defiance of New Orleans' health laws—or did your pet cat trip and sprain her morals? The town's been dead for weeks. Not even a decent bawdy house raid to liven up things."

"A bawdy house raid isn't exciting—unless you're in it!" he retorted. "Besides, you ain't covering police. However this story is on the police run. It's a stiff over at the Bienvenu hotel, and being Morgan's out—"

But I was on my way out too, grabbing a sheaf of copy paper as I went by the desk.

"Why didn't you say what it was?" I asked aggrievedly. "Is it a man or woman? Suicide, murder, or accident? Hurry up, Mac, give!"

"Keep your pants on," he advised. "This is just another death due to natural causes. Fellow lived in the hotel. They found him dead in his room about half-hour ago. The bellhop called me, said it looks like the guy's heart gave out or he had some kind of a fit. Don't you go giving me trouble with any half-baked ideas about murder."

"I don't have half-baked ideas about anything!" I snapped. "Where's the corpse? What was his name?"

"He was a doctor by the name of McGowan and he was in room—"

"McGowan!" I almost screamed. "Not *Ned* McGowan?"

Dennis nodded. "Yeah. You know him?"

"Hell yes! And he can't be dead! I talked to him late last night, about 1:30, and he was alive then. Plenty alive!"

Dennis tilted back in his chair and gave me a look. "My you're bright!" he jeered. "Well, he's plenty dead now. He contracted an incurable case of rigor mortis sometime during the night. His room number is—"

"I know the room number."

"Oh! You do! I might have known! Well, beat it over there and don't stop to weep for him."

"I'm practically there." I headed for the elevators.

Going down in one of the rattling wrecks that served the Phipps' combine of morning and evening papers for lifts, I debated on whether I should drive or walk the seven blocks to the hotel. In one of his periodic economic purges, the old penny-pincher who owned the two rags had cut down on mileage allowances—so I walked whenever possible or took a cab and put it on the expense account. Outside the March sun was pleasantly warm and I had well over an hour to get the story. I decided to walk.

As I strode along I mused on the instability of life and the unfairness of newspaper publishers. For almost seven years, I recalled, with conscious self-pity, I, Margaret Slone, had been bounced back and forth between the two papers. As soon as I got comfortably settled on the morning sheet, safely out of Dennis's way, I'd be shipped back to the afternoon paper. I'd been perfectly happy the past three months covering general assignments on the A.M. rag, but yesterday an inter-office memo from the old goat sent me back to the P.M. deal and McCarthy. Just like that. And, just like that, Ned, who'd been alive last night, was dead this morning. I don't know where I drew the comparison from, but that was my trend of thought as I neared the hotel. I began to search the pigeon holes of memory for what I knew of the doctor. Mentally I itemized the knowledge something like this:

Good looking—almost too much so. Full of personality.

Eligible as hell—the answer to a debutante's prayer. Threw a swell line—to which you listened even when you didn't believe it. It made swell hearing. One of New Orleans' most promising younger surgeons, he was assured of a really brilliant future. A specialist in heart and kidney diseases, he had been lauded by older medical men as a first-class diagnostician as well as a surgeon. Recently he had been written up in a national medical journal for having successfully performed a delicate cardiac operation.

His personal life was not as laudable as his professional. There had been ugly stories about his affairs with women, and at least two nurses had been dismissed from hospitals because of him. Off-color rumors about him and a wealthy, well-thought-of society woman circulated around town. Nothing definite, just whispers that she financed him when he opened his elaborate and beautifully outfitted offices in the Medical Building and that his entree to many of the city's best homes was due to her patronage. I'd never paid much heed to those stories, only to feel sorry her name should be linked in such a way with his.

Strangely enough, men liked him. As a rule they resent his type but even my own brother, Brett Slone, an air pilot, was Ned's admirer. Brett had taught him flying, and the third time he soloed he did a ground loop and tore up himself and the ship. As soon as he was out of bed he went to the field and took off in a plane. Men dote on physical courage, and, when he paid the damages on the wrecked ship, Brett's heart was won completely.

McGowan was a pretty regular visitor to the house where Brett, my two single sisters, and I lived with my mother and a motely assembly of Negro dependents whose ancestors had been slaves of Mother's family. The house, a relic of ante-bellum days, took up a city block and was all that remained of a once great plantation. Keeping it and the Negroes up kept us broke.

Ned often spent the night and bunked in with Brett—in the room next to mine. When he stayed over I locked the connecting door. I knew his line and I knew his type, so I took no chances. I was not jail bait.

Dennis had said Ned's death was probably due to heart trouble or some kind of a fit. That seemed unlikely. He was always doing things which no one who knew he had heart trouble would pull. Certainly no one who had as much to live for as Ned would foolishly risk his life when he knew care would protect it. That thought brought me sharply around to the talk I'd had with him the night before.

The city room had been quiet as a tomb and it was my last night on the morning paper. I was reading a gossip column and came across an item hinting at Ned's engagement to the popular and lovely Creole, Olivette Merceron, deb daughter of a fine old French family. He'd been rumored on the verge of making affairs legal several times but, having nothing better to do and bored doing nothing, I thought I'd do the society ed a favor and check on it.

I called Ned about 11:45, but he was out and I left my number. It was around 1:30 when he returned the call. I asked him if it was true he'd been hooked at last and got an affirmative. He'd give no details, said the dope would have to come from Vette. I thought, too, his voice sounded strange, his replies guarded—almost as though someone was with him and he didn't want to talk too much. I grinned at the idea he might be telling me he was getting married in the hearing of some girl he'd been dishing out a heavy line all evening. That would be funny!

I kidded him about losing his standing as an eligible bachelor and said something trite about the trail of broken hearts his marriage would leave. Then I asked how the world was treating him. He replied, in a rather strangely defiant tone, that he was sitting on top of it and had it geared to his speed. I told him anyone holding that seat deserved congratulations, warned him to keep the speed steady and not slide off, said good-by, and hung up.

I finished a memo to the soc desk to check with Vette for dates and wedding plans, just as the final edition came off the presses. A quick look at the paper showed all my stories okay and I signed out for home.

As I backed my car out of the lot the dashboard clock said 2:15. I had to be back to work for the afternoon paper at 8:30. I thought: Fine thing! The old stinker might have given me at least one day off to change over from one sheet to the other!

When I reached home I put the car in the garage, let myself quietly in the back door, and slipped upstairs. I rapped lightly on Brett's door, then peeked in. No one home. I remembered he'd said he was flying a late charter and wouldn't be home that night. In my room I checked to make sure Ida, the maid I'd inherited and whom I paid salary, had laid out fresh things for the next day. She had, so I took a quick shower and went to bed. That had been about seven hours ago.

I looked at my watch, 9:32. Eight hours ago Ned had the world geared to his speed. Now I was going to the hotel to cover his death. Callously I reflected that if written properly it would be something rare in obits. Then I felt a little ashamed realizing this would be a blow to Brett.

Under the marquee of the hotel a couple of cabbies were tussling good-naturedly and I stepped back just as one was thrown, crashing close to my legs. He scrambled to his feet, smiling broadly.

His grin was infectious and I returned it. "You should take a few lessons in wrestling!" I laughed.

"Aw, it ain't that!" He chuckled. "This guy couldn't budge me if I didn't have a gimpy leg. I'd toss him in a second flat!"

The victor was still jeering over that as I went through the revolving doors and headed for the phone booths to call

Brett, who should be home by this time. I meant to tell him about Ned before anyone else got to him. At the very moment of entering the booth I saw something that sent my good intentions glimmering. The coroner was making for the elevator and there could be only one place he was going. I hurried to join him.

"Good morning, Dr. Rollins!" I greeted him. "Going up to the tenth?"

"Good morning, Margaret." His voice was grave. In the clipped, precise manner, which seemed so out of tune with his roly-poly figure and apple-cheeked cherubic face, he continued. "Yes. I am going to the tenth floor. Too bad. Too bad indeed. The news gave me quite a shock. It is a terrible thing and the medical profession of this city has suffered a great loss. Dr. McGowan stood on the very threshold of a truly brilliant career."

"He was certainly headed for the top," I agreed. "Last month's *American Medical* had an article saying not more than five men in the world could have successfully performed that cardiac surgery he did at Touro hospital. And that reminds me! The hotel people seem to think Ned died of heart trouble."

"That's hardly possible!" Rollins answered. "I've known the boy since he interned at State hospital. He showed no signs of cardiac. None at all."

"He sure died suddenly though. Must have had some kind of a fit."

Rollins smiled ruefully at the term I'd used. Then he sighed. "Many diseases kill swiftly, you know. Besides there is only One who knows how far the span of life will reach. Young or old, it usually comes to the end before we are ready or willing to go."

"Why, Doc!" I half-teased, "I didn't tag you as a philosopher."

"My dear child, all of us are philosophers in our own ways."

"Really?" I smiled at him. "Even I?"

"Of course." He smiled back. "In fact you have rather a quaint sort of philosophy. I'll tell you about it someday. No time now."

We had reached the door of Dr. McGowan's room. He rapped, then opened it, stepping aside to let me enter first.

In spite of Dennis's low insinuations, it was the first time I'd ever been in that room, a large double one with nothing unusual about it except the present occupants—police and reporters. The Bienvenu caters to both transient and permanent residents. Doctors and nurses favor it because it's handy to two hospitals. The room furnishings could have been duplicated in any hotel of the same type: double bed, night table, desk, one easy chair and two uneasy ones—all done in Grand Rapids veneer. The only incongruous piece was a roller-fitted, white enameled cabinet with glass doors. It was full of boxes, bottles, and vials, and securely fastened with padlocks. Three of them—two on each bottom drawer and one fastening the doors.

I looked around. French windows faced east and opened out on a small private balcony with deck chairs and a glass-topped table. Nice for warm weather and cozy for entertaining outside the bedroom.

Newspapers littered the floor beside the bed and the reading lamp was lit, a sickly beam fighting the sunlight. The bed had not been slept in, although rumpled covers showed someone had rested on it. I glanced at the paper. It was the third edition which comes out around midnight and hits the street corners half-hour later.

The quiet which rules at scenes of death prevailed. The few people who'd arrived before me were grouped on the far side of the room speaking in hushed tones. I walked over to join them.

LeFevre, the hotel manager, an excitable little man of Gallic descent, who wore a pot belly and three chins, was talking to Officer Grady. He wrung his hands, quivered his chins and tummy, and softly bewailed the fact that this should happen in his hotel. He seemed to feel Ned had done him a dirty trick by shuffling off his mortal coil in this room. That brought to mind the body which was not in sight. I knew it had to be near by and the sight of the coroner disappearing into the bathroom located it for me.

I started after Rollins, so did the others, but the way was barred by the huge hulk of Detective Sergeant Joseph Shem. That didn't worry me. Joe was my pal.

"Hi, sweetheart!" I said, flippantly. "Did he die in his little white tub?"

The usual cheerful Irish grin was missing. "Doc's on the floor in there, kid. He musta been standing by the basin when he had the spell. I sure hate this." He was talking to himself as much as to me. "Doc was a swell guy. Why, he wouldn't take a dime from me when he operated on Molly. Not a dime."

I dropped the levity quickly. "I didn't know that. What do you suppose caused his death?"

"I ain't a doctor. Guess his heart just kinda give out on him."

"He never acted like he had the kind of heart trouble doctors treat," I objected. "Besides, he was a specialist and would have known what to do."

"That doesn't cut any ice." Joe frowned at me. "Lots of doctors die from ticker trouble. They work too hard and wear themselves out, I guess. And let me tell you, kid, when the old pump goes out she sometimes blows just like that!" He snapped his fingers.

"Could be." I shrugged. "Can I have a look at him, Joe? My deadline is coming up pretty soon."

"If Doc Rollins wants to let you in, it's okay by me."

"Ask him, Joe. I'm in a hurry."

"Sure." He called in to the coroner. "Doc! Can these reporters come in? Margaret Slone is in a hurry."

"If they want to they may," Rollins answered. "But it

isn't a very pretty sight, especially for a young woman."

"Maybe you hadn't better go in, kid," Joe advised. "Why not let the others look and get the dope from them?"

"I'm as good a reporter as anyone here and I'd thank you to remember it!" I said indignantly. "Of course I'm going in. I can take it!" And in I went, the others crowding behind me.

It wasn't a pretty sight. It was just plain awful.

McGowan's pajama-clad body was sprawled alongside the tub, to the left of the washbasin. The knees were drawn up and one arm hung inside the tub, as if he'd tried to use its side for leverage in one last vain effort to rise.

His face was a blotched, congested purple, and the facial muscles were horribly contorted—the lips drawn tightly back from the teeth, eyes bulged almost out of the sockets, and veins strained like hastily woven cords on his neck and forehead.

Things I'd heard about heart failure being an easy death passed through my mind. Easy, hell! Not if this was it!

I turned away, faintly queasy, and started to take notes. As I took them my subconscious recorded the scene. Twelve years of living have gone by since then but I can still close my eyes and see that bathroom.

On the tiled floor, to the right and lying between the basin pipes and the commode, was a toothbrush, dried paste adhering to the bristles. In the basin were shattered pieces of a glass, and on the bottom shelf of the built-in medicine cabinet was a bottle of mouth wash, open and with the cork lying beside it. The cabinet door was open.

"Well, I'll be damned!" I said. "He must have died while he was brushing his teeth."

I took a hasty look at the corpse to confirm that idea. Dried paste on the edges of the lips and between the exposed teeth proved I was right.

There was a peculiar, pungent odor in the small room, and I bent over to sniff at the broken water glass in the basin. The scent of an oddly strong antiseptic assailed my nostrils and I straightened up in a hurry.

Dr. Rollins had completed his examination and packed his kit. The group followed him out of the door.

Back in the bedroom, I ankled over and took up a stand where one quick grab would put me in possession of the phone. No one spoke for fully a moment and then it was Joe Shem who huskily voiced the question which was in everyone's thoughts.

"What did he die from, Doc? Ticker trouble?"

Rollins smiled at the slang term. "It looks like that, Joe. I only made a superficial examination and I can't make a definite statement until after the autopsy. But, as nearly as I can determine, heart spasms are indicated as having caused death. There may have been kidney complications. The color of the skin and the contorted facial muscles point that way."

"Now ain't that something!" exclaimed Johnny Morrow, police reporter for the afternoon paper of the Mangen combine and my direct opposition.

"And him a heart specialist!" added Art Herrot, beat man for the Mangen morning sheet. "Wouldn't you think he'd know better than to die of that?"

Rollins angled a stern look at both of them. "Many doctors die of the diseases they specialize in curing," he told them. "As for heart and kidney troubles, no one, doctor or layman, is immune to them."

Both reporters apologized hastily, saying they'd meant no disrespect and were not casting slurs on McGowan's ability.

The coroner inclined his head gravely. "I'm sure you didn't, boys."

"Look, Doc." These amenities were wasting time. Tempus was fugiting like hell and I had a story to get in.

"Yes, Margaret?"

"How long has he been dead?"

Rollins pinched his lower lip and pondered while I fidgeted.

"I can't say exactly," he answered at last. "However, judging from the advanced condition of rigor mortis, it must be between eighteen and twenty hours since death occurred. However you can safely place the figure at about fifteen hours. It can't be less than that."

Automatically I reached for the phone. Then I happened to notice the time my watch showed: 10:10. I did some rapid mental arithmetic.

"But that's impossible!" I exclaimed. "I talked to him just nine hours ago! He can't be dead longer than that!"

2. *Time Is Important*

~~~~~~

THE coroner flashed a startled look at me, eyebrows climb-
ing to meet a receding hairline. I giggled nervously, thinking that nothing could look as funny as a surprised, slightly
bald cherub.

"You spoke to him nine hours ago?" He shook his head.
"That's impossible, Margaret! Utterly impossible. You must
have your time figured wrong. Think again."

"There's no need to think again," I retorted, a little
nettled. "I know perfectly well what I said and I didn't
dream up that conversation."

"But, Margaret, Dr. McGowan couldn't have been alive
nine hours ago. I'd stake my professional reputation on that.
I'm positive of it!"

"Only a fool is ever positive of anything," I said tartly,
then added hastily, "And you're no fool. But you are wrong
this time and that's something *I'm* positive about. I'm not
mistaken and I haven't figured time wrong."

"You'd better explain, Margaret," he said quietly.

Shem, Morrow, and Herrot crowded closer to me, fixing
me with eyes as intent and questioning as the coroner's.

"I'll explain," I said. "I called Ned last night to ask if it
was true he was going to marry the Merceron girl, Olivette.
He'd been rumored engaged several times—wishful thinking on some girl's part—but I knew he had been dating
Vette for a long time. So I decided to check on it as a favor
to the society department—goodness knows they need
several favors.

"When I called around midnight he didn't answer, so I

left a message. He rang me back about 1:30 and said he was engaged but Olivette must be the one to give the details. It hadn't been announced yet. I'd just put the memo for soc on Anne's desk when the copy boy came through with the final edition. It rolls off the press about 2:00 A.M."

Rollins studied me, his expression grave. "You're sure of this? You're certain it was Dr. McGowan you spoke to?"

"Of course I am," I said impatiently. "I know Ned McGowan's voice when I hear it. I talked to him for at least five minutes. I'm sure of the time because I know too well when that paper comes off the press. Besides, when I got in my car to go home my dash clock said 2:15. I remember that because I griped to myself all the way home over not getting a day off to switch from the morning to the evening paper. Figure it out for yourself, but no matter how you figure you can't make it total more than seven, not nine, hours since death. The hotel people found him around 8:30."

"This is very strange and very confusing." He pinched his lower lip again. Anyone but Dr. Rollins would have found a stronger way of expressing its strangeness.

Another memory struck me. "If he'd been dead any fifteen hours he'd have had to die around 5:30 yesterday evening and I know that can't be so. He and my brother went somewhere to dinner together last night, someone's home. They would hardly have dined before 7:00 or later."

"You're sure of that too?" Rollins asked.

"I couldn't swear to it, no. I didn't actually *see* them eating." I was getting a little irked. "I can find out by calling Brett, but I hate to wake him. He took a charter out late last night and didn't get home until heaven knows when."

"Please call him," Rollins requested. "He can go back to sleep, but I must get this time element cleared up."

"I should think my having talked to Ned would do that," I said irritably, but I picked up the phone and called my home.

As I waited for the connection to be completed I watched Doc's worried face and began to feel sorry for him. I knew he hated to admit having made such a drastic mistake, but I didn't intend to hold any long conversation with Brett to prove he had done so. I was momentarily expecting a call from McCarthy wanting to know what the hell gave.

Bertha, the milk-chocolate shaded head of our house, answered the phone and refused at first to wake Brett. Finally she brought him to the phone.

"Brett, did you meet Ned McGowan and go to dinner with him last night?" I asked.

"What kind of an idiotic stunt are you pulling, waking me up for a question like that?" Brett was sleepy and annoyed. "What's it to you?"

"Never mind what," I snapped. "Just answer me yes or no."

"Sure I did, the four of us went to—hey!" The voice was wide awake now. "What's up?"

"You mean you, Olivette, Toni, and Ned when you say the four of you, don't you?"

"Yes, but what's this all about?"

"Never mind. What time did you leave Ned?"

"Around 10:00. My charter was due to leave at 11:00 and I figured an hour to change clothes and get to the airport. But why all this interest in Ned? What's he done?"

"Nothing," I said and thought: Unless you can call dying doing something. "I can't explain now, I'll call you back in a little while though."

"Now listen—" I cut off his argument by hanging up.

"Well." I turned to Rollins. "Ned was alive at 10:00 last night, and unless it was his ghost I spoke to, he was still healthy at 1:30 this morning. What do you think of that?"

"I think it's damned confusing," he said promptly.

I gaped at him. When our precise and well-spoken coroner says *damned* he's confused past belief.

"I simply can't accept the idea of being wrong by the margin of time you set forth, Margaret. It's incredible."

"It's not an idea, and incredible or not, it's a fact," I pointed out, and just then a real brain wave hit me.

"Hey Doc!" Then I stopped to think. If I put forth this theory and was wrong I'd never live it down and Dennis would be giving me the bird for years and making me eat it—feathers and all.

"Yes, Margaret?" Rollins was watching me anxiously.

I gave it another second of thought, but the desire to start some action was too strong for caution. I took a deep breath and plunged.

"Aren't there certain poisons which produce rigor mortis a short while after being taken?"

The coroner's eyes widened. So did everyone else's.

"Of course there are! Notably calcium cyanide and curare, the latter a product of one of the strychnos plants, *Strychnos toxifera*. Both of these poisons cause motor nerve paralysis which creates a false rigor and has all the symptoms of genuine rigor. But why do you ask Margaret? Surely you aren't suggesting Dr. McGowan died of poisoning?"

"Who, me?" Elaborately innocent. "I'm not suggesting anything. I was just curious, that's all. Of course if by any chance he did die of either of those poisons it will show in the autopsy, won't it?"

"It will now," he promised grimly. "Ordinarily we wouldn't look for such a thing and the post mortem would be cursory, but since you have suggested Ned took poison—"

"I did nothing of the kind!" I denied hotly.

"It sounded so to me," he said, and Shem, Morrow, and Herrot nodded an agreement.

"Well, you're all wrong. I don't think Ned took poison deliberately. The last thing he said to me was that he had the world geared to his speed and was sitting on top of it. No man feeling that way is going to kill himself."

"Then you're suggesting he was poisoned by mistake or accident?"

"I told you before I wasn't suggesting anything. All I know is that he was alive seven hours before his body was found, and if death by natural causes won't create such rigor, then something else must have done it."

"Death by natural causes couldn't do it. Not even if he was diabetic," Rollins said.

Shem started to say something, but Grady, who had been put on the door to keep out the morbidly curious, stuck his head in the room and called out: "Hey, Doc. The morgue basket is here. You all finished?"

"All finished, Jim," he answered. "Let them in."

The two white-coated attendants marched through into the bathroom carrying their long wicker basket. Doc went after them. They came out in a few minutes and left. Rollins picked up his bag and turned to Shem.

"Don't let anyone touch or move anything here until the post mortem report comes through," he said. "This may be an unnecessary precaution but I feel it should be taken. And you reporters," he turned to us. "Don't give out any stories of poisoning until we are sure. Shem, you had better keep Grady on the door. Let no one in unless he has business here."

"Okay, Doc." Shem gave Grady his orders and closed the door on the coroner's chubby figure. Then to Herrot, Morrow, and me: "You kids be careful what you touch in here, understand?"

"But, Joe!" I wailed, clutching the phone which already had my prints all over it. "Can't I call Dennis? I've five minutes to deadline!"

"We-l-ll." He hesitated, then saw my hand gripping the

phone and grinned. "You've printed your mitts all over it anyhow; go ahead and make your call."

"Thanks, pal." I grinned back at him and made a face at Morrow who was hightailing for the door. Johnny's deadline was the same as mine and he had to go to the lobby for a phone. He'd catch it.

I picked up the phone, then remembered something and looked around for LeFevre. He was gone.

"Hey, Joe. Who found the body?"

"The manager. Seems he had to be the one to unlock any door in case of anything suspicious. The maid got worried when she couldn't rouse the doctor òr get in the room, and she called him. He came up with the pass key and found Doc."

I put my call in and in a second Dennis's voice bawled in my ear.

"City desk! McCarthy spea—"

"I know who is speaking," I cut him short. "This is Margaret.. I'm set with that McGowan story."

"It's about time you were!" he beefed. "Migawd! Over an hour tò get an obit and you call yourself a reporter!"

"But this is no ordinary obit," I said. "This is a honey."

"Well, give it to Carter. I'm busy."

"Oh no you don't!" I stopped him. "I want you to take it."

"Why f'God's sake?"

"Because it's different."

He sighed resignedly, muttering about the trials of a city editor, and told me to go ahead and make it snappy.

I gave him strictly routine copy.

"The body of Dr. Edward McGowan, aged thirty-seven, was discovered in the bathroom of his quarters in the Bienvenu hotel shortly after 8:30 today. The body was found by the manager of the hotel, Jules LeFevre, who entered the room with a pass key after the maid had reported she was unable to rouse the doctor, who usually left the hotel before 7:30."

I got that far when Dennis interrupted. "Now listen, dammit! Carter can take this crap as well—"

"No he can't." I went on hurriedly: "Dr. McGowan, a native of Temple, Texas, was prominent in medical circles in the city and had resided here since he entered State hospital as an interne ten years ago. He recently attracted worldwide attention when he successfully performed a delicate cardiac operation."

"Godammit!" Dennis's venom sang along the wire. "What in the hell are you trying to do? Make a monkey out of me?"

"Nature saved me that job," I retorted. "Now shut up and listen."

"Dr. Arthur Rollins, Parrish Coroner, pronounced death as probably due to heart disease and kidney complications. The body was removed to the morgue for autopsy. Period. Paragraph."

The wire was ominously silent. I went on: "Dr. McGowan is survived by his parents, Mr. and Mrs. Jason McGowan of Temple and a twin brother, Fred McGowan of this city. Details of the burial will be announced later."

The wire continued silent. "You still there, Dennis?" I asked.

"I'm here." He sounded grim.

"Did you get it all?"

"I got it, and if that's all you're fired. No, by God! I'll transfer you to society!"

I grinned in unholy glee. "But it isn't all, darling. It's all you can print until the autopsy report comes in, but, unless I miss my guess, there's a lot more to come."

"What are you up to?"

I forgot I'd meant to stay nonchalant. "Dennis! This is going to be a story! Rollins said Ned had been dead fifteen to twenty hours and at least, the very *least*, fifteen. But I know he couldn't have been dead more than seven hours when they found him."

In a slightly bewildered tone Dennis asked me how I knew that.

"I told you I talked to him last night, dope! That was 1:30, and if he was able to talk he sure wasn't dead, was he?"

"I suppose not—and don't call me a dope," he answered. "Well, so what? I still want to know what you're trying to make of it."

"Who, me?" Again I played innocent. "I'm not trying to make anything of it. But only in algebra will two and two equal anything but four and I never got past simple arithmetic. So if he was alive seven hours before they found his body, it follows he couldn't be dead for fifteen hours or more. Therefore, if he couldn't get as stiff as he was from natural causes he must have got that way from unnatural ones. Catch on?"

"You're screwy!" He was profoundly disgusted.

I burned. "Oh! Am I now! Well, I'll bet you a pint Ned McGowan died from some kind of poisoning. How do you like them apples?"

"I don't like 'em, but you're on. For odds though. Your quart against my pint. Maybe this will teach you not to go off half-cocked and blow your top. Just because the guy talked to you the night before he cashed in does not prove he was poisoned."

I got good and mad. "As a city editor you're a good Sunday one!" I told him. "If you'll just let me finish—"

"I haven't time to listen to any more of your wild dreams. You stay there and when the report comes in proving he wasn't poisoned you come on back and I'll dust off a nice desk in soc for you and give you a drink from that quart you'll owe me."

"Now see here—" The bang in my ear shut me up, but I shook my head and grinned widely. I knew McCarthy. If he hadn't thought I was on the trail of something good he'd have ordered me back to the city room.

I looked around and beckoned to Shem who was standing forlornly by the balcony windows.

"Joe, just how well did you know McGowan?" I asked the question more to make conversation than out of any desire to know.

"Pretty well, kid," he answered. "I met him when he first went to State hospital. He was riding ambulance and I was on night duty there. I rode on his first call. It was a girl who'd bumped herself off; she was dead when we unloaded her. He was pretty upset about it. Later we used to talk about how much good a doctor could do in this world. We used to plan about how one day he'd have a clinic for poor patients and the rich ones would pay for it. He had a lot of dreams, that kid."

"They got lost, didn't they? All he talked of when I knew him was how much he could charge for an operation without getting a squawk from the patient."

"You're wrong, Margaret. He was still talking about that clinic when he operated on Molly six months ago. He almost had the dough to build it. Aw hell! He was a swell guy! When I tried to pay him for Molly's operation he told me he never took dough from a pal. Said I'd done plenty for him. Me? I'd never done nothing for Doc. Nothing."

Joe's grammar swamped in emotion and to my embarrassed surprise tears began rolling down the ruddy cheeks of the supposedly hard-boiled policeman.

The sound of the phone bell cut off anything I was going to say. He reached for it—but so did I. I got it first.

It was a woman and she wanted to speak to Dr. McGowan. There was a surprised note in her voice as if she wondered what the hell a woman was doing answering his phone that hour of the day.

"He's not able to come to the telephone," I said, cagily. "Who's calling, please?"

"Who's speaking, please?" she came back at me.

"I'm a reporter," I told her. "I'm here on a story."

"A story?" She was politely disbelieving. "What kind of a story?"

"I don't know that's your business!" I retorted snippily. "Who is this?"

"This is his office nurse." She sounded slightly smug.

"Oh! Oh, hello, Miss Cheng!" I knew the doctor's little almond-eyed nurse, a pint-sized and capable Oriental who'd been with him since he began his private practice. Damned attractive too, if you went for the lotus bud type. "This is Margaret Slone," I told her. And stalled right there.

"Oh, how do you do, Miss Slone?" The voice went polite and professional." I'm sorry to disturb your interview but there are several patients here and the doctor is quite late."

"I suppose he is," I said drily.

"Then may I speak to him?"

"I'm afraid not. Hasn't anyone called you or told you anything?"

"What do you mean? No one has called me to tell me anything. Is something wrong?"

I took so long groping for an answer she spoke before I had any ready.

"Miss Slone! Either let me speak to the doctor or tell him he has four patients waiting."

"You can't speak to him. I can't tell him anything—and he won't see any patients today or any day. He's dead." I cringed over my own bluntness.

"Dead!" Her voice hit a new high in squeals.

"Yes, he's dead, and you better send those patients home or to another doctor."

"But how can he be dead? He was fine yesterday!"

"That was yesterday." I unconsciously repeated Dennis's words to me. "He died early this morning. The coroner took the body for an autopsy."

3. *It's Murder, She Says!*

"AUTOPSY!" Her vocal chords hit high C. "Then it's murder! He's been murdered!"

An alarm bell began ringing in my mind. "What makes you say that?" I parried.

"What else could have happened? The doctor was a healthy man! If he's dead and there has to be an autopsy, then someone has killed him!"

The bell was still sounding. "Nonsense!" I said. "No one killed him. The coroner said he probably died of heart spasms and you should know, being a nurse, that bodies of people found like he was always get autopsied."

She disregarded the last part of the sentence. "Heart spasms?" Her tone reeked puzzlement. "Dr. McGowan had no heart trouble."

"Dr. Rollins also said it may have been kidney complications."

"That's ridiculous!"

"How come you're so sure?"

"Because I knew as much about his health as I did about his business. I'm his nurse."

The remark about her knowing his business gave me an idea.

"Maybe you had better come on over here," I said. "You knew his business, you may be needed here."

"I'll be there as soon as possible!" she assured me.

I hung up and turned to confront Shem, whose face was clouded with annoyance.

"What's biting you?" I asked, knowing damn well what was biting him.

"You ought to have let me take that call, Margaret. Who was that you told to come over here?"

"Didn't you hear me call her name? It was Miss Cheng, Ned's nurse. It seems no one thought to call her and tell her he was dead. He had some patients waiting in the office so she called here."

"Yeah? Well, what was that crack you made about no one had killed him? Does she think he was murdered?"

"I didn't mean anything and I don't know what she thinks, exactly. Let her tell you when she gets here."

"Okay—and the next time that phone rings you let me answer it."

The phone obliged and so did I. I couldn't help smirking when he gave it to me. "It's for you. Your boss, I guess."

My smirk widened into a grin. "Hello, darling! So your curiosity bump *is* still working!"

"Can the smart remarks," Dennis retorted. "Now finish that crackpot yarn you started to tell me."

"Crackpot, is it? You'll eat that without mustard! But here's the take. When I got here Dr. Rollins examined the body, then said Ned had been dead at least fifteen hours. I said he couldn't be dead that long on account I'd talked to him less than eight hours before the body was found. So Rollins said he'd stake his professional rep Ned had been dead longer than eight hours. So then I said the hotel people had found him at 8:30 and I'd talked to him at 1:30 and that only really made seven hours even and then Rollins said—"

"F'crissakes!" Dennis exploded. "He said, you said, I said, he said! All at the rate of a hundred words a minute! What t'hell are you giving me? Skip the he saids and get to the point. Make sense!"

"I'm trying to," I said acidly. "I have to tell you what was said to make any sense. Anyhow after I told Dr. Rollins I'd talked to Ned at 1:30 I got a bright idea—"

"Yeah! I'll bet it was bright all right. Your ideas usually are!"

I sizzled. "Okay, Dennis. If you don't want to hear the rest of this, say so and I'll come on in. It's no skin off my nose if we get taken on a good story. You're the editor."

"Finish it," he said tersely.

"Well, don't interrupt again. I asked Doc if there weren't certain poisons which caused a body to become rigid faster than normal. He said, and I quote, 'Certainly. Calcium cyanide and curare, a product of the strychnos plant, will cause motor nerve paralysis which produces an appearance of rigor mortis.' That started the thing—Hey! Hold it a minute, will you? I've got troubles here."

LeFevre had come back and was tugging excitedly at my arm, his chins jiggling up and down.

"What is it?" I asked him.

"The door! The door was locked from the inside with the burglar latch! If he died from poison he took it himself!"

"Don't get your jowls in an uproar," I advised him and resumed my talk with Dennis.

"The manager, who's just one jump ahead of a fit, says the door has a burglar-proof latch and the lock was on from the inside. You know what they are—they can't be opened except by the person inside the room unless the master key is used and all hotels keep that key in the safe. So, if no one could get in once Ned locked the door and no one could set the lock from outside, LeFevre wants it understood murder did not happen in his hotel. If it is poisoning it has to be either suicide or an accident."

"What do you think?"

"I've already bet it's poisoning. Of course it may easily be accidental."

"I still think you're going off half-cocked and it turns out to be a natural death."

"If it does I'll eat dirt!" I retorted. "There have been other times you thought I was going off half-cocked. How about that guy they fished out of the river?"

"He had a bullet hole through his head, remember?"

"Yeah! And you said it was suicide—remember?"

"Never mind. Just because that was murder doesn't mean this has to be poisoning, and if you've wasted a whole morning on a natural death I'll have something to say to you."

"Well, what the hell do you want me to do? Come in?"

"Hell, you've spent this much time on it, you may as well stick around awhile longer. But remember the next edition goes to press at 1:30. Try to call before two minutes of deadline."

I let that dig go by and hung up.

My watch hands pointed to 11:30; the autopsy would take another hour at least. I pulled the easy chair over close to the phone and sat down to wait in comfort. I lit a cigarette, relaxed, and looked around the room with the idea of gathering impressions that would look good in print. But people do not imprint their personalities on hotel rooms the way they do in homes and apartments. Except for the mussed bed and a pile of change and stuff on the dresser, the room was as neat and impersonal as could be. Smooth the bed, remove the photos and other things from the dresser, take away the white cabinet, and a new occupant could be roomed. I thought, with wry humor: Of course they'd have to clear out the drawers and closet and clean the bath.

As though he had caught a thought wave from me, Shem came over and sat on the edge of the bed.

"Seems funny that just a few hours ago Doc was alive and walking around this room." He sighed heavily. "Now there's nothing left of him but a few clothes and things. Clear those out and the joint can be rented in an hour. It gives me a sort of creepy feeling. Funny how different it is when you know the guy who kicked off. This hits me where it hurts the most."

"I suppose it does," I said absently, hearing his words

with only half of my attention. A nagging something was tugging at my memory cells and I tried to pin it down. The closest I could get to it was that something about the room was out of step with Ned McGowan's habits as I knew them. I was still puzzling, mildly irritated, when there was a commotion at the door.

In a moment Grady's head popped into the room.

"There's a dame out here says she's Dr. McGowan's nurse. What'll I do with her?" he asked.

"Let her in, Jim," I sang out.

"Just a minute, I'll handle this!" Shem glared at me and moved with great dignity out into the hall. In a brief moment he was back, the nurse with him.

"Hello, Miss Cheng!" I hailed her cheerfully. "Have a seat and don't mind Joe; he's upset about the doctor. Shem really has a heart of gold."

"I know Sergeant Shem." She managed a smile—then proceeded to relieve me of another illusion. I'd read that Orientals never gave vent to their real feelings, and here was one sobbing and dripping all over her uniform.

"Oh! Miss Slone!" She choked out my name between sobs. "Only yesterday the doctor was so fine and happy and now—and now he's—" Her voice trailed off in a loud wail.

"See here, this won't get you anywhere or do anyone a a bit of good." I hoped my voice was matter-of-fact. "You'll have plenty of time later to cry all you want, but if you're to be any help now you'll have to get yourself together. Suppose you start by telling me why you made that crack about Ned being murdered. Why did you say such a thing?"

She made a conscious effort at self-control, swallowing sobs as though they were stuck tight in her throat.

"W-e-ll—" She hesitated as if trying to marshal her thoughts into words.

I had a hunch she'd thought it over and decided to play it close to the chest. "Well?" I prompted.

"I don't really know what made me say that unless it was

the fact that you said an autopsy was necessary. Somehow murder and autopsy seem to go together."

That didn't go down with me. I could see it rang false to Shem as well. He took over, planting himself squarely in front of her.

"I don't have to tell you how much I thought of Doc," he said. "I want to know the truth about how come you thought he was murdered just because there had to be an autopsy. Your explanation won't go with me. You're a nurse and you know better than that."

She smiled appealingly at him. "I suppose it was just that I was so shocked when I heard he was dead. All I could think of was that someone must have killed him."

"What give you that idea?" Joe insisted ungrammatically.

"Really, Sergeant, you know yourself how healthy the doctor seemed! And yesterday, why he—he— Oh! I still can't believe it! Not Ned!"

She spilled over again and subsided into strangling sobs. Joe and I looked at each other and in mutual agreement wandered off. Joe went out to sit on the balcony while I walked aimlessly around inside.

The weeping nurse and I were alone in the room. Morrow had gone to phone in his story and get some coffee. Herrot had taken himself off just after the coroner left. LeFevre had departed to his hotel duties.

I stopped in front of the dresser and stood studying the top of it, thinking it was the most disorderly thing about the room. Again that teasing something pulled at my memory strings. I began checking the things lying in front of me, half hoping they'd make what was puzzling me come clear.

There was a set of military brushes and comb, nail file, and shoe horn. They were tortoise shell with initials in gold on the backs and handles. A bottle of men's cologne, half full, sat in a tortoise holder. The photos were of Olivette and Ned's parents. A snap of his brother was tucked in the side of the mirror. A soiled handkerchief had a smudge of dark lipstick on it.

Dumped helter-skelter in the middle of the dresser top was a motley mess of stuff which must have been the contents of the doctor's pockets. I grinned, thinking of the gags pulled about what women carry in purses.

The heap included a watch with gold wristband, a gold tie clasp, gold pocket knife, gold cigarette lighter, all matching, all initialed, "E McG," and beautifully made. There was an oversized horseshoe-shaped key holder, also gold and carrying six keys. Three were for Yale type locks and the others for small padlocks. There was another key holder, leather and buttoned with a snap. What looked like an ignition key stuck out of one end. I took an interested second look at a cigarette case, obviously new and very smart. It was gold too and matched the other monogrammed things. I thought: Those little items cost someone a pretty penny and I'll bet a hat it wasn't McGowan!

The rest of the stuff was what had called forth my grin. It resembled the contents of a small boy's pockets. Three pencil stubs, a jacknife, four packs of matches—evidently Ned had no faith in his lighter—a fountain pen and pencil, five capsules filled with brown powder, four bright red pills, a pad of prescription blanks, blue leather address book, a one dram vial, empty; two colored toothpicks such as you get with Manhattan cocktails, and a wallet, brown leather and generously stuffed with green money.

The wallet seemed to be lying on top of something, I couldn't see what. I took my pencil and gingerly lifted the billfold aside to see what was under it. I looked at it in some wonderment, and what crazy impulse prompted my next move I'll never know—but I picked the damn thing up and shoved it in my suit coat pocket.

That move not only got me in the doghouse with the police, nearly got me fired—it damn near cost my life!

4. *Heavy Hangs the Pocket*

ALMOST as soon as I'd taken it I had a burning desire to put it right back again. I would have too, if it hadn't been too late. Joe had hoisted his frame from the deck chair and was coming back into the room. Miss Cheng had turned off her tears and both of them were looking at me. I wondered if either had seen me lift the thing and decided not. They'd have said so if they had.

I went back to the easy chair, the filched article heavy in my pocket and on my conscience. A pall of silence, thick as a London fog, settled over the room. Joe and Miss Cheng were sunk in thought and I sat fiddling with my pencil and wishing I could go eat. It was past noon, that report should be coming in any minute—I hoped. Dennis had been damned emphatic about that deadline.

I stood the nervous quiet at long as I could, then turned to the nurse. I had to talk to someone or go nuts.

"Miss Cheng, when did you last see the doctor?"

She dropped her thoughts with a start. "What did you say?"

I repeated the question.

"Why, when he left the office yesterday afternoon. That was about 5:30. He usually left about then."

"Did he see many patients yesterday?" I was only making conversation.

"Not many," she answered as though she was wondering about my interest in McGowan's office routine. "It was a light day. Some personal friends came in. Your brother was one."

"Brett?"

"Isn't he your only brother?" She smiled and I nodded. "He came in at about noon and the doctor left with him, for lunch I suppose."

"What were Ned's office hours?"

"They were 10:30 A.M. to 12:30 P.M. and 2:00 until 5:00 P.M. Why?"

"Nothing particular. What does a doctor do on a light day when only a few patients come in?"

"Oh! Dr. McGowan always found plenty to do. He worked on papers for medical publications, he was preparing one on toxicology. He," her lips trembled, "he was much interested in that and I helped him in both research and experiments."

"Is that so?" I murmured politely—then the full import hit me and I sat up all attention.

"Toxicology? That's the study of poisons, isn't it?"

Joe sat up too, all ears and interest.

"It is the scientific term for that study." Her smile was a tiny bit superior. "We had been working with the rarer toxics, those which leave little or no trace in the body." She indicated the rolling cabinet with a nod. "That case is filled with different poisons—some common, some rare. He did very little work here, however, as he had a well-equipped laboratory for his experiments. Once in a while he did some things up here. The working materials, test tubes and such, are in the drawers."

"You don't say!" I gave the cabinet an interested glance, then looked at Shem—my eyes question marks. His answered affirmatively. I took a deep breath—there was no telling what effect my words would have on her. I could only hope for the best. I felt for an opening and chose an entirely irrelevant one.

"Miss Cheng, did Ned ever complain of being sick? Wasn't there anything wrong with him at all?"

"Never!" She was emphatic. "His only trouble," she

smiled ruefully, "was with his teeth. Only day before yes-terday he had one removed. It was a badly impacted molar, a lower one. The dentist had to cut around the bone and under two other teeth to get it out. Dr. McGowan made a lot of fuss about it, but really he was in quite a lot of pain. He hated pain."

"All men do." I smiled, remembering how Dennis had fumed about a boil on his neck. "They're regular babies."

"They are," she agreed. "But you aren't going to suggest the doctor died from a tooth being pulled, are you?"

"Lord no! What I really wanted to tell you was that the coroner said Ned had been dead fifteen to twenty hours. He'd have had to die between 1:00 and 6:00 P.M. yesterday to make the time come right."

There it was out! I sat back to await her reaction. It came at once.

She leaned forward, almond eyes glittering like jet.

"That's impossible! I spoke to him after he left the office, I called him here about 7:00 to ask about an operation he had scheduled for Saturday. He said he'd discuss it with me today, that he was just leaving for dinner."

"I know as well as you do that it's impossible," I told her flatly. "I talked with him much later than that. I spoke to him about 1:30. He was all right then. He told me of his engagement to Vette Merceron. I suppose you knew of it?" I watched her narrowly.

"Of course. It was what made him so happy this past month. He loved her very much."

I nodded and thought: No jealousy here. Not so you can notice anyhow.

"Well? It doesn't exactly add up, does it?"

"What doesn't add up?"

I wondered if she could be that obtuse.

"None of it. If he was alive at 1.30 A.M. he couldn't have been dead more than seven hours. They found the body at about 8:30. Yet Dr. Rollins, a first-class medical examiner, was willing to stake his reputation Ned had been dead no less than fifteen hours."

"What are you trying to tell me?"

I lost all patience. After all, she had been the first one to suggest murder.

"I don't know that I'm trying to tell you anything. I'm only trying, with your help, to arrive at a logical solution of what appears to be something of a problem."

"Naturally I'm glad to be of any help." Her tone was stiff.

"All right then. Let's try to figure this out. You saw him at 5:30 and talked to him at about 7:00. Then he met my brother— Oh! Lord help me!" I stopped abruptly. I'd just remembered I'd promised to call Brett hours ago!

"I've just thought of something!" I ignored their surprised looks and reached for the phone to call home. Brett answered immediately.

"Look, darling, you'll have to forgive me," I said appeasingly. "I got tied up and couldn't call back."

"That's okay." He didn't sound like it was. "Of course I've only been sitting on the phone for three hours."

"Two," I corrected.

"Never mind that. Just tell me what's wrong with Ned. I've called you at that damn paper five times and got nowhere. What's he done?"

"Nothing—except to die," I said bluntly.

There was a gasp, then an incredulous question.

"What the hell are you saying?"

"I'm saying that Ned McGowan is dead. Quite dead. They've taken his body for autopsy. He was found in his bathroom this morning and they don't know just what he died from."

"But he was perfectly healthy!" Brett sounded stunned.

I was getting a little tired of being told that.

"So I've heard—from everyone," I said tartly. "Well, he isn't healthy any longer. He's cashed in his chips, all of them. I saw the body."

"Where are you?"

"In his room, waiting for the report on the autopsy. It better be poison too, or I'll be poison around my city room."

"Poison!" he yelled in my ear. "Who poisoned him?"

Joe was waving distress and warning signals at me. I decided I'd better shut up. I looked fearfully at Miss Cheng, but she was lost in thought again and apparently hadn't heard what I'd said.

"I can't talk to you any longer," I said abruptly and hung up the still squawking receiver. I shook Miss Cheng's knee gently.

"Now, where were we? Ned met Brett and the Merceron sisters, and they went to dinner at someone's home. Do you know where they went?"

She shook her head slowly. "No. I didn't keep the record of the doctor's social appointments."

"It doesn't matter a lot," I said. "I can always find out from Brett. Ned was with Brett until about 10:00, when Brett left to take out a charter to Memphis. Damn fool," I grumbled, "he must have turned right around and flown home without any rest."

"I beg your pardon?" She looked puzzled.

"I was just griping about Brett. Now then, where Ned was from the time Brett left him until he got back to the hotel I don't know. I do know he was still out at 11:30 because I called him. I'm not sure he was in his room when he returned my call but I'm assuming he was. That was 1:30."

"I don't see where this is leading us." She sounded annoyed.

"Well, I do!" I retorted, annoyed myself. I decided to spill the whole business right then and with no further stalling. "You say he fooled with poisons. Well, it's entirely possible he died from one of them."

She tensed in every muscle and horror dawned in her eyes. Horror and something else: Suspicion, hatred—an emotion I couldn't quite analyze.

"Poisoned!" She bit the word out. "Poisoned! Of course! I should have known!"

"Now, Margaret," Joe was peeved. "You got no call saying that. The report ain't in yet."

"T'hell with the report!" I snapped. "Ned McGowan died of poison and I'm sure of it! Ouch!" I squawked inelegantly as five amber fingers bit into my arm. "Hey! Leggo of me! What's the big idea of pinching me?"

"He was murdered! Just like I said he was! Murdered!"

"Stop hissing at me and don't be so damned dramatic." I rubbed my arm. "No one murdered him. He probably got a dose of poison by accident. He had them all right here."

"Oh no! The doctor knew too much about poisons for that! He was murdered!"

"Don't be a fool! Maybe he took it on purpose. Who knows?"

Her eyes narrowed to almond slits. "I know!" she said sibilantly. "The doctor did not commit suicide. A happy man does not kill himself. He was murdered, I tell you!" Her voice rose to a shriek and this time I pinched her. Hard too.

Morrow had just come in, looking sleek and well-fed. And here I was—starving.

"Be careful what you say in front of this guy," I warned her.

"What goes on?" he queried. "Am I missing something I shouldn't? Who yelped just then?"

"I did," I told him. "I hit my funny bone."

"That the best you can do?" He wandered over to the dresser and stood looking at the disarray of articles. I wondered if he'd seen the one which weighted down my pocket. Even as I thought about it he lifted the wallet.

"Watch out, Johnny!" Joe warned. "Don't touch anything!"

"Sorry, Sarge. I forgot." He leaned against the dresser and crooked a finger at me in a beckoning gesture. I had a sinking feeling.

"Joe, watch my chair while I'm gone. I'm taking no chances with firsts on that phone. I got there first and it's mine."

Joe put his size elevens on the seat and I walked over to Morrow.

"What do you want?"

"Anything happen while I was gone? That report come in?"

"Nothing and it hasn't and it's almost 1:00 now."

He poked idly with a pencil at the things on the dresser. "Was I gone that long? Hey, kid. Who's the Oriental lovely in the nurse getup?"

I felt a sense of relief. So that was what he wanted!

"She was Dr. McGowan's nurse—and the *getup* is authentic," I stated with dignity.

"Hmmm! Not bad. Not bad at all! Slone, is it true what they say about—"

I kicked him in the shins.

"Shut up you fool!" I glared at him. "Must you be so goddam crude!"

He laughed and sauntered out on the balcony. I went back to my chair.

"Okay, Joe. Lift the hoof. And thanks. That guy's a heel."

Joe grinned. "You and Morrow! Skip the thanks. I'm always glad to do a favor for a pal." Sudden memory blotted out his grin. "Gee, that's about what Doc said to me about Molly. Margaret, do you think there's a chance Miss Cheng could be right about him being murdered?"

I shook my head. "Dr. Rollins said only the fastest acting poisons induced that false rigor. Ned locked the door himself. He had to, it didn't lock by itself. There's no logical way anyone could poison him and get out. Ned would have been dead before he could get to the door; that sort of stuff acts inside of seconds. He must have got it by accident." I gestured toward the cabinet. "Those things are poison to fool with." The pun was in bad taste and I knew it.

Joe ignored it. "How could it have happened?"

"Oh, maybe handling something, then putting his finger in his mouth to bite off a hangnail—something like that."

Miss Cheng leaned forward, eyes intense.

"The doctor had no hangnails!" she informed me. "Nor was he so careless as you suggest. He always worked with rubber gloves. He knew how deadly the poisons were."

If I'd been minded to argue with her, the sight of Tommy Gross, Chief of Detectives, and Les Beton of the Homicide squad standing just inside the door would have stopped me. Homicide! Well!

"Well, hello!" I said. "If it isn't the Rover boys themselves!"

Joe's greeting topped all existing records.

"What you guys doing here?" he asked.

"My brass-buttoned friend, we're detectives." Les was elaborately sarcastic. "Plainclothes police, you know. We believe Dr. McGowan did not die from natural causes. We believe that because the city chemist has discovered that he died from poisoning."

Expected though it must have been, the word dropped like a bombshell in the room. Morrow streaked for the door, but Joe and Miss Cheng just stared open-mouthed at the detective.

I looked at my watch. It said 1:20. Without waiting to find out what kind of poison I reached for the phone. All city desk phones were busy and minutes stretched out like hours before I heard the familiar yapping of McCarthy.

5. *Poisonous Palaver*

"NOW, don't squawk, Dennis!" I cut short the beef before it got past his windpipe. "This is worth waiting for. McGowan died from poisoning."

"What kind?"

"Huh? Oh! Just a minute, I'll find out." The ear cup of the phone rasped away as I turned to Tommy.

"Tommy! What kind of poison was it?"

"I don't know," was the surprising answer. "The chemist hadn't completed his tests and he wasn't sure what it was. He was going to call in Dr. Medier who specializes in poisons at Tulane Medical school. I have to call him in about an hour."

I returned my attention to the still rasping phone.

"Aw stop cussing me, McCarthy! Tommy doesn't know the name of the poison."

"Tommy who?"

"Gross, of course. He and Beton are here."

"Homicide, eh? So it must be murder."

"Now don't go off 'half-cocked!" I said sweetly. "Why must it be murder?"

"If it isn't what's Homicide doing there?"

"Just checking to make sure what it was."

"Oh. Well, what have you got that is worth listening to?"

I had my story in fairly good order in my notes, and I gave it to him as rapidly as I could. I finished it up with the nurse's information about McGowan's research in poisons and told him about the cabinet in the room.

"There goes your mystery," he said as soon as he 'heard that part.

"What do you mean, mystery?"

"Hell, it's as clear as glass! He got hold of the stuff by accident."

"Could be. But his nurse doesn't think so."

"What does she think?"

"That he was murdered. She has very definite opinions about that too. She's been howling murder for hours. But you can't print that."

"Why can't I? I can say the 'nurse alleges,' can't I? What's to stop me?"

"Nothing. You can do it if you want, but I wouldn't advise it."

"Why wouldn't you? Not that I value your advice."

"There's the fact of the burglar-proof lock which was fastened from the inside. And that the poison was one that works almost immediately. But go ahead and make an ass of yourself and the paper if you want to."

"It's your story, you'd be the ass."

"See here, Dennis McCarthy!" I yelled. "Don't you dare put anything like that under my byline!"

"I don't know about that." Dennis was enjoying himself. "What do the detectives think?"

"I don't know. I haven't talked to them yet. I called you as soon as I knew it was poison."

"How long will it be before they know the kind of poison?"

"Tommy said about an hour," I said. "Shall I hang around?"

"You might as well. Call me if you get anything in the meanwhile that might make decent reading. If I want you I'll call you there."

"Okay." I started to hang up, then remembered something. "Dennis! Wait a minute. You owe me a pint of good liquor!"

He gasped with well-simulated shock. "I owe you what? You're nuts! I made no bet with you!"

It was my turn to gasp, but honestly. "Why you certainly did! A pint against a quart that it would be poison! You said I was on and made the odds yourself!"

"You're dreaming. I knew all along it would be poison."

"You lousy welcher! You knew nothing of the kind! This is strictly my beat and you know it!"

"So all right," said Dennis. "It's your beat and you're stuck with it. Call me when you have anything new." He hung up.

I slammed down the phone and expressed in loud tones my opinion of one Dennis McCarthy, city editor.

He was, I allowed, a louse and a skunk, a welcher and a bum. He stank to high heaven and I hoped he roasted in hell. Only I hoped it was hotter than advertised by the revivalists. I only regretted I couldn't be there to turn the carcass on the spit.

"What's the matter, Margaret?" Tommy grinned at me. "You and Dennis at it again? It's a wonder you two haven't cut each other's throats!"

"Why that stinkin' no-good son-of-a-a," I took a deep breath, "son-of-a-linotyper!" I finished. "I'll fix him for this! The welching dog!" That off my chest I grinned back at Tommy. "Well, Sherlock! What do you do next?"

"Next? We haven't done anything first yet. First it's a matter of finding out whether he took the poison deliberately, got it by accident, or had it fed to him."

"I think you can eliminate the first and last," I said. "The suicide theory won't hold water, neither will a murder one —much as I'd like to work up a good mystery. It's a locked door situation, a burglar-proof lock. Of course," I waxed ironic, "the transom was open, someone may have climbed through it. You might make it murder if you try hard enough."

"Who wants to try?"

I indicated Miss Cheng, who had grabbed his arm. "She does."

"Captain Gross!" She was as tense as stretched hemp. "Dr. McGowan was murdered. I know it!"

"Oh nuts!" I said. "She's been harping on that for hours. No one killed Ned McGowan, neither did he commit suicide. He got some poison by mistake."

She transferred her attention to me, pinching both arms.

"Miss Slone! I've told you such a mistake is impossible! He was murdered!"

I shook her off. "You see what I've been up against?" I appealed to Tommy—but I got no sympathy there.

"She was his nurse, wasn't she? She should be able to help us. To tell us who saw him yesterday and last night, if he had any enemies or was in trouble or bad health—stuff like that."

"I can be as much help there as she can, maybe more," I retorted. "I could easily be the one who spoke to him last."

"Is that so?" Beton showed interest. He'd most likely be accusing me of murder next.

"Yes, that's so."

"How come?"

Again I told the story of my talk with Ned, his dinner date with Brett, and, in particular, the state of happiness Ned appeared to enjoy, ditto the state of his health. I ended with his crack about how he had the world geared to his speed.

"Does that sound like a man who'd be likely to commit suicide?"

"No, it doesn't," Gross admitted.

"As for enemies—that's a cat of another color," I continued. "He must have had a number of them, mostly women. Ned McGowan was a male chippy, a sensualist. He fell for every pretty new face and he had a good line, but his love wore off as fast as it came on. So lots of women and girls hated his guts. Funny part is that chaser and cheat though he was, he started out sincerely enough. He really meant his lovemaking just in the beginning. But when he was through, he meant that too. He broke quite a few hearts around this town. Oh no!" I shook my head at an inquiring gleam in Beton's eyes. "Mine wasn't one of them, although I did have a date or two with him."

"Do you know any of these girls?" Beton asked.

"Several," I replied wryly. "My kid sister, Vangie, was one. She lasted six months and moped for another six. I used to want to beat her, she'd make me so mad. I tried to warn her, but she thought I wanted him myself! Little nit-wit! However he must have decided he'd found the real thing with Vette."

"Who were some of the other girls he fooled around with?" Beton asked.

I thought for a couple of minutes. Then, "Well, there was Lucille St. Clair, she's a nurse; little Marie Chauvin, she was c-c-crazy about him—she's crazy anyhow. Agnes Gilchrist, Molly Burke, and Chrissy Wilson all fell for his line. Now, let me see— Oh sure! There was Katie Ledson, Marie O'Brien, and Angela Elwood, and, this is a funny one, there was Toni Merceron, Vette's sister who was always considered Brett's girl—but Ned dated her. Then there was Catherine Kelly, a nurse. She got kicked out of the hospital because of him. Amelia Crisler and Elsie—"

"That's enough!" Beton threw up his hands in surrender. "He must have been one of them Lothario guys!"

"Definitely!" I was emphatic.

"How come you know so much about his love life?"

"He double-dated with my brother a lot and they often brought the girls to the house. Vangie used to have fits when they did, but she got over it in time. To tell the truth, if it hadn't been for that lock I'd have figured this for murder right away. It would be easy to fit a jealous, jilted woman into the picture."

"Too damn easy," Gross remarked drily.

The phone bell rang and Shem leaped for it. "Hullo! No,

this isn't Ned. Just a minute." He cupped a hand over the mouthpiece and whispered, "Woman—wants the doctor. What'll I tell her?"

"Why not let Miss Cheng answer?" I suggested. "She knows all of his patients and most of his friends. She'll know what to say."

Gross nodded and motioned the nurse, who'd sat glaring at me through my recital of Ned's philanderings, to take the call.

"This is Miss Cheng, Dr. McGowan's nurse," she informed the caller. "What is it, please?"

I watched her and decided all stories about Chinese being deadpan experts were a batch of lies. Her lips tightened and her eyes glittered venomously.

"Oh, hello, Mrs. Dellman. No, the doctor is not here. Take a message? I'm afraid that's useless. What do I mean?" Her voice became as soft as velvet. "Why, Dr. McGowan is dead, he's been poisoned, Mrs. Dellman. Didn't you know that when you called?"

I gasped and yanked the phone from her hands. "What are you trying to pull, you fool!" I hissed. "Have you gone nuts?"

"Hello, hello, Mrs. Dellman!" I spoke into the phone.

"Hello! What was that you said, Miss Cheng?" The voice was shocked.

"This isn't Miss Cheng, Mrs. Dellman. This is Margaret Slone, Brett's sister. You remember me?"

"Of course I do," she answered. "What's happened to Ned? For God's sake tell me quickly!" Hysteria sounded in her tones.

"Well—" I stopped. Damn this business of being the one to break the bad news. I looked appealingly at Tommy and Shem. Both shook their heads firmly. Damn, damn, damn! I turned back to the phone.

"It's just like this. Dr. McGowan's dead." There it was out!

"But how can he be? How did he die?"

"He just is. From poison."

"Who—who poisoned him?"

I thought: Oh, oh, here we go again! "No one did it. It must have been an accident. Something he got hold of by mistake. He had a lot of poison around."

"I know," she said, and I thought: Oh, you do!

"This is awful!" she exclaimed. "I was very fond of Ned. Is there anything I can do?"

"Not that I know of at the moment," I answered.

"Well call me if there is. I'll be glad to help if I can."

I assured her we would, said good-by, and hung up. Then I turned on the nurse in fury.

"You lame-brained idiot!" I exploded. "What the hell did you mean by making cracks like that at Mrs. Dellman? Are you batty?"

"You needn't use that tone with me!" she said tartly. "I'm not 'batty,' as you phrase it. That woman has chased after the doctor for nine years and she acted like he belonged to her, body and soul! He'd been trying for a year to get rid of her, and lately I've seen her watching him with hate in her eyes."

"Nuts! You've been reading too many novels or seeing too many movies. Mrs. Dellman is a fine woman, and everyone knows she and her husband are perfectly happy. You know who they are, don't you, Tommy?"

"Sure. They're both tops in the whole state. Swell people."

"You see?" I turned back to the nurse. "Stop going off half-cocked; it's a sure way to get in trouble." I looked at my watch, 1:45. "I'm as empty as a used container," I said. "I'm going to lunch. How long you going to be around?" I asked Tommy.

"God knows! We have to talk to the hotel gang. Have to stay here until that chemist report comes through so we'll know what kind of poison to look for."

"I'll see you later then. I'm going to forage for food. How

about you Miss Cheng? Don't you want a sandwich or
—something?"

"I couldn't eat a thing!" she answered.

"Oh fiddle!" I said impatiently. "You have to eat sooner
or later. Come on and keep me company anyhow." I wanted
to get her out—there was no telling what would happen if
she stayed around spilling 'her ideas and facts. I knew
Beton.

"All right," she said listlessly, and followed me out of
the room.

6. *A Woman's Weapon*

WE caught the elevator, went down, and walked along St. Charles Avenue until we found a small hash house. We hadn't spoken since we left the room.

The waitress, who looked like a fugitive from a cotton patch, took my order for Creole Gumbo. Miss Cheng said she wanted nothing but coffee. When we had been served, the first sip of coffee seemed to loosen her tongue.

She leaned toward me. "You think I'm crazy when I say the doctor was murdered, but believe me, and I know, it is the only way he could have been poisoned unless it was suicide and you have agreed that is impossible."

"Not impossible, unlikely rather," I corrected.

"Impossible," she insisted, deadly serious. "So it must be murder."

"Accident," I muttered.

"How can you be so blind! This is no accidental death!"

"How can you be so sure of that?" I countered.

"Because I've worked with Dr. McGowan for eight years, almost nine. I knew him as few people have ever known anyone. I knew when he had drunk too much and when he'd eaten too well. I met all of his girls and I always knew when he was having trouble getting rid of one."

"There's a name for your sort of person," I said. "They call them 'office wives.' "

She dismissed the comment with a shrug.

"I helped him with his research and he never started or completed an experiment without me. We Chinese are much interested in the science of poisons—"

"Toxicology," I murmured.

She smiled. "Toxicology. For centuries the Chinese have worked with rare poisons, plant and mineral. It's something of a heritage with us."

Through a mouthful of soup I gurgled what was meant to be an interested sound.

"Research was the part of my job I liked best. The office end was just routine. When we worked on an experiment we worked without thought of time, often past midnight."

I swallowed the last mouthful of gumbo and asked, "What has all this to do with the way Ned died?"

"You'll soon see. You inferred Ned—Dr. McGowan—"

"Oh go ahead and call him Ned," I said. "Anyone who worked as closely and for as long as you worked with him is entitled to relax formality."

"That's true. Well, you seem to believe Ned was careless enough to die from accidental poisoning. I know better. We never handled poisons unless we wore tight rubber gloves and special coveralls. We cleaned up after each experiment, we never left even a speck of poison around. We even used a special cloth to wipe off surfaces. All supplies were kept under lock and key."

"Then how could anyone but Ned or you get to them?" I asked quickly.

"Keys can be duplicated." She had me there. "And there was also the doctor's habit of sharing his work with his friends."

"What do you mean?"

"Well, he was so interested himself he used to try and get anyone he liked interested also. He taught more people about toxicology than many professors. Even your brother came in for his share of instruction."

"Brett? Funny, he never mentioned it to me."

"He didn't care much about it—but *others* did!"

"Who, for instance?" I began to see where this was leading.

Her eyes glittered. "Mrs. Dellman!" She spat out the name. "*She* was most interested! She even made minor experiments with us. Your sister, Evangeline, enjoyed studying about poisons. Miss St. Clair, being a nurse, was quite naturally interested. So was Miss Kelly. Both the Merceron girls worked with him, and Antoinette showed quite a talent for the science."

"Most of his students seem to have been women," I remarked.

She smiled, a bit wryly. "They were. But women are usually more intrigued by poisons than are men. Also they use it more often in murder. Poison is a woman's weapon. Men choose guns, knives, and clubs."

I laughed, but a shiver made a round trip on my spine. "That's probably all very true. But I still can't see murder in this case. All the physical evidences are against it. Mainly that double-locked door."

"You place too much importance on that locked door," she said flatly. "Locked doors won't stop a murderess. There are several ways she could plant poison so that death would not occur until she was safely out of the way."

"Is that so?" I asked interestedly. "How? And why the emphasis on the feminine pronoun?"

"Because a woman killed Ned. Any woman, Miss Slone, who was at all clever and knew something about poisons could have killed him, locked door or not. I could have done it."

"How do I know you didn't?" I questioned, irritably. This almond-eyed babe was getting me down. Murder by planted poison is no subject to aid digestion. "You'd know just how to go about it. You just said so."

"I had no reason to kill him," she said tonelessly. "All I wanted was the privilege of working with him and I had that."

"But you think others did have such a reason?"

"Others *thought* they had. Mrs. Dellman was one!"

"Baloney!" I said inelegantly. "There you go again! Why should Marta Dellman want to kill anyone?"

"She wanted to kill Ned because she was in love with him and she knew she had lost him to Olivette. Besides, he owed her a lot of money."

"The first, if true, might be a motive," I said. "As for the second, hell! She has scads of dough. Any money she loaned him would hardly make a dent in her bank balance. She must have known the loan was safe, Ned was on his way up. I've heard some silly tales about her and Ned, but she stands to lose too much by a murder scandal. She'd never take such a chance. Lovers are a dime a dozen for a woman that wealthy—if she's that kind of woman."

I picked up my check and rose from the table. "Come on. We'd better get on back."

"I think I'll go on back to the office. There will be calls to attend to. If you need me I'll be there."

"Okay," I said. "I'll see you later then." I started out of the door with her behind me. On the sidewalk she turned to me, eyes slitted.

"Miss Slone, Ned was murdered and I'm going to prove it!" She walked off without giving me a chance to answer her, and she was out of earshot before I realized I'd never found out how poison could be planted. Not that I believed such had happened, but she was so *damn* sure it was no accident.

What she'd said about cleaning up stuck in my mind. I had a mental picture of them tidying up after an experiment. Then I had another—and flash! I had the answer to what had been puzzling me about that room!

It was too damn neat!

No clothes were draped over chairs with no regard for creases—and Ned McGowan never hung anything anywhere but on the handiest chair.

This development started a new chain of thought that called for some thinking. I ducked back into the lunch

place and ordered a coke. Then I took out a cigarette and
searched for a match. I found none in my purse so I stuck
my hand in my pocket and what I felt there kicked everything else out of my mind. I pulled out the thing I'd pilfered
from the dresser and studied it with interest and distaste.

It looked innocent enough on the surface. A common key
chain with two keys. One was a large wrought-iron affair
—the kind that opens patio gates only. The other was for
a Yale lock. I stared at them, wondering what Ned was
doing with that iron thing. He had no patio. I read the attached metal disk. An address in the French Quarter, 605
St. Anne Street, Apt. Four. I thought: That's funny. What
was he doing with a key for an apartment there?

Part of New Orleans' charm is that it is two cities within
one. Canal Street divides them. "Uptown" is the modern
city of skyscrapers and swank home sections. "Downtown"
is an amazing collection of ancient buildings, antique
stores, quaint markets, call houses, waterfront dives, clip
joints, artists' studios, and the best cafés in America. The
"Vieux Carré" stretches from Canal to Esplanade Avenue
and from the river to North Rampart Street. Down there
is Le Petite Théâtre and its famous patio, Pete Herman's
Ringside Cabaret, Nora Warner's infamous bawdy house,
Antoine's and Turci's renowned cafés, and the first apartment buildings ever erected in America—The Pontalbas—
built by the Baroness de Pontalba during the Spanish oc-
cupation. In the Quarter such celebrities as Sherwood An-
derson, William Faulkner, and Ernest Hemingway had
resided.

In both the Pontalbas and other apartments non-celeb-
rities paid rent on what I called "Shame Shanties." But
McGowan was a bachelor. What would he be doing with
a shame shanty? Therefore why the key to a patio gate?

I sat sipping coke and trying to figure this new puzzle.
I considered and discarded the idea that he planned to
live there after he was married. That didn't jell. I shook my

head. I didn't get it—but I did get a look at a wall clock that said 2:30. I slapped down a nickel and went out in high gear. That report should be in by now.

I dropped the troublesome keys back in my pocket, told myself they were not my business and promised silently I'd replace them as soon as I had the chance.

In the hotel I caught the same elevator with Art Herrot.

"Hi!" I said. "Do they work you night and day too?"

"I'm on day side this week," he said. "King saw your story about the doctor having died from poisoning so he thought it should be followed up. Anything new happened since then?"

"I wouldn't know. I've been out to lunch. Gross and Beton are upstairs though—or were when I left."

"Gross and Beton!" He whistled. "This might turn out something good!"

"Oh, I don't know." I shrugged.

"What do you think?"

"I'm not paid to think," I told him. "Only to report the facts."

He was laughing at that when we got off at the tenth and walked down the hall to the room. A dozen feet away from the door you could hear voices and in front of it every word was distinguishable. Tommy was talking.

"Well, there's nothing here or in the bathroom, and he couldn't possibly have disposed of it. He didn't have time."

I glanced up at the open transom and grinned at Herrot and Grady.

"You couldn't raise much hell in this joint," I said. "Not with the transom open."

Inside the room I walked over to Tommy. "What's missing, Handsome?" I asked.

"How do you know something's missing? You been gone an hour!"

I nodded toward the door, lifting my eyes to the transom. He smiled sheepishly. "Damn! Was I talking that loud?"

"You were. Now what are you looking for?"

"What the poison came in. If he took the stuff himself it's got to be here. A box or a vial of some kind. Or a hypo needle and syringe."

"A hypo needle? How come?"

"The chemist said he died from a poison the Indians in South America put on arrows and darts when they hunt. It must enter the bloodstream to kill; no amount you swallow will do anything but make you sick. So it isn't an accident. It's either suicide or murder!"

LeFevre came bustling over, looking like an excited comic balloon.

"Captain Gross! Murder is impossible in this hotel! Besides, the door was locked from the inside. The doctor must have locked it himself, and only this key could open it from outside!" He waved a key attached to a large brass ring.

"I know, Mr. LeFevre. I know," Tommy said soothingly. "But to prove it suicide we must find whatever the poison was in."

"Nothing has been touched!"

"I'm sure of that," Tommy said. "We'll find it here somewhere."

"But why a box or vial?" I asked. "If it has to enter the bloodstream then only a hypo could do it."

"Oh no! An open cut or wound would serve. We found a pin near the door of the bathroom and the body had a long deep scratch on the left arm. But that poison acts as soon as it hits the blood, so there has to be something here that the stuff came in."

"You won't find it in the bathroom," I said.

"Why not? He died in there, didn't he?"

"Yeah, but all the poisons are in that cabinet over there." I gestured toward the white case. "He might have put some in his hand, then put the box or whatever back in the cabinet. I don't see the suicide angle at all, though."

"Why not?"

"Because I knew Ned and he wasn't the suicide type."

Beton gave me a suspicious look. "You know a whole hell of a lot about that guy for not having been one of his dames!"

I bridled angrily. "I've been learning about him for years—from his dames!" I retorted.

Tommy and Shem walked over to the cabinet and inspected the padlocks.

"Locked tight," Tommy said. "Guess we'll have to break it open."

Again I talked out of turn. "You'll probably find the keys on the dresser. There are two holders there."

The third holder was where it had no business being.

Beton gave me another look, picked up the chain and handed it to Gross. The first small key he tried opened the case.

"If I were you I'd put on gloves before I handled any of that stuff," I advised. "Some may be the kind that only a touch of it on the tongue is needed and you bite your nails, Tommy."

He considered that. "I haven't any gloves with me. How about you, Les? Joe? No?" He glanced at Morrow and Herrot. Both laughed.

"Who ever heard of a reporter on a New Orleans' paper with enough dough or swank to own gloves?" Morrow jibed.

"Here's one who has and does," I said. "I've a pair with me and I'll handle the stuff if you want me to."

Tommy nodded and I fished out my good white gloves, hoping I'd remember to wash them before wearing them again.

"What are we looking for?" I asked. "I don't want to haul all of these things out. They're all clearly stamped or have labels."

"We want something called c-u-r-a-r-e. Never mind the other stuff."

"Curare! That's one of the poisons Doc Rollins mentioned."

"Yeah, I talked to him. It's a resinous substance. See if you can find it."

"In that case it's more than likely in a bottle or vial," I said.

The cabinet had five shelves all filled with containers, small and large. I started on the top shelf, looking only at the bottles and vials. I took them in turn. No curare. I recalled the technical name Rollins had given it, *Strychnos toxifera,* and went over again. No soap. Then I checked the boxes, just in case. It wasn't there.

"What's the matter? Can't you find it?" Tommy squatted down by me.

"It isn't here to find," I said. "There's every poison here you ever heard of and a lot you haven't—but there's no curare."

I stared at the shelves and picked out one container. It was sealed tight.

"There's just this." I got up from the floor where I'd been kneeling while I went over the lower shelves. "Strychnine. And curare comes from a plant of the same family. But you can see this has never been opened."

I sat it on top of the case, then I went back to my chair and parked while I peeled off my gloves.

"This case is as clear as pea soup and getting clearer by the moment. I don't think." I looked around at the circle of faces. "Tommy says it can't be accidental. So it's suicide or murder and both seem equally impossible. Ned's dead from a poison but it isn't to be found in a whole cabinet of poisons. Nuts!"

Morrow chuckled. "Don't take it so hard, Slone. Beton, the ace of Homicide, will have it all figured out in a few minutes."

Beton glared at him and growled something. Tommy stood silently, a worried frown creasing his forehead.

I beckoned him over and he sat on the bed facing me.

"What did that chemist say about curare?" I asked.

"Said it wasn't exactly a rare poison but neither was it one you ran into often. Said it was native to South America and the Indians there take the juice and tip their arrows with it so wounded game can't escape. It kills but doesn't affect the meat of the animal. I've got the name of the plant written down—wait a minute." He fished in his pocket and brought out a slip of paper. "S-t-r-" he began to spell it out.

"*Strychnos toxifera*," I finished it for him. "I know. I even looked for it under that name, but it wasn't there."

"Ummm," he murmured absently, still studying the paper. "The stuff paralyzes the nerves almost immediately. There's some kind of a final convulsion and then the body starts getting stiff."

"Which accounts for the appearance of rigor."

"Yeah. But that's the only answer we have so far." He glared at the cabinet. "Why couldn't that stuff have been in there? If it kills all that fast he didn't have time to throw any container away, so it's got to be here. But it isn't. There's nothing fits the picture but that pin and the scratch on his arm."

"And neither mean a thing," I said. "He had on freshly laundered pajamas. The pin could have been in them, and if he scratched his arm he just pulled the pin out and threw it on the floor."

"I never thought of that," said Tommy. "But it could have happened."

"Listen!" Beton lit up with a sudden idea. "Why couldn't he have meant to make it look like murder? He takes the poison out, gets rid of the thing it came in, empties most of the dope down the drain, keeping just enough to kill himself, then scratches himself and puts the poison on the pin, washes off his hand and then uses the pin!

Why couldn't he have done that, huh? Lots of people commit suicide and try to make it look like murder!"

"It can't be suicide." The flat, positive statement surprised even me.

Beton and Tommy both gaped at me.

"Now listen, Margaret, why can't it be?" Beton asked querulously. "How can it be anything else? Remember that locked door!" The last sentence ended on a triumphant note.

"To hell with the locked door!" I said, remembering something I should have remembered long before and realizing with a sense of shock that the nurse was right. Ned McGowan had been murdered—and very cleverly murdered.

"But you were the first one to point that out!" Tommy said tartly.

"I know. But Ned didn't kill himself. I'll bet a month's pay on it. Anyone want to cover me?"

Beton stared at me hard. He knew damn well I wasn't making bets like that unless I was sure of winning.

"You sound mighty damn sure of yourself!" he said testily. "Get to the point. What the hell are you trying to put over?"

"Just this. A man does not commit suicide when he's in the middle of brushing his teeth!"

7. Toxic Toothbrush

I DROPPED my bombshell and sank back to await the explosion.

"Brushing his teeth!" Beton's voice hit high G. "Are you crazy?"

"Nope. At least not violently."

"Then what the hell do you mean?"

"Just what I said. Ned McGowan was brushing his teeth when he fell dead in the bathroom."

"How do you know he was brushing his teeth?" Beton's eyebrows were high.

"I was here. I saw the body. Toothpaste was caked on his mouth and gums. Look in the bathroom. The toothbrush is on the floor and there's a broken water glass in the basin."

Beton disappeared into the bathroom and came out a minute later with the toothbrush in his hand.

"Here it is! Just like she said."

"I hope you know you've spoiled any fingerprints which may have been on that thing." I looked at his big paw, wrapped around the handle of the brush.

He dropped it like a hot coal, then stooped and picked it up with a handkerchief.

"Oh well, the only prints on it must have been the doctor's."

"And perhaps one other person's—and now yours are there." I turned to Tommy. "What do you think now?"

"I think godammit! That's what I think. And that this is the very hell of a case!"

"So it is," I agreed. "But just what is it?" I knew when

to stop being too smart. Cops don't like too smart reporters.

Tommy shook his head. "Damned if I know. If he was
brushing his teeth it sure can't be suicide. The door was
double locked, so it can't be murder, and the chemist says
it can't be an accident. So I don't know what it is."

Right then I threw caution to the winds.

"I do," I said.

"Oh! You do!" Beton jeered. "Well, let us in on it. What
is it?"

"Murder," I said, much more calmly than I felt.

"Really? Well, where and how did he get the poison?"

I thought: Here we go—and let the bits fall where they
may!

"That's easy to figure," I said. "He got it off the toothbrush."

Jaws dropped as though let down on hinges.

"You're nuts!" Beton shouted. "Just plain nuts!"

"I am not!" I denied, violently. "I've more sense than you
have. At least I can see the nose on my face. Ned didn't
commit suicide. He didn't get poisoned by accident. Then
he was murdered. Killed with a toothbrush!"

Beton was disgusted. "Killed with a toothbrush! Who
ever heard of such a thing?"

"Shut up, Les," Tommy said mildly. "I remember reading a story once about a man killed that way. I suppose it
could be done with several poisons. I don't know about
curare."

"Et tu Brutus." Beton turned an injured stare on Tommy.

"The lad even knows Latin!" I said, nastily. "But he
doesn't know how to get out of the way when a brick
building starts to fall." I'd quite forgotten I'd needed a good
jolt myself to see the obvious.

"Now you shut up, Margaret. Or, wait, don't shut up. Let
me hear how you figured the toothbrush angle?" Tommy
was annoyed but interested.

"Miss Cheng had it figured for murder from the start," I said, sullenly. "Only she hadn't figured out how it was done—or had she? She spoke of how poison could be planted!"

"Planted?"

"Uh huh! She told me all about how she and Ned worked on experiments and how he let his friends in on the poison study. She said it was murder and she meant to prove it. And she went into long detail about how she and Ned always cleaned up after experiments so it couldn't have been an accident. Her talk about tidying and cleaning up gave me an idea."

"About what?" Tommy prodded.

"Well, it was the answer to something that puzzled me earlier."

"What?"

"Well, you see, it's like this—" I began cautiously but excitement gave caution a kick in the pants and I blurted, "It told me a woman had been up here when Ned undressed!"

"How can you say such a thing!" Beton sounded horrified.

"The act's good, but you can skip it," I said. "Tommy! I think I've got the whole thing in a bottle! Ned was killed by a woman, someone he knew and had no fear of—someone who was here with him when he came home last night!"

"But who?" He'd caught my excitement.

"How would I know? All I know is that Ned often spent the night at my house. Brett is almost too neat, and the contrast between his tidily hung clothes and McGowan's things draped over the chairs and floor was strong enough to leave a mental impression. This room is too orderly, except for the dresser."

"Maybe the maid hung his clothes in the closet," Tommy suggested.

"There were no maids on duty when he got home and undressed. The things were put away then."

"You mean—?"

"Exactly!" I anticipated him. "The woman who was here had to be one Ned was intimate enough with to disrobe before her. She hung up his clothes—that's strictly a woman's trick. No man would think of doing it."

"But the curare, Margaret? I told you taking it by mouth wouldn't kill. That washes out the toothbrush theory."

"On the contrary. It clinches it!"

"How?"

"That woman knew he'd been to a dentist and had a tooth pulled!"

"Who told you that?" He looked his amazement.

"Miss Cheng. Dr. McGowan had a tooth pulled from the lower jaw, an impacted tooth that called for a lot of gum cutting. The cavity provided the open wound through which the poison entered the blood!"

"That ties it!" Tommy snapped his fingers excitedly. "Maggie! You've hit the jackpot this time!"

"It's the first one I've ever hit—and don't call me Maggie."

"Oops! Sorry!" He grinned at me. "Well, Margaret, it looks like you've drawn the picture. All we need do is find out who knew he'd had that tooth pulled."

"That search should give you quite a few suspects," I said drily. "No doubt everyone he spoke to after it was out heard the whole story."

His face fell. "Yeah. Guess you're right. But," he brightened, "after all, he couldn't have seen so very many people in just two days."

"Not more than fifty, including patients," I deflated him.

His face dropped again. "Hell!"

"Cheer up, darling. It may not be as tough as it sounds. Let's try a little reconstructing, with me as the woman who did the job. How about it?"

"Okay by me." He grinned widely. "Let's see what kind of a poisoner you'd make."

"Poison being a woman's weapon, I'd probably do all right at it. But seriously, we must figure I'd be someone to whom he'd taught toxicology. I'd have to know he had curare and where it was and about his tooth being pulled. I'd have to be someone in love with him, someone jealous and filled with a sense of having been done wrong."

"How about his fiancee?"

"She's out. In that case he wouldn't have admitted the engagement. There wouldn't have been any to admit."

"Then it must have been some woman he'd been stringing along," he observed brightly.

I gave him a look. "For a smart guy you say the dumbest things at times! Well, say I came up here with him or followed him up and went off on a long tirade of abuse and recriminations about his treatment of me. While I raved on he found my message and called me."

"How could he call you if you were here with him?"

"Are you being funny?" I shot him a look, then realizing how strange the remark must have sounded I laughed. "Oh! That's right. He couldn't very well do that. Well, put it that he found a message to call a reporter he knew and did so. I listened to him make the call, heard him say he was going to marry Olivette, and wild with jealousy decided to kill him. Assuming I hadn't already decided on it before I got here. How'm I doing?"

"Damn good, so far. Now how did you manage to get the poison on his toothbrush? You had to have it or get it somewhere."

"Of course. Well, he undressed while the woman—I mean while I—was here. He emptied his pockets and put his stuff on the dresser. I took his clothes and hung them in the closet. I saw the keys on the dresser and I knew which ones fitted the cabinet."

"You couldn't get in there while he was in the room," Tommy objected.

"No, but I could when he went to the bathroom."

"How do you know he went to the bathroom?"

"If you're going to be smart, I'll stop right now," I threatened.

"Don't get sore, Margaret. I was just kidding. Go ahead."

"All right then. I'd take the poison out, put it in my purse or my pocket, relock the case, and put the keys back. I'd choose the curare because I knew how it worked, and knowing about his cut gum, I'd figure it would be almost impossible to trace murder to me.

"After some more argument, I'd go to the bathroom and put the poison on his toothbrush, knowing he would use it either that night or the next morning. Then I'd come out, argue a while longer to make it look good, and leave.

"Ned let me out, put the latch on—that explains away the locked door—and sometime later used the toothbrush and rang down the final curtain. How is that for a picture of what could have happened?"

"Very pretty. *Very* pretty!" It was Beton. "Very—pretty—indeed!" He dragged the words out. "In fact it could be just what happened and how else would you know so damn much about the method and means?"

It took me a full minute to realize what he was implying.

"Why you poor dumb flatfoot!" I blazed at him. "Haven't you been on the force long enough to learn about reconstructing a crime? That's what I was doing, you ass!"

"Oh is it? Well, if you ask me you know a hell of a lot about how the guy was poisoned."

"No one asked you," I retorted. "You're certainly screwy if you suspect me! That's why the police department in this town stinks—guys like you give it a smell that rises to high heaven!" Then I realized I was being silly. "Oh, nuts to you, my fine feathered friend," I said disgustedly.

He turned to Tommy. "It might be a damn good idea to check on what Miss Slone was doing when this murder took place. How do we know she didn't make a date with him when he called her last night? How do we know she didn't do the job herself? She had the opportunity and she sure seems to know just how it happened. Why can't she figure as the jealous woman in the case?"

"You imbecile! Of all the damn fool things I've ever heard of this wins the dough!" I was in a tearing rage. "I help to drop a nice murder in your lap and you have the brass to accuse me of committing it! You make me sick!"

Beton ignored me. "Funny how come she pulled that poison angle on the coroner so fast." He half-mused. "Sounds to me like she was just wanting to show off how smart she'd been."

"Now listen, you pluperfect jackass—" I started to rise but Tommy waved me back into the chair.

"Shut up, Margaret. And you too, Les. This is so stupid it isn't funny. We have a murder on our hands, a very clever murder—and you two are standing here spitting at each other like a couple of alley cats. We'll never get anywhere if you keep clawing at each other. Margaret was only theorizing. She didn't kill McGowan."

"Yeah? How do we know that? Can she prove she went right home to bed when she left work?" He leveled a finger at me. "Can you prove it?"

"Aw, can the melodrama," I sneered. "I told you I got in my car at 2:15. I stopped for nothing but traffic lights until I got home. I went upstairs, stopped by Brett's room, saw he was out, and went to bed. So there!"

He tucked his thumbs in his trouser belt and said smugly, "That proves exactly nothing to me. Who saw you come in? Did you talk to anyone when you got there? Who can back your story for an alibi?"

"Why you—" I stopped abruptly. No one could back me up! There wasn't a way in the world I could prove what time I got in! I knew it—of course—but proving it was something else. I couldn't!

Six pairs of eyes were fastened on me, six pairs of ears were waiting for me to offer some proof I'd told the truth.

I laughed—but even to my own ears the sound was forced and unnatural.

"This beats me," I said and turned to Tommy appealingly. "I can't really prove what time I got home. No one saw me come in. I don't think anyone even heard me." I laughed again, this time more naturally. "You'll just have to take my word for it."

He patted my shoulder. "Of course I'll take your word for it. You're not the killer type, Margaret. Although it's hard to say just what the killer type is at times. It depends on circumstances and motive."

I looked at him sharply. Was it my imagination or was there a rather speculative gleam in his eyes? I told myself: Some day you'll learn to keep your big mouth shut, Margaret Slone. You're always talking when you should be listening.

I shrugged my shoulders, as if to throw off the tenseness I felt in the air. "All this stupidity is getting us exactly nowhere," I opined. "I thought we were trying to catch a murderer."

"Well, if you ask me—" Beton began, but Tommy cut him short.

"No one asked you. And it might be a good idea if you waited until someone did."

Beton looked ugly, but he shut up.

I looked at my watch; 3:15 and deadline in fifteen minutes. I picked up the phone to call and Morrow looked at his own watch and hightailed for the door. LeFevre followed him. Herrot came and sat by me.

"I'll get my dope from you." He grinned.

I nodded and spoke to Dennis. "Well, McCarthy! I've really got a tale for you," I said.

"You'd better have a good one!" he snapped. "What in hell has got into you, waiting until dealine to phone in? Don't you know a deadline when you meet one?"

"I know a heel when I meet one!" I retorted. "And this

time I don't mean you. I mean Les Beton." I glared at the offending cop.

"What's Beton done to you?"

"Practically accused me of murdering McGowan," I said bitterly.

"Wh-a-a-t! Are you crazy? Why should he do that?"

"I may be a little nuts but even I don't know why he should pull that," I answered. "But here's your story and it's a murder story, Dennis. No doubt about it."

"So you managed to make it murder?"

"It managed to be murder!" I said tartly.

"All right. Start talking." I could imagine him settling to business. Dennis could always tell when I wasn't in the mood for ribbing.

"The poison he got was curare, a product of a strychnine plant. What? No, it wasn't strychnine, it was curare, c-u-r-a-r-e."

"How did he get it?"

"I'm coming to that, if you'll just give me time," I said impatiently.

"All right, but don't take all day."

"Curare kills only when it enters the bloodstream. It's not rare but neither is it used very often in murder. The Indians in South America smear their arrow and dart tips with it when they hunt. As soon as the animal's skin is punctured with the poisoned weapon it drops dead."

"Indians! Arrows! Animals! I thought we were talking about a murder, not a big game hunt!"

"We are!" I snapped. "Keep your Irish down. In McGowan's murder the poison was used by someone who knew their toxicology. NOT a South American Indian! It was planted. McGowan was quite an expert in poisons, it seems. He even wrote articles on the subject and he liked to teach his girl friends all about it. Which wasn't very smart of him."

"How was the poison planted?"

"Well, when he died he was brushing his teeth. The poison was either in the paste or on the toothbrush—most likely the latter. The suspicion is that the poison was put there so he'd get it when he was alone. Whoever did it figured he'd use the brush either that night or in the morning."

"Have they tested the brush yet?"

"They can't while it sits in Beton's pocket!" I said, throwing Les a dirty look. "I don't know what he expects to do with it, but no doubt he'll get around to sending it to the chemist eventually."

Beton's reaction, a hasty departure for the door, gave me a moment's pleasure.

"The brush is now on its way to the lab," I told Dennis. "Whoever did this clever job knew Ned had been to the dentist and had a tooth pulled. Curare won't kill unless it goes in the bloodstream; it only makes you sick to swallow it. The open gum provided entry for the poison."

"Suppose he had stomach ulcers?"

"Now look, smart guy, this is no time for your low humor."

"Well, after all, Maggie, if he had stomach ulcers couldn't the curare kill him?"

"Maybe it could. I don't know. But it didn't because Ned had no ulcers. He got it through that torn gum."

"Okay. Now that you've settled that point, who have they arrested for the murder? You?"

"You'd love that, wouldn't you?" I jeered. "But just because Les Beton is a crack-brained idiot who can't see past his nose doesn't mean I'm going to be arrested. Why should I?"

"I don't know, I'm sure. But he did accuse you, didn't he? You said so."

"I said he 'practically accused me.' There's a difference."

"What brought that on? Your big mouth?"

"Mind your own mouth!" I snapped. "We just had an

argument, that's all. Anyhow, no one has been arrested. We only figured it for murder a short while ago. We don't even have a real suspect yet."

"*We!*" He accented the word heavily. "Say, look, do you work for this paper or for the police force? Reporters who set themselves up as dicks give me a pain in the—"

"Now wait, McCarthy!" I cut in hastily. "Don't get on your ear. It just happened I knew a few things about Ned and certain things I knew didn't fit it with suicide or a natural death. The nurse was against accident and it worked into murder."

"Hell of a case, I'd say. No suspects, no definite evidence. What about the inquest? When will they hold that?"

"Inquest? Oh! The *inquest*! Just a minute, I'll ask Tommy."

"Blat, blat, blat," went the phone—much as it had earlier. I beckoned frantically to Tommy.

"The inquest, when is it?"

"Tomorrow morning. Around 10:00."

I spoke to the blatting phone. "It's at 10:00 tomorrow morning, dear."

"Don't give me that slushy talk. I'm not your dear. Okay, I'll get this much set and please try to call back—"

"I will! I swear it!" I interrupted the old story.

"See that you do." The phone clicked in my ear.

8. *Brett Blows Off*

I LEANED back and took a deep puff on my cigarette. Tommy bent over my chair and I gave him a look, eyebrows at top mast.

"Margaret—er, now look—" He hesitated.

"Yes?" Stiffly. And added, "It's come to a pretty state of affairs when a person can't voice an opinion without some dumb cop getting suspicious!"

"Now, Margaret—"

"That's my name. What are you trying to say?"

"I've been talking to Les."

"I saw you. I hope you gave him hell."

"Now, Margaret, he didn't mean to accuse you of murder. He just caught part of what you said and it sounded like you knew a lot about the way McGowan got bumped."

"As a detective—a chief of detectives—you're supposed to know something about the process of deduction," I snapped at him.

"Hey! Hold on! It was Beton who got you riled, not me! This is Tommy, remember me? I'm your pal!"

"Are you?" I narrowed my eyes, recalling the speculative look he'd given me when Beton was popping off at the mouth.

"Of course, I am," he assured me. "Now I think you've used some darn good deductive theory so far and I want your help and opinion on some other things. Will you play ball?"

When a chief of detectives talks like that! I all but purred!

"You know I will. I've told you about all I know, though."

"You said he and your brother went somewhere for dinner. Where?"

"I have no idea, but I can find out." I called my house again and Bertha answered. Brett, she told me, was not home.

"Where is he?" I asked.

"He headin' fo whar you is," she said succinctly.

I replaced the receiver.

"Brett's on his way over here."

Beton was standing near me, shifting from one foot to the other.

"Well?" I looked at him inquiringly.

"Uh, Margaret. I didn't mean to call you a murderess. But you did talk sort of suspiciously, you know."

"Your sudden contrition wouldn't have anything to do with the fact that you know my big brother is on his way here, would it?" I asked nastily.

He reddened angrily. "Why, you damned red-headed snip! I ain't scared of your brother! And I ain't scared of that rag you work for either! For two cents I'd run you in and have you held on suspicion!"

I fumbled in my change purse, found two cents, and jumped to my feet.

"Oh, you would!" I thrust my hand with the pennies right under his nose. "Well, here's your two cents. Go ahead and take me in! I dare you! I'll have your badge so fast it won't be funny! I'll—"

What else I'd do was cut short by Tommy, who stepped in between us.

"Godammit! I'm sick of your bickering! Now behave or I'll slug both of you! I mean it."

"I'll behave. Just make that lug lay off of me!" I settled back into my chair, glowering at Beton who glared right back.

Joe Shem walked over to me.

"Look, kid. There's no call for you to fight with Les. He's a good guy and a good cop. Go ahead and tell him you're sorry."

I was about to tell Shem where he could go when Grady popped his head in the door and announced a Mr. Slone was out and wanted in.

Gross ordered him admitted and Brett blew in the door. I stared at him, mouth agape. His hair was every which way, his collar open, and he wasn't shaved. He looked like hell.

"Whew!" I whistled. "You're a sight!"

"So what? You say you'll call back and you don't and I try to get you and can't, so I call McCarthy and he tells me you've been accused of murder! I beat it over here without stopping for anything."

"McCarthy's brand of humor stinks," I said bitterly. "Why couldn't you get me? I've only left the room once and I wasn't gone long then."

"The operator said she had orders not to accept any incoming calls to this room unless it was the police."

"Tommy, do you know anything about that?" I asked.

He shook his head, puzzled. "Nothing. I didn't give them."

"Call the operator. That's what she told me." Brett's jaw was jutting a bit.

Tommy picked up the phone and questioned the girl. She said a call had come from the district attorney's office setting down those orders. Tommy hung up and shook his head bewilderedly.

"I don't get it. Why should the D.A. give such an order without telling me about it?"

"Call and ask him." I suggested.

The D.A. knew nothing about it either. Light began to dawn.

"It's a gag!" I exclaimed. "Brett, you know Johnny Morrow. Did you see him downstairs?"

"Sure. He was in the lobby talking to a couple of guys. I said hello to him."

"Is that all you said?"

"All I had time for—the elevator was waiting."

I began to laugh. "That's rich! Morrow figured Dennis and others would call me here, so he puts in that phony order from the booth downstairs thinking he might get a break on the story. Then he passes up a chance for some real information by letting Brett walk right by him! Dope!"

Tommy smiled. "I'd better call off that order." He did that, then turned to me. "Is this your brother?"

I looked at him blankly. "Don't you know Brett? Oh!" I turned to Brett. "This is Tommy Gross, a swell guy and a swell detective," I said. "And this is Les Beton—a detective. You know Joe Shem and Art Herrot."

The amenities over, he turned to me.

"Now then, what's all this about? Are you in dutch?"

"Of course not," I answered the last query first. "Ned McGowan has been murdered though. And in a devilishly clever way."

"Ned murdered? So someone finally washed him out. How?"

I heard his matter-of-fact acceptance of murder with some surprise.

"Yeah, someone washed him out all right." Tommy's satire was subtle. "Washed his mouth out—with a poisoned toothbrush. We think the poison was planted by a woman."

"You don't seem much surprised." Beton watched him warily.

Brett opened his mouth and put his foot in up to the ankle.

"I'm not. Not a bit. I've been telling that guy for years that some dame would kill him before he got distinguished gray hair at the temples."

Beton jumped like a cat on a mouse.

"Now did you! How come you told him that?"

"Because of the way he treated women."

"Whadda y' mean? How *did* he treat women?"

I started to say I'd told that sorry story, then shut up. I'd said enough.

"It's a little hard to explain," Brett said slowly. "Girls, well, they were just a sort of amusement with Ned, and he didn't stay amused with the same one for very long. He played the field, but he did it so every field runner thought she was favorite in the betting. I didn't like that trait in him, but that may have been because I'm a one woman man and my girl knows that. She ought to, she hears it often enough." He grinned.

Tommy smiled warmly. "And when you tell her so you mean it. Right?"

"You're damn tooting I mean it!" Brett's grin widened.

"Who is she? Or is it any of my business?"

"If you'd known me an hour you'd know who she is. I'm surprised Margaret hasn't told you. Her name is Antoinette Merceron. She's the sister of the girl Ned was to marry."

Tommy and Beton both looked at me, somewhat accusingly.

"I did tell you she was Brett's girl!" I defended myself.

"You said she was one of the dames McGowan ran with!" Beton accused.

"Well, she—"

Brett interrupted me, his voice rather tight. "Margaret has never liked Toni, but it's true she did have a few dates with Ned. I was away at the time, working for a private outfit in Chicago. As soon as I came home she stopped going out with him and he took up with Vette."

I sighed with relief but thought: There was a damn sight more to Ned and Toni than that, my lad!

"This McGowan—he was always chasing women, huh?" Beton asked.

"Always chasing them and always brushing them off,"

Brett answered. "I used to tell him that someday he'd try to brush off the wrong woman."

"You did, huh?"

"Sure. Lots of times. When Ned got ready to brush off a woman and she didn't brush easy, he could be a skunk!"

Beton's eyes narrowed. "You didn't like this guy too much, did you?"

"Of course I liked him," Brett asserted. "I just didn't like the way he treated women. Maybe that's because I have several sisters."

"Say, that's right!" Beton exclaimed and I cringed, knowing what was coming next. "Didn't he play around with one of your sisters?"

Brett smiled wryly. "He tried to play around with all of my sisters at one time or another. The youngest one went for him for a while but I soon stopped that."

I smirked, thinking: If he believes that, let him!

"How many sisters have you?" Beton asked.

"Six. Three married and three single at home."

"Did this McGowan date the married ones before they got hitched?"

Brett was getting tired of questions. His jaw jutted out again. "Hey, what's the gag? Am I on the witness stand or something?"

"Of course not." Tommy took over smoothly. "What we really wanted to ask you was where did you and the doctor have dinner last night? If you came back to the hotel with him you may have been among the last to see him alive."

Brett relaxed his jaw into a smile. "I didn't come back. I left him where we had dined, at Mrs. Gerald Dellman's."

"Mrs. Dellman's!" I squawked. "Why, that's who Miss Cheng said—" I stopped, wishing I'd bitten my tongue before I squawked.

"Yes, Margaret?" Tommy queried. "What about Miss Cheng and Mrs. Dellman?"

"Nothing much. You heard those cracks Miss Cheng made to her and also about her and Ned. You were here. Then when Brett said that was where they had dinner it—well, it just sort of surprised me."

"I see. Does Miss Cheng really think Mrs. Dellman is mixed up in this?"

"She does—and she's nuts," I said firmly.

Brett broke in, in an unexpected manner. "You've a nerve calling Lili nuts!" he said angrily. "She's a damn nice girl and plenty smart."

I was amazed and furious. "You shut up! What the hell do you know about it? Were you here when she was holding forth?"

"I must have missed that." Beton looked his curiosity. "What did she hold forth about?"

"Oh, a lot of damn silly nonsense. She accused every woman Ned had ever known of murdering him. Mrs. Dellman knew him."

"It seems to me you've been conducting this investigation!" he sneered.

"That ain't so!" Joe Shem blurted belligerently. "I was right here and heard every word Miss Cheng said before you guys came in. She kept whooping that Doc had been murdered. We didn't think so then and Margaret told her she was nuts. That's all Margaret did."

"We understand, Joe." Tommy hid a smile. "By the way, Margaret. You took that phone away from Miss Cheng. What did Mrs. Dellman say to you?"

"Nothing important." I threw an irritated glance at Beton and Brett. "She was shocked and surprised and wanted to know if there was anything she could do, that's all. Suspecting her would be as stupid as suspecting me. She's not the the killer type either."

To my surprise Beton agreed. "Of course she ain't! She's a real lady and she always buys a couple hundred dollars of tickets to the police ball."

That seemed to settle Mrs. Dellman's innocence as far as Les was concerned. But not so Tommy.

"We have to suspect every woman he was friendly with, married or single. We can't leave anyone out."

I wondered if that sweeping category included me and started to ask, but for once I kept my trap shut. The questioning resumed a static routine.

"What time did you leave the doctor, Mr. Slone?" Tommy asked.

"About 10:00 last night. I had to get to the field and I figured an hour to get home, change clothes, and get to the field. My charter left at 11:00. Toni drove me out, then she went back to rejoin the party."

"Oh! It was a party?"

"Just a small one. Five for dinner, including Mrs. Dellman. Mr. Dellman is out of town. A girl who is a sort of companion-nurse to Marta joined us for coffee."

"I didn't know Mrs. Dellman needed a nurse," Tommy remarked.

"She doesn't, really. She has migraine and she's very nervous. But the girl is more of a companion, even though she is a registered nurse."

"I see. Now one more thing. Who do you know who might want to kill McGowan?"

Brett smiled grimly. "You should have asked how many ex-girls of Ned's might want to murder him. I'd say pretty nearly all of them. That's a large list of suspects."

"I suppose so! Well, put it this way. Was he afraid of anyone?"

Brett snorted. "Him? Hell no! I used to warn him and he laughed in my face. One day he said to me, 'Bub, all women can be had and if they can be had they can be let go when you're ready. Women like to think they're tigresses but actually they're kittens. Let them know you mean scat when you say it and they'll scat.' "

"So that's the way he had it figured."

"That's the way."

Tommy rocked on his heels, back and forth. "Mr. Slone, you said Miss Merceron drove you to the field?"

"She did and we sat in the car talking while the ship was being serviced and warmed up. When the passengers started going aboard I left her."

"And she went back to Mrs. Dellman's?"

"I suppose she did." Brett was getting impatient.

"I realize this questioning is tiresome." Tommy sounded apologetic. "But it is important. If your girl went back, then both sisters must have been seen home by Dr. McGowan. If so, they must have been the last of his friends to see him alive."

"I suppose they could have been. You couldn't call the one who killed him a friend." Brett grinned ruefully.

"The killer doesn't necessarily have to have been the last one to see him alive. That poison could have been planted any time yesterday. We don't know. But we do know the two sisters were with him until late. Is that right?"

"I suppose so."

"You *suppose* so?" Beton stressed the word. "Don't you know? Haven't you called your girl since you heard of your friend's death. Seems to me you'd have done that as soon as you got the word."

Brett looked at him steadily. The look was not friendly.

"I called but they weren't home. They'd gone shopping. Trousseau shopping. Poor Vette, she won't need a trousseau now."

"We'll get in touch with them later," Tommy said.

"Then may I go? Or have you more questions?" Brett asked.

"No more questions and you may go when you wish." Tommy smiled. "You're not under suspicion, you know. We're looking for a woman."

There was no answering smile from Brett.

"I'm glad to hear that. Your buddy seems to be willing to suspect anyone, man or woman."

"Oh, him!" I said airily. "Pay no attention to that dope."

Beton glared at me and opened his mouth to speak. I unsheathed my claws and waited. But Tommy cut us off with a stern look and a warning.

"All right now, you two! You know what I told you."

We subsided sullenly as Ed Jolly, another Homicide man, walked in. He went at once to Tommy and spoke in a low tone. Low as it was my sharp ears caught the murmur.

"That toothbrush was still coated with that poison."

"That cinches it for murder then!" Tommy said. "No man would go to all that trouble to commit suicide."

I flashed a triumphant look at Beton. "Did you hear that, ninny?"

"Hear what?"

"What Jolly just said. It was the poisoned toothbrush, just like I said! Now maybe you won't be so goddam smart when someone tries to tell you something!"

"Yeah? Well, I'd still like to know how come you knew so damn much about how he got it!"

Brett doubled up his fists and glared at the detective. "Listen you—!"

Tommy interfered. "Now, look here, Les!" he said angrily. "If you don't stop being so damn funny I'll take you off the case. I've had just enough!"

I giggled at Beton's discomfiture but sobered as another thought struck me. "Hey, Jolly! Was Johnny Morrow in the lobby?"

He nodded. "Sure. Why?"

"Did you tell him about that brush?"

"Yeah. The D.A. said it was okay to let you guys have it."

I groaned and looked at my watch. Then I brightened. I could get it in in plenty of time for the Pink. I asked Brett to wait and called Dennis.

"The brush was poisoned," I told him. "Coated with curare. Good alliterative line, that. Anyhow it ties up the case as murder."

"Fine. Come on in and do a feature on it."

"Feature?" I howled. "Now? You're screwy! It's 5:20 and I'm off in ten minutes. I'm going home."

"I said to come in and do a feature on it. I want one for the Streak."

"But I'm—"

"You heard me," Dennis said quietly.

"Oh all right!" I slammed down the receiver, grumbling, "I'll do him a feature! Some day I'll do him dirt!"

I started for the door but Tommy motioned me to wait.

"What do you want?" I asked ungraciously. "I'm in a hurry."

He reddened self-consciously. "I just wanted to know if you were going to be home this evening."

I grinned impudently. "I 'spect so darlin'. Why? Are you planning to make a social call or am I to be tailed?"

"Don't be nasty. I just wanted to know where to reach you in case I needed you, that's all."

"I don't know why you should need me for anything, but I'll be home—in my bed." At the time I meant it.

Brett and I left and caught the elevator. Outside on the sidewalk I stopped and looked at him.

"You going any place but home?"

"I guess I'll have to go out to Toni's. Vette must be pretty broken up. She loved Ned and I believe he really loved her. They'd probably have been very happy."

"I doubt it," I said cynically. "But you can't tell. Some of the worse chasers develop into ardent hearth-huggers. What time will you be home?"

"Early. I'm tired out."

"I'll see you later then—and before you go anywhere comb your hair and get a shave. You look like the wrath of God!"

I left him and walked over to the newspaper building, taking my own sweet time about getting there. I strode defiantly into the city room and got the shock of my life. Dennis beamed on me and the copy desk men placed me in an admiring circle! I was the hit of the evening!

So completely did I wallow in it, I even let McCarthy talk me into doing a complete résumé of the story and a feature. It wasn't until I'd worked up a sweat getting it all done that I began to wonder if I hadn't been rooked by a smart Mick. I was harboring that suspicion when I left the city room.

Downstairs I stood for a moment, undecided whether to go home or stay in town for dinner and a show. There was a picture at Loew's I wanted to see. I decided to stay down. If Tommy wanted me he could damn well wait until I got home. With a fine sense of freedom, I got in my car and started for Kolb's.

In the restaurant I ordered, then called home and told Bertha I'd not be there for dinner. I ate leisurely, enjoying the first free evening I'd had for weeks. Finished with the meal, I took a cigarette—preparing to idle over coffee.

There were no matches on the table and none in my purse so I reached into my suit coat pocket. Once more my hand closed over that filched pair of keys.

"Damn!" I spoke aloud and took them out. Once more I studied the chain and the two keys, my curiosity mounting by the second.

What could they mean to this murder? Whose apartment did they belong to? What in time was Ned McGowan doing with them?

To all three questions I told myself sternly: None of your damned business. I made up my mind again to get rid of them at the earliest moment possible, slipped them back in my pocket, paid my check and left—intending to walk over to the theater.

I never got there.

9. *Keys to Trouble*

~~~~~~

I DON'T know just when I decided to at least have a look at the place those keys belonged to. Perhaps I'd been sub-consciously meaning to do it all along. But I found myself driving there instead of walking to the show. I stopped on St. Ann Street and parked directly across from the house.

It was typical of French Quarter buildings. They all look like hell from the outside unless you are keen enough to notice and appreciate the beauty of the delicate wrought-iron balcony trim. It's as lovely as lace. The houses gen-erally are badly in need of a coat of paint and this was no exception, from what I could see in the gleam of the street lamp. You must go inside to find the grace the old architects put into such places. I sat debating whether or not I should go inside this one.

My dash clock said 7:45. I looked at the metal tag on the key chain: Apt. Four. If the building followed true to form that should be third floor front. I glanced up at the win-dows. Dark. In fact, the whole front was dark and a To Let sign hung over the second floor balcony rail.

Suddenly I made up my mind, took a small pocket flash from the glove compartment, got out, and crossed the street. With a sense of urgent excitement prodding me, I fitted the large key into the patio gate lock and, heart thudding, slipped through the shadowed courtyard and up the stairs to the third floor landing. There had been a dim bulb on the second floor but none on the third. I used my flash and located Four just where I'd figured it to be.

I controlled a strong impulse to turn and run, took my

courage in both hands, and moved slowly to the door. It was fitted with an oddly worked brass knocker: an elephant's head with raised trunk. Irrelevantly I thought: I've never seen a knocker like that before. I lifted it and rapped smartly. If anyone came I could say I had the wrong place.

There was no answer but I thought I heard a movement inside. I rapped again and listened intently. Right then was when I should have left, but I counted to twenty and tried the other key. The tumblers turned easily. I took a deep breath, opened the door softly, and faced pitch darkness. A faint odor of some odd perfume came wafting out of the dark room. Behind me was the feeble beam of the light on the second floor landing. Before me—blackness.

A queer premonition rose in me and I hesitated a second, then clipped my flash back on and stepped inside. I meant to find a wall switch and get some light, even if it meant being arrested for breaking and entering. But my flash happened to be turned down on the floor when I went in and it got no higher. Ringed in its small circle of light was a head, an ugly stain spreading under it and darkening the light carpet.

My first thought was to get the hell out of there and quickly. The second was to see who lay there and how badly hurt she was. That impulse took me, with reluctant, dragging steps, over to the prone figure. I bent down and played my flash on her face.

Lili Cheng lay there, bleeding and unconscious. My mind revolted against the possibility of anything worse than that.

"Oh my God!" I exclaimed and added, as if she could answer, "What the hell happened to you?"

I knelt down and started to lift the small Celestial and there was a celestial explosion inside my skull.

I awakened to a splitting headache and a fast forming resolution never to mix homebrew and gin again. Then I tried to remember where I'd drunk homebrew and gin. If

I hadn't, what was causing this head? And what made the bed so lumpy? My mattress at home wasn't like this. In that case, where in hell was I and how had I got there? I groaned and turned over, rolling only about three inches from bed to the floor.

I lay there a minute, trying to collect my wits, and suddenly the whole picture came back to me: The dark room, Miss Cheng's head in the beam of the flash, and the explosion in my own head.

I told myself: Someone conked me on the head; hit me from behind, the skunk! But why? And who did it?

Because I'd found Miss Cheng—and the same person who hit her had hit me too. I must have fallen over the nurse; her back was the lumpy bed I'd been laying on. I knew I should try to get up and do something, but my head was a roaring mass of pain, so I just lay there another moment or two. Or maybe it was an hour.

After a while I began to wonder what hour of night it was. It must be late because the moonlight was casting weird shadows around the room and the moon was past full. Vaguely I sensed a discordant note about the room. The heavy drapes were pulled back from the windows which opened to the balcony. That's where the light was coming in. When I'd been outside I'd have sworn those drapes were drawn together. I decided they must have been because now a faint glow reflected from the street lamp as well as the moon, and the room had been pitch black when I entered.

My mouth went dry with fear as a new and terrifying thought struck me. Perhaps the person who'd assaulted us was still in the room! Frankly, I was scared witless and hadn't sense enough to figure that whoever wielded whatever it was that had brained me must have gone long since. Long moments dragged by before I worked up enough courage to move at all. Then I simply edged over an inch or two—the floor felt solid and friendly and heaven only knew what might be lurking in the shadows!

My eyes gradually adjusted themselves to the dimness and finally I decided to sit up. I couldn't, I told myself, just lay there all night. Movement brought a flash of pain and I groaned, then cringed back—expecting disaster. But the only sound was my own loud, terrified breathing.

I felt cautiously of the back of my head. There was an egg-sized lump there and it hurt like hell. I rubbed it tenderly, relieved to discover the skin hadn't been broken and I wasn't bleeding. But Miss Cheng! She *had* been bleeding! I thought: My God! She may have bled to death by now and me just laying here and letting her bleed!

I struggled to my feet and groped along the wall until I located a switch and snapped it on. For the first time I really appreciated Thomas Edison!

Light, beautiful light, flooded the room. Weird, menacing shadows became prosaic chairs, tables, and other pieces of furniture. But the sprawled and alarmingly still figure of Miss Cheng gave the lie to the otherwise harmless appearance of the room. So did the wicked-looking poker which lay a couple of feet away from her.

I realized it was what we'd been hit with and started to pick it up. Then I remembered prints and drew back hurriedly. The motion brought a twinge of pain and I felt of the still swelling lump, giving pious thanks that I'd never bobbed my hair. Undoubtedly the thick knot had cushioned the blow. But—the thought chilled me—the nurse had short hair.

I knelt beside her and searched for a pulse. There wasn't any. She was not only quite dead, she was growing cold.

Fear rolled back like a tidal wave. I stood up and moved hastily toward the door. Then I stopped and grimly pulled myself together. I thought: I must get the police and get them right away!

I looked around for a phone but saw none—it must be in one of the other rooms. But maybe the murderer was hiding in one of them? I wished I had a gun and the wish was father to a bright idea. I began looking for one in the large walnut desk near the door.

I searched through it. No gun. Then I crossed the room and began going through a chest of drawers, keeping a weather eye on the doors and balcony windows. In the third drawer I found a .38 revolver, fully loaded. My fingers curled gratefully around the cold metal.

Bold as brass now, I stalked over and threw open a door leading to the bedroom, calling loudly to anyone in there to come on out, I had 'em covered! No murderer appeared. I repeated the performance at the dining room door, then went on to the kitchen, turning on all lights as I marched. I tried the bath last, but turned up nothing more lethal than a sleepy tom cat, who almost scared me into a fit when he leaped up from the floor and scatted out, brushing against my legs as he ran.

I returned to the kitchen and at once realized what Miss Cheng had meant when she said the doctor had another place where he carried on his experiments. This kitchen was a lab, a darn well-equipped one too.

"Well!" I spoke out loud and the sound of my voice comforted me. "Now I know what he was doing with those keys! But it's a hell of a funny place to have a laboratory. Mebbe he used it for other purposes too!"

I went back through the apartment, looking behind curtains and in coat closets. No one was there but me; the cat and Miss Cheng's body—and I had to do something about the latter right away.

The phone was in the bedroom but it did me no good. The line was dead. I'd just have to go downstairs and find a phone or a cop—and I dreaded the trip through that dark courtyard. But dark patio or light, what I most wanted was a strong arm of the law right beside me, and the sooner I

found one the better. Back in the living room the sight of
the dead nurse strengthened my desire for a shield-wearer.
I opened the door and fled down the stairs, taking some of
them two at a time.

Outside I scurried across the courtyard, which wasn't
dark at all but was bathed in the silver of the late moon.
When I reached the patio gate I had a moment that should
have turned my hair snow white—it wouldn't budge and I
knew damn well I hadn't locked it!

I stood there shaking and trying to remember what I'd
done with the keys. I thought, frantically: I can't, I won't
go back to that apartment alone! Then I thought of my
pockets and went weak-kneed with relief when I found the
keys tucked in one of them.

Trembling like gelatine, I got the gate open, went through
it like all hell was behind me, shot across the street, and
jumped in my car. Not until then did I realize I didn't have
my purse and it must still be on the floor beside Miss
Cheng! My car keys were in it.

This last blow was too much. I dissolved in helpless, hysterical tears, whimpering, "I can't, I won't go back in there!
I want a cop!"

I bawled for several minutes before I realized this was
not getting me anywhere. I stopped crying and turned on
the dash light. It said 2:15 and I'd gone in that building
before 8:00. I must have been out for hours. Irrelevantly I
thought: It's exactly twenty-four hours since I started home
after talking to Ned. Now both he and his nurse have been
murdered and I've got to get a cop.

"What a mess!" I spoke aloud and again the sound of my
voice was remotely comforting. At least I was still alive and
could talk. My mind began to function again and I looked
in the glove compartment where I always kept a dollar bill
for emergencies. Well, this certainly was one! I found the
bill, pocketed it and got out of my car turning my footsteps
toward Royal Street.

St. Ann Street was quiet and deserted. Which suited me fine. I think I'd have fled screaming at the sight of anyone but a policeman. On the corner of St. Ann and Royal I saw a parked cab and started for it. The driver stepped up to open the door, then stepped back hurriedly. In the light from the street lamp I saw his face go ashen.

"What's the matter?" I asked impatiently. "What are you staring at?"

"You—you, you've got blood all over you!" His voice was frightened.

"I'm not surprised," I answered. "Let's get going."

He made no move to get going, but stood rigid—his eyes popping wide. I followed his gaze to my belt line. The pistol was tucked in it. I'd thrust it there when I'd made sure the apartment was empty.

He backed off a foot and looked like he was going to cut and run.

"You—you sh-shoot someone?" he quavered.

"Good God no! Do I look like a murderess?"

"N-n-no. But you got a gun and you're all bloody and *you* ain't bleeding!"

I fought for control, lost the fight, and went off into a gale of semi-hysterical laughter.

"Don't be a bloody ass!" I advised, when I could finally speak. "I haven't shot anyone. Just you get in and drive me to police headquarters as fast as you can."

That convinced him murder had been done and most likely by me.

"How about the Third Precinct?" he asked. "That's closer."

"I don't care if it is," I said irritably. "You're being paid to drive, not to think for me. I want headquarters. Now get going."

I climbed in the cab and after a momentary hesitation he got in and drove off. It was the fastest cab drive I'd ever had.

Inside I headed for the detective's office. It was empty, so I made for the pressroom. I'd probably find them all in there swapping lies with the night side reporters. I was right.

Standing in the security of the pressroom door, facing the familiar faces, I went suddenly weak in the knees and clung to the jamb, my legs wobbling.

Alarm and concern painted itself on the faces around me while waves of weakness rolled over me and threatened to wash me out.

Someone grabbed me by the arm and got me to a chair. Then came a babel of voices, all asking questions.

"F'crissakes, Slone! What happened to you?"

"How'd you get all bloody?"

"What are you doing with that gun?"

"Jeesus Keerist! What kinda brawl you been in?"

"What the hell you been up to now?"

My head started to throb again. I found my voice.

"Shut up!" I yelled at them. "Shut up, all of you!"

They shut. I looked around the circle of astonished expressions and singled out Rudy Gross, Tommy's brother— only recently promoted to a plainclothes man. I got up and motioned to him.

"Come into your office. I've got to tell you about something."

I started for the hall and the floor came up and hit me in the face.

Lights hurt my eyes and I closed them again quickly. As if in a dream I heard a bedlam of excited voices.

"Wet this handkerchief again!"

"No, just pour the water on her face!"

"Hell, pour some of this gin down her throat! That'll bring her around!"

"Didja feel that lump on her noddle? Big as an egg! Someone musta beaned her!"

"Stand back, you guys! Give her some air!"

"Gimme that gin, she's coming to!"

Through half-open eyes I could see a spinning white circle. I opened my lids wide and the circle slowed and gradually swung to a stop, resolving itself into a group of worried faces. I struggled to a sitting position on the press-room couch, looked around me, and laughed out loud.

"Don't look so upset, children. I'm all right."

"Yeah? What the hell happened to you?" Rudy asked.

"Uh huh! Where did you get that wallop on the head?" Barney de Sales, our morning paper police reporter, wanted to know.

I looked at the eager expressions on the two beat men's faces. Instinct reasserted itself. Why should I make them a present of this story? Hadn't I suffered and nearly died for it? In a few minutes it would be too late for their papers and I'd have it exclusively. I'd keep it. To hell with them!

"I had a car accident," I said. "Hurt my head and had to leave my car on the street. A cab brought me here and I was going to report it."

"Report a car accident to a *detective?*" Ed Walker, who worked night-side for the opposition, snorted.

"Yeah! And what about that gun? And the blood?"

"The gun is one I keep in my car," I lied. "I didn't want to leave it."

"That egg is on the back of your head," De Sales pointed out. "And your hair isn't bloody."

"So what? It's not your business, but mine." I turned to Rudy. "Will you please take me home? I'm completely pooped."

"Sure kid," he said. "Come on, let's go."

I followed him out and once away from the pressroom I tried to break into a run. But Rudy had tight hold of my arm—he thought I needed to be helped to the car.

"Leggo of me and let's get the hell away from here!" I hissed at him. "I'm in the very hell of a mess and that's not the half of it! I damn near got killed and Miss Cheng did!"

"What?" he asked, startled out of his solicitude.

I jerked away from him and broke into a trot. He jogged alongside of me, asking questions I only half heard.

"Where's your car? I'll tell you all about it in a minute."

He pointed to a closed car on the far side of the lot. "That black Chrysler over there."

I speeded up and climbed into the car. He followed me. Inside and beside the muscular arm of the law, safe and sound, I broke down and really let go.

"She's dead!" I bawled. "Deader'n hell. I don't know who killed her and klunked me too, and I don't know how long she's been dead. She may have been alive when I first got there but when I came to she was dead."

He shook me, none too gently. "What the hell are you talking about? Who's dead? How did you get that lump on your head?"

I pulled myself together with an effort and told him the story. I left out only one thing: How I happened to have keys to the apartment.

He listened without interrupting. When I stopped talking he asked, "Who hit you, a man or a woman? Or don't you know?"

"I'm not sure, but I think it was a woman."

"Why?"

"There was a scent of perfume in the apartment. Of course, it might have come from Miss Cheng, but I don't think so."

"Where is the apartment?"

I looked at his dash clock, 3:05 and too late for the morning papers even if the boys followed us. I gave him the St. Ann Street number and we pulled out of the parking lot. He drove off and I tried to get my nerves unknotted.

We drove up and parked in front of the house, got out, and went in through the still open gate. I couldn't remember whether or not I'd left the door upstairs open; if not I'd have to expose the keys. When we got there would be time enough to start worrying about that.

I followed him up the curving stairway and brought up at the door to number Four. It was ajar, a patch of light outlining the opening. Rudy unlimbered his police special and went in. I trotted after him.

The place was just as I'd left it: lights all on, doors standing open, drapes pulled back, and, on the floor, Miss Cheng's body.

Rudy bent over her and examined the wound. I picked up my courage and looked too. Then I felt better about the time I'd lain scared witless on the floor. The blow must have killed her instantly. The wound was big enough to put a fist in.

"Has she any perfume on?" I asked.

He sniffed, his face close to the body. "Nope, she just has a nice clean smell."

"Then another woman has been here. I don't waste my scent on working hours and I can still smell perfume."

He straightened up, sniffed and nodded. Then he looked at the prone figure again. "Someone sure busted hell out of her. Doesn't seem possible a woman would have the strength to strike a blow like that."

"I've read that Chinese have very thin skull structure," I said. "And she had bobbed hair. My knot caught part of the blow I got, but even so I must have been out for hours."

He spotted the poker, wrapped his handkerchief around his hand, and picked it up. Blood and strands of hair were matted on the handle end.

"Hmmm. It was held by the stirring end. There may be prints. Guess I'd better call Tommy and have him get Doc Rollins and come on over here."

"You'll have to call from outside. This phone is dead."

"Wires cut?"

"I didn't look. It's in the bedroom if you want to check."

"It can wait. I'll go on out and find a phone. You stay here."

My protest was loud and fervent.

"You'll be all right," he said, handing me back the gun I'd dropped in the pressroom. "Just keep this handy and if anyone tries to come in let 'em have it. But," he grinned, "for Pete's sake don't shoot me! When I get back I'll whistle, like this—" he whistled "Yankee Doodle Dandy."

I was still protesting as he went clattering down the stairs. Left alone, I wandered about the big room, my back hair raising every time I heard a creak which, in that old house, was often. I retrieved my purse and began planning my story in my mind. I wondered how Dennis would take it. He'd sure want to know how in hell I got mixed up in this mess.

I stopped in front of the chest where I'd found the pistol and saw the drawer was still open. I started to shut it when I noticed a sheaf of paper slips. I took them out and leafed through them. Notes, payable on demand and made out to Marta Dellman. I added the total and whistled with surprise. Sixty-eight thousand dollars!

I started to replace them, thought better of it, and put them in my purse. Might as well be hanged for a sheep as a lamb—if I got caught. They might save her embarrassment if I could get them to her without it being known.

A second packet of papers caught my eye and I pulled them out too. Letters this time. All tied together. I untied them and glanced through. All were addressed to Ned, either to the office or the hotel, and had been mailed from all over, some were from abroad. The handwritings were feminine but not in the same hand. I'd turned them over to look at return addresses when a stealthy step on the stairs brought me alert. I dropped them in my purse too, and crept to the door, gun in hand.

Breathless, hidden behind the partly open door, I waited for the intruder and grimly decided to shoot first and ask questions later. But the sounds halted, stopped, then started again—this time going rapidly downstairs. I scurried out and took after the fugitive. Rounding the second floor landing, I looked down the stairwell and saw a woman kiting down the last few steps.

"Stop!" I yelled. "Stop or I'll shoot." But she was already in the patio.

I raced into it, just in time to hear the gate slam. A split moment later I threw it open, but she was already turning the corner—out of range of gun or recognition. A faint scent seemed to linger in the air.

Panic swept over me and I thought: I'm getting out of this bloody place! To hell with it—I'm going home!

A powerful motor zoomed down Chartres Street, narrowly missed a sedan turning the corner, and roared off toward Canal. The sedan skidded into St. Ann and came to a screeching stop in front of the patio gate. It was Rudy's and he was raging mad.

"Did you see that damn fool woman?" He howled, leaping from the car.

"I saw her all right and I'm—"

"Why, goddammit! She nearly wrecked me! There ought to be a law! Did you notice what kind of car she had?"

"Only that it had plenty of power. But I'll bet the driver was the woman whom I just caught sneaking up the stairs. I chased her but she got away."

It dawned on him that instead of being where he'd left me, I was parked on the curb—gun in hand.

"What? Did you see who she was?"

"No. She ran too fast for me. I heard the car start and a second later you almost crashed with her car. She—she may have been the murderess!"

As the import of the last words struck me, I began to shake.

"I've had enough," I said flatly. "I'm going home. Right now."

"You can't do that!" he protested quickly. "Tommy's coming right over. He wants to talk to you."

"If he wants me he knows where I live. I'm going home, do you hear?" My voice rose to a hysterical scream. "Don't you dare try to stop me! I won't stay here! I won't do it. I want to go home!"

"Shhh." He put an arm around my shaking shoulders. "You'll wake the whole street. You can go home. I'll take you as soon as Tommy gets here."

"I'm going right now! This minute!"

"You're in no condition to drive. You're shaking all over."

"I can drive. I can drive anywhere so long as it's away from here!" I headed for my car, Rudy tagging after me.

"I wonder if the landlady lives there?" he queried conversationally. "Looks like all the ruckus tonight would have roused someone."

I turned on my ignition before answering. "I don't know. She may be in the rear. Those walls are thick, noise doesn't carry far. The first and second floor fronts seem to be empty." I stepped on the starter.

"Yep. Well, we'll have a look around when Tommy gets here. I wish you'd wait."

"Not a chance. I'm scramming." I handed him the revolver. "Take this damn thing and f'crissakes explain how my prints got on it or Beton will be accusing me of something else."

"Les? What did he accuse you of?"

"Murdering Ned McGowan—that is, he practically accused me of it. I'll tell you about it someday. Right now I'm leaving. Good-by!" I shoved the gear in first and rolled off.

Turning into Royal Street, I looked at the clock—4:05. I'd been back in that place an hour. Indeed, I'd practically spent the night there! I giggled nervously: Fine thing! Spending the night in Ned McGowan's apartment!

10. *Morning Melodrama*

I PUT the car in the garage at home and opened the back door. A cluster of anxious faces greeted me. Mother, Vangie, Marian, and Brett all threw questions at me.

That was all I needed.

I'm still apologizing for the things I said that morning but, at the moment, the sight of them and the sound of their yapping was too much for me.

I called them assorted and fancy damn fools, refused to answer any questions, and stalked to the phone alcove to call Dennis. I knew it was the hell of a time to awaken anyone but I had no intention of going to work at any 8:30 and I wanted to give him the story.

Rudely awakened, he started yowling like a sore bear, and set off another explosion of temper.

"All right dammit! If that's the way you feel about it you can go to hell! It may not mean a thing to you that I almost got my head caved in tonight. But it's my head and it means plenty to me! I'm through. I'm quitting. No job in the world is worth the trouble—not to mention the danger—I've been through tonight!"

I slammed down the phone and had my foot on the second floor landing when the phone bell shrilled.

"If that's Dennis tell him I've gone to China where it's nice and quiet!" I called to my mother. "And tell him to mail my check and get the story from the police. And," I added viciously, "you can tell him he's welcome to that pint he welched on—he can go soak his head in it!"

I marched to my room, locked the door, and plumped down on the bed. I thought: T'hell with it. I'm through with the whole kit and kaboodle. I'm going to bed and to sleep.

I kicked off my shoes, took off my hose, and removed my jacket. I'd just started to get out of my skirt when someone rapped on the door.

"I'm not home!" I called out.

"It's me," said my youngest sister, without regard for grammar.

"Well, go away," I answered.

"Please, Margaret! I've got to see you!"

Something urgent in her tone propelled me to the door. I opened up and she slipped in, her pointed little face drawn and haggard, big blue eyes filled with tears and trouble.

"What's the matter?" I asked. "Can't it wait until later?"

A burst of tears answered my question.

"Oh, Lord!" I exclaimed wearily. "Now what? All right, tell me."

"Margaret," she choked through tears, "Margaret, she killed Ned! I know she did. I heard her threaten him!"

"I don't give a damn who killed him," I said brutally. "He's dead and good riddance to him. He was no good and what the hell are you bawling about?"

She backed off, a hand over her mouth, eyes stricken and staring at me as though I were some kind of a monster.

I thought: Very dramatic pose—and grew annoyed with her.

"I never thought my own sister would refuse to listen to me; would speak so about the man I loved!" Her voice throbbed huskily.

"You can stow the melodrama!" The words gritted between my teeth. "I've had enough real drama today to last me for a lifetime. I don't mean to take any nonsense from you. Ned McGowan probably deserved what he got and you can be grateful the cops aren't suspecting you of his murder. As far as I'm concerned I hope whoever did it gets away with it! Now beat it!"

She backed off a step, eyes wide and accusing.

"How can you be so cold-blooded?" Her eyes narrowed speculatively. "Or is it possible you were the one I heard threaten him?"

I actually heard the last thread of my patience snap. I grabbed her and started shaking her. A moment or two later Brett was holding me while Mother held onto Vangie.

I jerked away and felt the sides of my neck where she had used her too-long-for-good-taste nails on me. The scratches stung and over the sound of voices I could hear the phone ringing. Dennis, I supposed. Let him ring.

I gathered the raveled threads of my nerves together and faced my family. "Get that hellion out of here!" I snarled. "I can't take any more. So get out, all of you, and let me go to bed."

Brett took Vangie from Mother and half-carried, half-dragged her out of the room. Mother lingered, a question in her eyes.

"No!" I said tartly. "Positively no! I'll tell you nothing and I'm not home to anyone until I get some rest. Then I'll be able to cope with people again."

She left and quiet settled over the room. But Vangie's muffled sobbing was like a troublesome conscience. I resisted the impulse to go comfort her.

"Damn fool kid!" I muttered. "I suppose I shouldn't have jumped her like that, but, good God! I've had enough!"

I got out of the rest of my clothes and too tired to put on a gown, climbed in bed in my birthday suit.

Dawn was sending its gray tones into the room. I stared at the window for a minute, then got up and pulled the shutters closed and piled back in bed. I closed my eyes and willed myself to sleep, but my mind refused to obey and continued to race around in scattered thoughts.

My head began to ache again and I felt the back of it. Now the lump felt like a golf ball and was tender to the touch. I snapped on the bed lamp and looked in the night-table drawer for aspirin. There wasn't any, so I got up and looked in the dresser drawers. None there. I knew there had to be a bottle in the bathroom but I hated to make the effort so I got back in bed. The pounding and throbbing got steadily worse and driven by near desperation I got up, pulled on a robe, and went to the bathroom.

Vangie stood by the basin, shaking and sobbing and holding a bottle of mercury tablets in her hand!

I lunged for her and grabbed the bottle.

"You fool!" I grated. "What do you think you're doing?"

"Give me that poison!" she demanded. "It's my life isn't it? I don't want to live with Ned dead!"

I hauled back and let her have it and she went for me like a wild cat, fighting silently and viciously. But I had twelve pounds the best of her and in the close, panting struggle I soon had her winded. I shoved her aside and emptied the tablets into the commode. Then I turned on her in a rage.

"What the hell would your death solve?" I demanded. "Do you want to bring shame and disgrace on a decent family by killing yourself over a man who never gave a damn about you?"

She sneered at me. "Now who's being melodramatic? What do you know of my affair with Ned?"

"I know he was going to marry another girl—not you!" I exclaimed vehemently. "Just wait until Mother hears about this little stunt!"

"You wouldn't dare tell her!"

"Oh wouldn't I though! Just wait!"

"She'll be wild!"

"What do you think she'd have been if you'd managed to swallow that stuff? Tame?"

The fight went out of her like air out of a leaky tire.

"I must have been crazy. I didn't think of that. Please, Margaret, don't tell Mama on me."

She was my kid sister again. I took her cold hand and held it in mine.

"Look, baby, tell we what this is all about. I knew you had a crush on Ned but I thought that was all over. It seems I was wrong."

Several seconds dragged by before she spoke. Then, "Let's go in your room," she said in a small, tense voice.

I sat on the bed and pulled her down beside me, but she slid off and crumpled at my knees—sobbing uncontrollably.

"Why," I inquired of the furniture, "must things like this happen to me?"

At last she quieted down and started to talk.

She was anything but over Ned McGowan, and when she heard he was going to marry Vette she was wild with jealousy.

"I went to the hotel last night and he wasn't home," she sobbed.

"Last night? But he was dead then!"

"I mean night before last," she whimpered. "He wasn't in and I sat on the exit stairs to wait. He had to pass by them and I knew I'd see or hear him go by."

She described how she'd waited several hours until at last she heard the elevator stop and his voice asking the boy to bring him some cigarettes and the morning paper.

"He walked past the stairs and he was humming. I started to follow him in a few minutes but the elevator stopped again and I ducked back out of sight. A woman got off and went down the hall. I waited until I figured she had time to get in her room, then I came back out and went toward his."

"Did you go in his room?" I asked tensely. Much depended on the answer.

"No!" She looked at me impatiently. "That's what I'm

trying to tell you. That woman was going to Ned's and she was in there when I got to the door. The transom was open and I could hear every word she said. I heard her tell him she'd kill him."

"Who was she?"

Vangie shook her head. "I don't know. I never saw her face."

"But you heard her voice. You heard them talking. Didn't he call her name while you were listening?"

"No. He just told her not to be silly, that he wasn't worth the trouble she'd get into if she killed him."

"Well, he told the truth that time!" I said bitingly.

I felt Vangie's withdrawal and went on hurriedly. "What did you do, just stand there?"

"No. I knew the elevator boy was bringing Ned some things and I didn't want him to catch me listening at the door. I left and walked down four flights and caught the elevator on the sixth floor. Then I walked down St. Charles three blocks and caught a cab."

"Thank God you had sense enough for that!" I exclaimed. "Who, besides the elevator boy, saw you?"

"I don't think anyone did. But I was so upset about Ned I didn't notice."

"Upset about him marrying Olivette or because a woman threatened to kill him?"

"Well, both. I even thought of calling the police and telling them what I'd heard."

I didn't say she might have saved his life if she'd done so. I didn't really think so. But she might have put the police on a fresher trail if she had called. I didn't mention that either. She had enough grief without adding self-reproach.

"What time did you get to the hotel?"

"Around 9:30."

"What time did he come in?"

"It was after 1:00 I know. I got home just a few minutes before you came in. I heard you come upstairs. That was about 2:30."

"That's good," I said, remembering Beton and his screwy ideas. "One more thing. Did the same elevator boy take you upstairs and bring you down?"

"I didn't notice."

"No one ever seems to notice bellboys, waiters, and such," I remarked. "But they have a bad habit of noticing everything. I wish you'd have told me about this sooner."

"I wanted to call you but I was afraid."

"Afraid of what?"

"Well, I was scared Mama might hear me talking."

"Hmmm. Where did she think you went that night?"

"To a show."

"A show—" I thought a second, my mind racing in circles. "What shows have you seen this week and did you go alone to them?"

"Loew's and the Saenger. I went alone to the Saenger."

"Listen, hon. You went to the Saenger night before last. Understand?"

Her smile was a little grim. "Alibi?"

"In a way. If anyone gets curious your story is that you went to the show, stopped in a drug store, had a soda, and came home. If you knew who that woman was it would be different, but you don't. The police are going to suspect every woman Ned went out with and I don't want you mixed up in a nasty scandal."

She started crying again. "I don't want to be mixed up in a scandal! But if my story will help find the murderess, I'll be glad to tell it!"

"You'll do nothing of the kind!" I said sharply. "Now stop blubbering and go to bed. He's dead and your bawling won't bring him back."

"But it's awful to know he's been murdered and I can't help catch who did it!" she wailed.

"Well, you can't help. Can you describe the woman at all? How tall she was, the clothes she was wearing—anything?"

She thought a second. "She wore a wide-brimmed hat and a coat with a big fur collar. The coat was black or navy. She was short and plumpish."

I smiled, remembering her accusing words to me. I'm five-six, in socks.

"That description is about as good as none at all," I said. "Now go to bed and remember—you went to a show!"

She left and I crawled back into bed, my body one ache of weariness. But there was to be no sleep for me that day. I'd just settled under the covers when the doorbell pealed loudly, then pealed again and went right on howling through the house like a banshee. I cursed heartily and looked at the clock—6:10—it could be Dennis, it was about the time he'd be going in.

The ringing stopped and a grumbling, frightened Bertha rapped at my door and stuck her head in.

"Miss Marg'ret, dey's two pleecemen wants you. I tole 'em you wuz asleep but dey sez git you up."

I struggled into a robe, silently cursing all cops. Rudy and Tommy Gross were waiting in the living room.

"How come you ran out on me?" Tommy asked.

"F'crissakes I was dead tired and just before a fit!" I exploded. "I had damn good reason to have fits! And I didn't run out, I told Rudy I was going home and get some sleep, but," with heavy disgust, "sleep is what I'm not to be allowed. Was it necessary for you to put your finger on the bell and wake up everyone in the house?"

They ignored the last question.

"I don't see why you got so rattled and left before I got there," Tommy said blandly. "You had a gun and Rudy was with you."

"I wanted to go home," I snapped. "And you'd have been rattled too if you'd been through a night like I had. When that woman tried to sneak in it was just one thing too many for me."

"It's too bad you didn't shoot her when you had the chance."

"I don't go around shooting people!" I retorted. "Besides I *didn't* have the chance. She moved too fast and I'm not expert enough to hit a running target."

"How did you get in that apartment in the first place?" Tommy asked. "The landlady, who lives in the rear, said the gate was kept locked."

"I got in with some keys I had," I said sullenly.

His eyebrows arched. "Keys you had! Where did you get them?"

"I took them off the dresser in the hotel room," I muttered surlily. "So what?"

"So what? A man is murdered in his hotel; a woman is murdered in his apartment; you lift the keys to the apartment from the murdered man's room and find the woman's body, getting klunked on the head yourself—and you ask so what! My God, Margaret! You can't be that dumb!"

"I'm not dumb at all!" I snapped. "I took them because I was curious. I couldn't figure what Ned was doing with them and I meant to have a look at them and then put them back. But I forgot to replace them and later, when I found them in my pocket, I decided to have a look at the place. That's all."

He shook his head reprovingly. "Playing detective again. Now you're in the very hell of a jam."

"I don't see why. I told you what happened."

"Sure—and I believe you. But there are others who won't."

I gaped at him. "What do you mean?"

"The D.A. will be damn curious, for one. Les Beton won't hesitate to point out that you have no alibi for night before last or last night."

"Is that so?" I asked angrily. "Well, I do have an alibi

for night before last! My kid sister heard me come in and knows what time it was. And I've a lump on my head that is alibi enough for last night! Besides, why try to pass the buck to Beton? It looks to me like you're the one who's trying to make a case against me!"

"You know better than that, Margaret. I'm just trying to show you how you have placed yourself in a spot to be suspected of these murders."

"I suppose I bopped myself on the *back* of my head with a poker!"

"You could have. Lots of killers wound themselves to divert suspicion."

I stared at him as if he'd gone crazy.

"In books and movies, maybe," I sneered.

"No, ma'am. In life. It's an old dodge."

"Well," I shrugged irritably, "I didn't. Nor did I poison Ned McGowan and bash in Miss Cheng's head. And I don't see that this line of reasoning is helping to find the real killer!"

"It isn't." He looked at his watch. "But you'll have to tell this whole tale to the D.A., so you better get dressed and come down with us now. The hotel people are coming in before the inquest to testify. As the person who found Miss Cheng's body your testimony is important. Damn! I wish you'd left those keys alone!"

"So do I!" Rudy exclaimed fervently.

"What do you guys think I wish?" I asked sarcastically and started for the door.

Tommy grinned at me. "Better wash that blood off your face. Beton would make plenty out of that!"

"I always wash my face in the morning," I stated tartly and left the room.

I took a warm shower, then let the cold water beat on me, took my time making up my face, and dressed in a blue tweed sports suit. I gazed with disfavor at the bloodstained jacket of my new beige wool outfit, threw it in the corner, and went back downstairs. I found the whole family and the cops drinking coffee in the dining room.

Bertha poured me a cup, rolling her eyes and slopping the coffee into the saucer.

"What's the matter with you?" I asked. "You haven't been out killing anyone, have you?"

She walled her eyes at me. "Lawd no, Miss Marg'ret! I ain't nevah kilt a livin' soul!"

We all laughed and the tension lifted.

I drank coffee, keeping a wary eye on Vangie who looked like she was wound on a spool and might unwind any second. I didn't want her breaking down and confessing. One suspect in the family was enough.

Tommy finished his coffee and sighed. "I sure wish you'd have sent for me when you found the nurse's body, instead of going to headquarters."

Vangie leaned tensely forward. "Nurse's body? What nurse?"

I gave her a warning look. "Miss Cheng. I didn't want to upset you but I found her body last night. She'd had her head smashed in with a poker in a building where Ned had a lab."

"The dirty killer!" Brett jumped to his feet. "Why Miss Cheng?"

Tommy shrugged. "She must have caught the murderer in the place, so she had to be silenced. Your sister came in a few minutes later and got hit over the head too."

Four pairs of eyes turned on me in surprise.

"Why, Margaret! You didn't tell us about that!" Mother looked baffled.

"I was going to tell you the whole story after I'd rested," I said. "But I haven't rested and now it will just have to wait."

Vangie stared at me, panic in her look. I finished my coffee hastily.

"Come on, Tommy, let's get going."

He stood up. "Okay. You want to ride with us or take your car?"

"I'll take my car. That way I can leave as soon as I'm through."

We drove off, Rudy riding with his brother. I smiled, thinking I wasn't much shakes as a suspect if they let me go on my own. But I realized, with a slight sense of quaking, that I was in a tough spot. I decided I'd better call Dennis as soon as I reached a phone. There are times when a fellow needs a friend and the paper was an important one. Although Dennis might tell me I'd quit and to hell with me. I grinned wryly at the thought.

I drove into the police parking lot and braked right behind Tommy. We went up the steps arm in arm, the three of us.

"By the way, did you ever talk to the Merceron girls?" I asked.

He nodded. "Yep. Last night and again this morning while you were dressing. Your brother is going to bring them down this morning. After we get all the statements we'll really get to work. This is going to be a tough one to crack."

"It seems so," I agreed. "One thing sure—when this is over I promise never to stick my nose into another murder. I'm through playing with fire."

"I hope you mean that." He smiled, then frowned. "If you'd have left those keys alone you'd have been okay. You should know better than to touch anything at the scene of a murder."

"I didn't know it was murder then!" I retorted, nettled. Then I remembered the notes and letters I'd taken from the apartment. I let go of Rudy's arm and pulled Tommy to one side in the hall. I'd better come clean!

"Er, er, Tommy! There's something else you should know about. I took some other stuff—from the apartment."

"*Now* what?"

"Papers. Notes and letters. They were in the drawer where I found the gun. I don't know why I lifted them."

"I don't either." He sighed resignedly. "Well, where are they?"

"Right in my purse," I said, and added virtuously, "I didn't read the letters but the notes were made out to Mrs. Dellman for sixty-eight grand."

"Sixty-eight grand!" He whistled. "Well, hand them over."

"The notes?"

"And the letters. I could wring your neck, damn little meddler!"

I handed them over without another word. By that move I involved Vangie and got myself in deeper.

Tommy gave them to Rudy. "Here. *You* took these from that chest. I'll tell you when to turn them in."

We went on up to the district attorney's office. No one was there and I looked at my watch. 7:35. Tommy went out, saying he was going to look in on the coroner and find out how the inquest preparations were coming along. I picked up the phone and called Dennis.

"Where in hell are you?" Dennis greeted me amiably. "I called and your mother said you'd left with two police-men. Are you coming in or not?"

"I'm not due in until 8:30," I snapped. "Right now I'm in the D.A.'s office and I have to wait for him."

"Why? Oh, t'hell with him! You come in! Why didn't you tell me last night that you'd found that Chinese girl's body?"

"I tried to but you wouldn't listen. You kept screaming at me."

"Never mind. Just come in and make it snappy."

"I can't," I reiterated.

"What's stopping you?"

"The police," I said bluntly.

11. *Questions and Answers*

"BUT why?" Dennis yelled. "What have you done?"

"Nothing much." I giggled nervously. "I swiped some keys from the hotel room yesterday and they turned out to be for that apartment in the Vieux Carré. After dinner I decided to have a look at the place and I found Miss Cheng. Then someone smacked me down and I passed out."

"Leave it to you to get behind the eight ball! I ought to fire you!"

Quick anger prompted me to say I'd quit already but a remnant of sense shut me up. I'd need the paper and, far as I was concerned, Dennis was it!

"I thought I'd get a good beat," I said meekly.

"So you got beat!" he retorted. "Well, nothing showed in the morning papers and you still have a feature if you come in and write it. I can't do anything with what you tried to tell me in the middle of the night."

"It wasn't the middle of the night!" I denied. "It was morning."

"I don't give a damn! I want to know what the cops got on you that they won't let you go! All I know is what I got from De Sales and the desk sergeant."

I lost patience. "Stop shouting at me!" I yelled. "I've enough without you giving me hell. The police and the district attorney want a full statement from me. There are others coming in about the doctor's murder and I'll have a story for the City edition, but I can't leave here now. I don't know how long it will be before they'll let me go.

I don't know if they'll let me go at all. They're just likely to accuse me of both murders!"

Dennis gasped sharply. "Are you kidding?"

"Hardly! It hasn't come to that yet, but I'm going to have to do some fast talking about why I took those keys and that's not all. I swiped some papers from that apartment— but I turned them over to Tommy."

"It would serve you right if they held you. It might even make a good story."

"Thank you, *dear*," I said sweetly. "That's just what I'd expect you to say! If you want to send someone else over here, it's okay by me. I'm fed up with the whole show."

"Oh nuts! Stay with it. They haven't got anything on you and you may as well earn your salary."

"What salary?" I asked.

He ignored that. "Write me a story for the City and send it by messenger. I'm taking nothing by phone."

"Oh sure!" I hung up, promising myself I'd do nothing of the kind. By the time I called in McCarthy would be damn glad to take it by phone.

I looked at Rudy, eyebrows raised mockingly.

"You newspaper people must lead the *most* interesting lives!" I sang in a high falsetto.

Rudy smirked. "Why don't you join the force? You seem to like doing detective work."

I gazed at him reproachfully. "That was unkind."

"Sorry." He grinned, not looking sorry at all.

"At that I might not make such a bad detective!" I retorted with some spirit.

"You'd probably be damn good."

"Well, I'd be a damn sight better than some coppers I know and what's—"

The entrance of Howell Nelson, district attorney, and his secretary put a stop to my speech.

"Good morning!" he greeted us. "How are you, Miss Slone?"

"As well as can be expected, all considered," I informed him.

"You should go to bed nights instead of wandering around falling over dead bodies," he told me.

"I see you've heard all about my little adventure."

"Yes indeed. Chief Gross told me about it."

He motioned me into his private office and waved me to a seat facing him. He'd been in office about four years. I recalled that when he went in he hadn't been so fat and he'd entirely lacked the pompous air he now wore.

The secretary seated herself next to his chair and waited, pencil poised over her notebook.

Nelson cleared his throat, smiling benevolently at me.

"Now then! Just tell me the whole story!"

"Starting from the very beginning?"

"Starting from when you took those keys—and you might tell me why you did that?"

"Following an urge common to my calling, I suppose," I said wryly.

"Curiosity?"

I nodded and began the story. He didn't interrupt until I reached the point of having entered the apartment. Then he asked, "How did you know which apartment to go in?"

"The address and apartment number was stamped on a metal tag. I did knock first and when no one answered I opened the door. The room was dark."

"Weren't there hall lights?"

"Only one and that was on the second floor. It was a small light and didn't do the third floor much good. When I went in I turned on my flash and the first thing I saw was Miss Cheng's head."

"Was she dead then?"

"I can't say for sure and I never got the chance to find out. As I bent over her someone bashed me on the head and I passed out."

"How long were you unconscious?"

"I'm not sure of that either, but I went in there before 8:00 and it was after 2:00 when I left. Of course I spent some time lying on the floor after I came to, scared to move. And then I prowled around the place for awhile with a gun in my hand—after I found the gun."

"Why didn't you phone the police from the apartment?"

"The phone up there did me no good. The line was dead."

"Wires cut?" he asked, as Rudy had earlier.

"I don't know. I didn't stop to look."

"I see." He pursed his lips. "Now, then. Didn't it occur to you when you took those keys that you were interfering with the police?"

"Not at that time. There was still no proof of murder. I figured the keys might show Ned led a double or triple life and make a good story."

"Where are those keys now?"

Instinctively I reached into my suit pocket, then I remembered.

"Oh Lord! They're still in my other suit pocket!"

"Never mind. How soon after you became conscious did you ascertain the nurse was dead?"

"Quite a while. I'd fallen over her body and when I rolled off I just lay there, too frightened to get up and do anything."

Nelson smiled bleakly. "A natural reaction. And then?"

"When I finally got up I found the light and saw she was dead. I really got into a lather and all I could think of was to find something to protect myself with. I found the gun, then went through the apartment to see if anyone was hiding there. Of course no one was, except a yellow tom cat who nearly scared me witless."

"Was your attacker a man or woman?"

"I was hit from behind, so I couldn't see who struck the blow. But I did get the idea it was a woman."

"Why?"

"There was an odor of perfume in the air. It didn't come from Miss Cheng. We made sure of that later."

"Hmmm." He hmmed. "Women don't often use such forceful means as pokers."

"It must have been the only weapon she could find. Anyhow, after I'd made sure no one was in the apartment I developed a great yearning for the police. I hightailed out of there, found I'd left my purse with my car keys in it, so I got a cab to headquarters."

"Where did you get money for a cab if you didn't have your purse?"

"Out of the glove pocket of my car. I keep some money in there."

"Why didn't you go to the Third Precinct instead of headquarters?"

"I don't know. I guess I must have been too rattled to think straight. I found Rudy and then I passed out again. Rudy got me to his car and I told him the story. I wouldn't talk before because there were reporters hanging around. We went back to the apartment and Rudy left me there while he went to call Tommy. While he was gone someone sneaked up the stairs. I waited but something must have warned her because she took off and ran like hell."

"You saw a woman on the stairs?"

"Uh huh! I *saw* her that time. I ran after her but she beat me out of the patio gate. A minute or so later Rudy almost had his car wrecked by a woman driving like mad out Chartres Street."

"You didn't follow beyond the patio gate?"

"No."

"You just stood there and let her get away? Why? You had a gun."

"Yeah—and I had a full dose of trouble and headaches too! I wasn't looking for any more. As soon as Rudy got there I left for home. This morning he and Tommy came after me and here I am. I guess that's all."

Nelson shook a finger at me. "I hope you learn a lesson from this!" He said. "Don't go around stealing keys that don't belong to you."

I sighed with relief. Apparently he wasn't going to get tough about it.

"Don't worry, I won't!" I assured him.

Tommy came in with the coroner's report on Miss Cheng. She had died instantly from a blow on the head by a blunt instrument. While they were discussing the murders the buzzer sounded and Nelson flipped the button on the office communications box. Rudy's voice said Beton was there with the hotel crowd. Nelson said to send them in and told me I could go.

I reared up in protest! After all! This was my story and I'd suffered for it! I thought I should be allowed to sit in on the questioning!

Tommy queried Nelson with his eyes. The attorney considered a moment, then said I could stay—if I sat quietly and minded my own business. I agreed and settled back in the chair as Beton came in with a group of people.

LeFevre was there—unhappy about the whole thing. A bright-eyed but scared Negress came next in line, then a chipper kid in uniform—a bellhop or the elevator boy. There was a hennaed stylish-stout with a wad of gum in her mouth and a mousy little man who turned out to be the night clerk. Morrow brought up the rear.

Johnny walked over to stand by me.

"I hear you got yourself into a mess, sweetheart," he said.

"My, my! News does travel fast, doesn't it?"

"Yeah. You know, I figured you'd swiped those keys. I saw them on the dresser once and then they disappeared."

"Why didn't you tell on me?"

"Me?" His query was injured. "I'm no squealer! I meant to follow you when you left the hotel and see what you were up to. But I missed you and I didn't know what doors those keys opened so I just skipped the whole thing."

"I wish you had followed me." I meant it. "You'd probably have saved me a fine headache and a lot of aggravation."

The questioning had started so we shut up and listened. Nelson was taking the maid first.

"All right, Ivy. Just tell us what happened that morning when you tried to get in the doctor's room to clean up."

"Ah couldn't git in," was the simple and succinct answer.

I giggled nervously and Nelson warned me with a look.

"I know that," he said patiently. "But what made you get worried? Lots of people sleep later than 8:00."

"Well, suh, Ah 'spects some folkes does but not de doctah. He wuz up and gone mos' mawnin's by den. He allus gone when Ah gits to he room. Ah sees he jes oncet a week, dat bees on Sundays. Ah does he room late dat day an he tip me foh de week. Effen he out he left a lil change an a note on de dresser."

She paused and went on dramatically: "Well, suh! Ah tries to git in dat mawnin' but dey ain't no tottin!"

Nelson looked puzzled. I grinned. She meant there was "nothing doing."

"De doah wuz lock wid de latch and Ah wuz outside and couldn't git in," she continued. "So Ah figgered mebbe he ain't got no operations dat day and wants to sleep an Ah goes on off and cleans some yuther rooms. Ah comes back and tries agin to git in. Den Ah knocks and dats when Ah stahts gittin worrit.

"Ah goes to de linen room an looks at de clock. Hits after 8:00. Miz Armstrong, de housekeeper, she ain't around so Ah goes back and pounds real good on de doah. Suddint, clare frew mah bones, Ah knowed somepin is wrong. So Ah calls de office man. Him and Mr. Lee Fever comes up and dey fines de doctah—daid!"

I beckoned to Tommy who came and bent over my chair.

"Ask her about the doctor's habits," I whispered. "You know, neatness and all that."

He nodded and spoke to the maid.

"Ivy, did the doctor hang up his clothes when he went to bed at night or did he just leave them laying around?"

She snorted. "Dat man nevah hang up a thing! He wuz plain ca'less about he cloes. Ah wuz allus pickin up after him."

Nelson was looking a question at Tommy and Gross explained the point of the query. Nelson nodded and I beckoned Tommy again.

"Ash her if any women ever stayed overnight in the hotel with Ned."

Tommy frowned but asked the question.

The Negress grinned widely. "Nossuh! But de doctah he spend nights out a lot. Times Ah comes in an de baid ain't teched!"

"That'll do, Ivy!" Nelson looked annoyed. "We're not interested in where the doctor slept or in his morals."

"De gemman axed me an Ah tole him," she said sullenly.

I put my oar in. "I should think his morals would be important," I said. "I'm told that poison is a woman's weapon."

He frowned unpleasantly. "I thought I told you to mind your own business?"

I subsided sulkily.

The maid was dismissed and LeFevre was questioned next. He merely corroborated the maid's story, adding that the lock was a burglar-proof one and that the master key was available only to him. He described again the finding of the doctor's body.

Nelson asked him how long the doctor had lived there, what were his general habits, and if he had many women visitors.

I thought: Humph! So you aren't interested in his morals!

LeFevre said the doctor was most circumspect in his behavior, that no one had ever complained of noise or parties in his room, that it was almost impossible to keep a check on visitors to the rooms of permanent guests.

Nelson told him he could go, but he said he'd wait until the others were finished and drive them back to the hotel.

The mousy little man said the doctor carried his key with him and came to the desk for messages only—or to pay a bill. He hadn't seen him come in the night of his death, so he must have been in before 2:00 A.M. as the clerk went on duty at that hour. He explained that the shifts swung on hours, working one week 6:00 P.M. to 2:00 A.M. and the next from 2:00 A.M. until 10:00. He had, however, been in on the finding of the body and he told of that.

Nelson thanked him and said that was all. Mousy joined Mr. "Lee Fever" by the door where the manager waited to take his workers back with him.

The girl with the hair and gum was the night operator. Her only addition to the story were several duplicate slips of incoming messages and outgoing calls. There were two sets of call records kept for the phone company, she explained, both starting at the hour of 6:00 and running for twelve hours; A.M. to P.M., and vice versa.

The messages were from me, the hospital, Catherine Kelly, and Mrs. Dellman. The outgoing calls were to me, at the paper, to my home—probably to Brett—several to hospitals, the Merceron number, the Dellman number, and Catherine Kelly. That one was important. It had been made at 2:29 and established that he was alive at that hour.

The operator said several calls had come in from women who would leave no message. Nelson dismissed her and the uniformed boy took her place in the chair beside Nelson. His name, he said, was Bob Sullivan.

"Doc had a late visitor," he said quietly.

I sat up all ears. I knew of that visitor, the police only guessed at her.

"How do you know that?" Nelson asked.

"I took her upstairs and brought her back down." The boy's look was eloquent of his opinion for the attorney's intelligence. "Doc came in about 1:15 or 1:30. I work a full twelve-hour shift, but from midnight on I'm not too busy.

When Doc came in he was feeling pretty good, not drunk, just a little high. I started to carry him upstairs—I mean take him up in the cage.

"We were almost to his floor when he reached in his pocket and said he was out of cigarettes. I told him I'd get him some so he gave me a buck to get two packs of Camels, a tube of toothpaste, and the morning paper. He told me to keep the change. I went down and was starting to leave the cage when a dame breezed up and said she wanted the tenth floor. I took her back up.

"I was pretty sure she wasn't a guest, the tenth has mostly permanents, so I kept an eye on her when she got off and saw that she went to Doc's room. I figured that was okay so I went back down, got his stuff and started up to deliver it. The buzzer showed for the sixth floor and I stopped to take on a girl. I asked her if she minded riding up and waiting while I delivered a package."

I swallowed a gasp: Vangie!

"She told me to go ahead, so I left her in the cage at the tenth and took the package to Doc's door. The transom was open and I could hear what was being said in the room."

"What did you hear?" Nelson and everyone bent forward attentively.

"The woman said, 'You'll never get away with this, Ned. I won't let you treat me like this.' Doc said he didn't know what she meant, that she must have known it had to end sometime. Then she told him it had gone too far to end. 'I won't let you go!' she said real loud. 'Not if I have to kill you.' Doc sort of laughed and said that was the third time that night she'd said she'd kill him. He told her he could have her jailed for saying that and, anyhow, he wasn't worth the trouble she'd get into."

"That's when he told the truth!" I said viciously and all eyes turned my way.

"That's a fine way to speak of the dead!" Beton exclaimed.

"Sorry." I leaned back in my chair. "The opinion is purely personal."

"I knocked," Sullivan took up his story, "and Doc opened the door just wide enough to take the package. Then I went back to the cage and took the girl who'd got on at six downstairs."

"When did the woman leave Dr. McGowan's room?" Tommy asked.

"About 2:30. I brought her down and she started to go out the back door that leads to the parking lot. I called to her that it was locked so she turned around and went out through the side."

"What did she look like?" Nelson queried.

"I don't know," he answered, and a sigh of disappointment went around the group.

"But you must have had a good look at her!" Nelson's voice was edged.

"No, I didn't. She had on a coat with a big fur collar pulled around her face and a wide-brimmed hat pulled down over her eyes. All I can tell you is that she was real short, plump—and nervous."

"Nervous? How?"

"She fidgeted and she pulled on a small white handkerchief until she had it almost torn to ribbons. And here's another funny thing—although I don't know if it has anything to do with Doc's murder, but it may tie in. You remember I told you about a girl getting on at the sixth?"

I braced myself and thought: What now, oh Lord! What now!

"We-e-l-l," he drawled the word. "I've seen *her* before—*with* the doctor. And I'd seen her earlier that night when I took her upstairs—to the tenth! Going down she was on the sixth. She couldn't have known that floor has been closed for a week for redecorating."

I cursed soundly and silently: What a lousy break!

12. *Ink and Issotta Fraschinis*

"DID you see *her* face?" Tommy's query was sarcastic.

"Oh sure! I recognized it too. I don't know her name but she went with Doc for several months. She looks," his eyes turned squarely on me, "something like her, only younger. Enough like her to be her sister."

Beton's eyes popped. "Enough like her to be her sister!" he parroted. "Why, hell! That's just about who she *was!*" He turned to me. "You said yourself that your sister had carried on an affair with Dr. McGowan."

"You're a filthy liar!" I spat the words at him. "I didn't say she had any affair with him and you'd better mind your language and choice of terms! I said she'd had a crush on him, that's all!"

"From what I've heard about that guy no dame who went out with him more than once stayed a virgin," Beton sneered.

The inkwell was the handiest thing and I hurled it at him, splashing ink all over him: face, shirt, and new-looking light tan suit. The paper weight was due to follow but Tommy grabbed me as I drew back my arm to fling it.

"Damn it, Margaret! Behave yourself! Do you want to go to jail?"

"I've taken as much from that lying, stupid, bullying, flat-footed lug as I intend to take!" I blazed, struggling to free myself from Tommy's hold. "First he accuses me of killing that would-be Casanova, now he slanders my sister! I'll kill him! Leggo of me!"

Tommy held tight until I was reduced to panting quiet.

"So I'm a stupid flat-footed lug and a liar, am I?" Beton shouted, his face blue from fury and ink. "Well, I'll bet my dough you and your sister both had plenty to do with these murders! You're all-fired quick to threaten to kill someone! I'm going to see to it that you're held on suspicion!"

"Aw shaaaddduppp!" I gritted, through my teeth. "You just try it!"

Tommy gave my arm a jerk. "You shut up. You too, Les. You both make me sick."

"Let go of me, Tommy." My voice was quiet but venomous. "I won't throw anything more at him."

I turned to Sullivan, who was goggle-eyed at the brawl he'd brought on.

"Did that woman in the elevator, who went to Ned's room, look like me?"

"Not a bit!" His voice was emphatic. "You're much taller and skinnier."

"See!" I jeered at Beton. "Besides, I can prove where I was."

"Yeah?" he jeered back. "Sure! With twenty-four hours to cook up an alibi! You couldn't prove it yesterday. You admitted you couldn't!"

"Look, Mr. D.A.," Sullivan's voice was timid. "This may not be important but you should know about it."

Nelson glared at me, then turned back to the boy. "Well, what is it?"

"When that dame went out of the side door I followed her. She went to the parking lot and got in a car and drove off. I couldn't see the make, it was too dark in the lot, but I did see that the whole hood was like silver and shaped like a Rolls only bigger. It was a convertible."

Excitement whipped inside of me. Only two cars in the city answered that hood description. They were imported Italian Issottas and they both belonged to the Dellmans! One was a town car, the other a convertible!

I started to tell Tommy, then changed my mind. If Marta

Dellman had killed McGowan, why should I lead the cops to her door? Then I thought of Miss Cheng—and my own sore head. Still I kept silent.

Nelson looked around the room. "Anyone here know who owns a car like that?"

No one spoke and I smiled smugly while keeping my mouth shut for once in my life.

He turned to his secretary. "Check with the traffic department. A car like that should be known on sight by every motorcycle man on the force."

"Is that all?" he asked Sullivan, a bit wearily. The boy nodded and Nelson told him he could go.

He filed out with LeFevre and the other hotel employees. I asked if I could go and was given enthusiastic permission. I followed the others out with Morrow following me.

In the hall the kid called me aside.

"I didn't mean to get you in Dutch," he said. "But that girl does look like you."

"It's okay. Don't let it worry you."

"Could she have been your sister?" His eyes were bright and inquiring.

"I hope not." I forced a smile. "But I have a kid sister who went out with Ned—as you heard that louse Beton say."

"If I'd have known that I wouldn't have said anything."

"Well, don't get upset. They're trying to catch a murderer, you know—and anything goes."

"Yeah, I know. I hope they get who did it. I liked Doc."

"I didn't," I said flatly.

He looked uncomfortable, then said good-by and rejoined his group. I turned to Morrow.

"Come on, Skeets. Let's go tend our knitting."

We went down the corridor and walked down the one flight of stairs to the pressroom. At the door he took my arm.

"Look, Slone. I'd lay off Les if I were you," he advised.

"He's got it in for you and he can get damn nasty. I know that guy."

"I'll lay off him if he does the same with me," I snapped and walked into the pressroom, where I picked up my direct wire and dialed for Dennis.

"Oh, it's you!" he yelled. "Didn't I tell you not to phone in your stuff?"

"I'll come in and write what I've got if you promise to let me go right home when I'm finished. I can't go much longer. I'm dead beat."

"I can't let you go, kid." His voice was gentle. "I've two out sick and you'll have to stick with it."

"Then you'll have to take it by wire and between naps." I cast a longing glance at the couch. "If I don't get some sleep you'll have three out sick."

"Okay. Let's have it."

I gave him the story, including the episode of the inkwell.

Dennis grunted angrily. "I'm surprised you couldn't have found something heavier to throw at the sunnuvabitch instead of just an inkwell!"

I wondered if Dennis was ill.

"I tried to pitch a paper weight but Gross stopped me," I said wryly. "And you may as well know right now that Beton would like to pin these two murders on me."

"He's nuts," McCarthy said curtly.

"I know that," I agreed. Then I went on with the description the boy had given of the woman in the elevator and of the car she drove.

"I hate to mix Mrs. Dellman up in this mess, but self-preservation is the first consideration in my life. And she has the only car that could fit. Besides, if she killed Miss Cheng she deserves anything she gets. Why not put a sneak camera on her cars? You can show the pix to Sullivan. McGowan owed her sixty-eight grand and he had the notes —uncanceled. They should have been in her possession."

"That's true. Who were the letters from?"

"I don't know, I hadn't the chance to check that. But sixty-eight grand is a lot of dough. Combined with jealousy, it's motive for murder."

"Combined with jealousy, yeah. Otherwise it's just peanuts to a dame with her dough." Dennis chuckled.

"True, but I still think getting pix of that car is a good idea. I told you yesterday the nurse suspected her."

"You did not," Dennis denied flatly.

I thought back and couldn't remember. "Maybe I didn't. I thought I had. I meant to, even though it sounded silly then. Miss Cheng said Ned and Mrs. D. had been carrying on since before he got out of interneship. What with two murders and my headache, her story sounds more likely now than then."

"Okay. I'll put a camera on the cars. Call in when anything new develops."

I hung up and called my home. Bertha answered and I asked for Vangie.

"She sleep 'n' Ah isn't gwine wake her." She sounded sullen.

I smiled. Bertha had helped "birth" Vangie and always regarded her as special and private property.

"You'd better wake her up before the police get there and yank her out of bed!" I said sternly.

"Is you crazy, Miss Marg'ret? Whut she done to git de p'leece after huh?"

"Never mind. Go get her—and hurry! I haven't all day to wait."

Grumblingly she complied and soon a sleepy voice came on the wire. I lit into her with all four feet.

"Why in hell didn't you tell me you'd ridden back to the tenth floor while the elevator boy delivered that order to Ned?" I asked.

"What of it? The boy doesn't know me and I got on at the sixth."

My squeak sounded like a sour flute note.

"He'd seen you with Ned before! And the sixth floor happens to be closed for redecorating! Out of fifteen floors you had to pick that one!"

She gasped, "Oh!"

I went on, bitterly, "To make the pattern complete, that boy recognized your resemblance to me."

"Oh!" She gasped again.

"Is that all you can say?"

"What else do you expect me to say? That, being sisters, we have no business looking alike?"

"We have no business being sisters, with you so damn dumb!"

"You're probably right." She refused to get riled. "Well, what do I do now?"

"The police will pick you up for questioning. That's sure. They may be on their way to get you now. Say nothing, admit nothing about going to the hotel until they prove it. Keep your trap shut and let them do the talking. If Sullivan identifies you as the girl he picked up—that's something else. I'm hoping he'll be sport enough not to do it."

I put down the phone and staggered to the couch.

"God! I'm tired!" I informed the reporters around. "I'm going to sleep. Kindly try to be quiet."

I'd barely found a semi-comfortable spot on the lumpy leather couch when a uniformed cop barged in.

"Where's Miss Slone? The D.A. wants her. Her brother and two girls are in his office."

I hauled my tired frame from the couch and plodded after him.

Brett met me at the door to the outer office. Toni was standing by a window, Vette was not in sight. Brett's forehead was deeply creased.

"Don't look like you've met the end of the world!" I said. "You've nothing to worry about."

"That's what you think. From what that cop said I've

plenty to worry about." He added, in a mutter, "A guy oughtn't ever have sisters."

"Now what? And what cop?" I asked.

"That guy who got so bitchy yesterday."

"Beton? Oh him!"

"Yeah, him. He said he had a strong hunch—and expected soon to have evidence—that you'd killed Ned and Lili."

"That louse is screwy!" I retorted. "Pay no attention." I smiled at him and Toni, then noticed she had a strange gleam in her eye. I decided to quench that at once.

"*You* saw Ned late that night," I said. "What time did you leave him?"

"He left *us.*" She accented the pronoun as I had. "It was about midnight. I heard the bells from the cathedral strike the hour as he said good night."

"He didn't get home until almost 1:30. About an hour after he took you home. Wonder where he went?"

"I wouldn't know," she said, coolly.

"I suppose not. He called me at the office about 1:30."

"Did he?" She raised well-groomed eyebrows.

I was not coming out ahead in this verbal battle—and I didn't like it.

"I seem to have started this mess," I said. "Just because I talked to him so late got us off on a murder chase. Too bad, isn't it?"

Her eyebrows arched again. "Would you prefer his murderer went unpunished?"

My eyebrows went up that time. "*Murderer?* It's generally agreed the word is *murderess.*"

She shrugged. "I know. That policeman seems to think you did it."

I shrugged too, annoyed as hell. Words were my business and I wasn't accustomed to coming out second best in a battle of them.

"Maybe I did, who knows?"

"In my opinion there's no maybe about it!" A voice remarked tersely and I turned to see Beton and his triumphant look stalking into the inner office.

A tug on my arm took my attention from the door. Morrow was yanking at me.

"What do *you* want?" I asked.

"Got to talk to you, right away," he muttered.

I went out in the hall with him.

"Those letters they got from that apartment! Holy hat! They've got you and your kid sister in the pan and the fire burns high!"

"What do you mean?"

"She wrote some of them and she threatened his life in several!"

"Are you kidding?"

"Hell no! The worse part is that she's got you in it too!"

"Are you completely crazy?" I asked explosively.

"F'crissakes, Margaret, listen to me! I told you Beton was out for your hide. He saw those letters. In several of them she said she'd tell you how he was treating her and you'd 'fix' him!"

I took a deep breath and counted to ten. And *I'd* been the one to hand those damn things over to the police!

"She threatened him, said she'd kill him if he didn't stop treating her so coldly. You Slone girls," he looked at me searchingly, "must be hard to get rid of once a guy gets under your skin!"

"Stow that crap! I've never bothered you, have I? How did you find out about the letters?"

"I saw Les and Rudy in a huddle in the corridor. They were reading some papers. I slipped up in back of them and read most of them over their shoulders before they caught me. Beton bawled me out but he also said he had you where he wanted you."

"Oh fine! Well, thanks, Morrow. This gives me a chance to think and I wouldn't have had it otherwise."

"That's okay. But give me a break when you can. I'm not a bad guy."

I smiled tenderly at him. "You're a swell guy and a swell reporter!"

"Stow that crap!" He tossed my own words back at me. "I only mean a break on this. I know you've got an inside track and I want to hang on the edges."

"You will," I promised—and added mentally: The outer edges.

I went back in the office and walked over to Brett.

"Your two sisters are in a hell of a mess," I said bluntly.

"I know that," he said shortly.

"You don't know anything. Vangie wrote letters! *Letters,* mind you! She threatened Ned in them."

"Why?" He was white to the lips.

"Why does any woman threaten a man?"

"But Vangie's just a kid!"

"Come off that stuff. She's eighteen and when mother was that age you were already a bright gleam in her eyes!"

"Do you think—think she—?" His tortured eyes finished the question.

"I don't think anything," I said curtly. "I only know that Ned McGowan was a louse and a heel and whoever killed him should get a medal!"

"Do you prefer bronze or silver?"

I wheeled around to face Beton, who'd come out of the inner office with Olivette in time to hear me pop off.

I opened my mouth to tell him off but Vette stormed at me.

"How dare you say such a thing! Ned was brilliant and fine and good! Whoever killed him should be hanged!"

"That's *your* opinion," I said acidly. "I haven't denied his brilliance, but as far as his personal life was concerned—I'm entitled to *my* opinion."

She glared at me. "If you weren't Brett's sister I'd scratch your eyes out!"

"Don't let that stop you!" I challenged, but Brett took her by the arm and led her to a chair where she subsided and began sobbing.

Beton motioned to Toni and she followed him into Nelson's private sanctum. She was out in only a few minutes and Brett got the nod to go in. I started to follow him but Beton barred the way.

"You stay here. When you're needed you'll be sent for."

"I was sent for!" I retorted.

"That's tough!" Beton closed the door in my face and I went back to a chair, to listen to Toni humming tunelessly and Vette sobbing loudly.

I stood both sounds for about two minutes, then: "F'crissakes, stop that bawling, Vette! And you, Toni, stop that noise you're making."

The humming and sobs stopped as both turned to stare at me. Vette was the first to speak.

"Who could have done this awful thing?"

I shrugged. "Any one of the couple of dozen women Ned had played hard and fast with."

She smiled pityingly at me.

"You didn't know him very well, did you? Ned loved only me."

"Is that so?" I looked my skepticism. "Such faith is touching. But you seem to forget he's been poisoned and most likely by a woman. There was a time when you were not in the picture and," I looked deliberately at Toni, "other women were."

"You don't understand. But I know Ned had not been out with any other girl for eight months."

"He may not have been out with them—where he could be seen. But certainly some woman visited him the night he was killed. She wasn't calling for medical attention and she wasn't threatening his life because he wouldn't treat her!"

"What woman are you talking about?"

"That's what the cops would like to know. The woman who killed him—and Miss Cheng."

"I heard nothing of this!"

"Why should you? You've a perfect alibi."

"I don't need an alibi!" she said stiffly.

"Every woman who knew Ned McGowan will need an alibi for what she was doing from midnight of Wednesday until about 3:00," I said. "And don't forget Lili Cheng was killed too."

"I'm not forgetting it!" she exclaimed indignantly. "But I can see no reason for either murder."

"I can see plenty of reasons for Ned's," I said drily. "As for Miss Cheng, she must have spotted the killer and had to be shut up. Unless—unless the killer was an insane, grudge-holding patient who had it in for both of them! That could be!"

"That would explain both murders!" Vette leaned forward eagerly.

I played with the theory for a minute, then shook my head.

"No, that won't wash. The murderer had no way of knowing she would be in that apartment that night. Ned's murder was planned. Hers was the act of a desperate, trapped person. I nearly got killed myself."

"Brett told us. Didn't you see anything?"

"Stars, bars, and comets," I said ruefully. "That's all. Next thing I knew was when I came to lying on top of Miss Cheng's body. Damned unpleasant sensation, that!"

"I should think so!" Toni exclaimed and shuddered.

"I did notice one thing and the memory has stuck with me. The odor of an odd scent. It wasn't on the nurse. Later, I almost caught a woman sneaking up the stairs but she got away. I got rattled and beat it for home as soon as Rudy came back from phoning Tommy."

"I don't blame you!" Toni said emphatically. "I wonder you had nerve enough to go back there the second time!"

"I had Rudy with me." I smiled. "It's easy to be brave when the law, with a .38 in his hand, is along."

"I suppose so." Vette smiled tearfully. "But going back to that place, with a dead body lying on the floor, must have taken courage."

"I hadn't much choice." Another thought struck me. "What did you know about that apartment?"

"I've known about it since I first started going with Ned," she said calmly. "It was his lab as well as a place of entertainment for his friends. He sublet it from a friend, Jerry Conover. We all worked on experiments there. Only a few intimate friends knew about it and the work that we did."

"Well, someone else knew it well enough to own a key to it," I said.

She nodded, then looked sharply at me. "How did *you* know? How did *you* get in?"

I felt and looked sheepish.

"I swiped his keys from the hotel room that morning. I guess I thought I'd uncover a juicy scandal. Now I wish I'd left the damn things alone!"

She started to weep again and I got up and walked out into the hall, wondering what kind of trouble those letters of Vangie's would bring on.

I hadn't long to wonder.

13. *Identifications Plus*

I'D been pacing the hall perhaps five minutes when the elevator turned out Vangie, guarded on each side by a detective.

She was bawling with fright, and the minute she spotted me she broke loose and started to run. Instinctively one cop unlimbered his gun.

I called out in real alarm. "Hold it! This is my sister!"

She threw herself on me as if I were the only person in the world who could save her. I smiled, remembering her unsheathed claws of a few hours earlier.

I held her off. "What's all the rumpus about?"

"They're trying to say I killed him!" she howled. "Just because I wrote him a few mean letters!"

"Serves you right for being such a fool," I said brutally. "You didn't kill him, however, so you've nothing to fear. Now stop bawling. There's been too many tears shed over that louse!"

She pulled away from me and in silent, injured dignity stalked into the D.A.'s anteroom. I followed.

"You needn't get on your high horse with me, Miss," I warned her. "We're both in a fine mess, thanks to your maudlin letters."

"What do you mean?"

"I suppose you've quite forgotten you threatened to have me *fix* Ned? You surely must have thought he'd scare easily!"

Brett was coming out of the inner office. Without answering me, she threw herself in his arms with a loud wail.

"Margaret's picking on me!" she bawled.

"Why don't you lay off the kid?" Brett asked reproach-fully. "Can't you see she's a nervous wreck?"

That got me! "For the love of Judas, what do you think I am? She ought to have her head bounced against a brick wall!"

Olivette was studying the scene with puzzled eyes. "What's the matter with Vangie?" she asked. "Why is she here?"

"Because she's one of Ned's jilted loves," I said bluntly. "She also wrote him some stupid letters and the police have them. They want to know how come she did that."

Vette's reaction was a surprise. She crossed over and took Vangie in her arms. "Don't cry, dear," she said—and kept on weeping herself. "I know how you feel. I loved him too, you know."

That was the signal for both to yowl together. Thoroughly disgusted, I strode out into the hall again.

Standing against the wall, I heard Beton call Vangie. I wondered if she'd tell the story I'd made up for her and half hoped she wouldn't. They'd break her in no time. I thought of Sullivan, and as if the thought had summoned him, he stepped off the elevator.

He came directly to me. "They sent for me to identify the girl who got on at the sixth floor."

"They've got my sister in there," I told him. "You might as well go in and get it over."

We went into the outer office and Bob knocked on the door. Beton let him in and again almost slammed the door in my face. The kid was gone only a few moments when he came back out, and I knew by the expression on his face that the cat was out of the bag.

"I'm sorry." He looked like he meant it. "She gave the whole show away. I was going to hedge about it, but as soon as she saw me she began to cry and said she'd tell the truth. I had to tell them she was the girl I'd seen."

"It's okay, Bob," I said wearily. "They'd have got it out of her anyhow. Vangie has no stamina."

"Your paper sent for me," he said. "They had a picture of a car. I'm pretty sure it was the one that woman was driving."

"Really?" I asked absently, my mind busy with wondering what was going on in Nelson's office. I walked away from Sullivan and over to Brett.

"You might as well know that Vangie was in Ned's hotel the night he was killed," I said flatly. "That boy has just identified her."

"She told me she'd been there," he said.

"Well, she's in a fine mess. Right up to her ears."

"But you don't think she had anything to do with these murders?" His eyes held frightened inquiry.

"Of course not!" I said, impatiently. "She didn't go in his room and she saw the woman who went in. That will jibe with what Sullivan told the police and should help her some. She also heard the woman threaten Ned in much the same terms as Sullivan heard. Damn!" I ended vehemently, "I'd like to beat the hell out of her! She needs it!"

"Does she know who the woman was?"

I couldn't help being amused. "All New Orleans would know it by now if she did. No. She only saw a woman and later heard her voice."

At that moment Tommy blew in and waved a paper under my nose.

"What t' hell!" I gasped, startled.

"This the hell!" he shouted. "Now explain this!"

It was the City edition of my paper which rolled at 11:00. I only needed one look to see that Dennis had jumped the gun and printed a story that could be libelous as hell. Pictures of the Dellman car were spread all over the front page, and the story, in no subtle manner, asked how come her car was at the scene of the murder.

I groaned.

"Well?" Tommy demanded.

I took refuge in denial and evasion. "I didn't write it. It looks like a good libel suit to me."

"Don't crap me! How did Dennis get this if you didn't send it in?"

"I didn't tell him to go bust out with anything like that! I simply told him the description of the car sounded like Mrs. Dellman's Issotta. That's all I said."

"That's all! Well, you sure tore the lid off the can of dynamite this time! You must have known about that car from the minute you heard it described. Why didn't you tell *me?* Why did you have to spill your guts to McCarthy?"

I froze up. "McCarthy signs my pay check—not you!" I said icily. "And I didn't spill my guts, as you so delicately phrase it. I merely suggested it might be a good idea to get a shot of the car and show it to Sullivan."

Tommy gave me a disgusted look. "Well, it's your little red wagon—yours and McCarthy's. I hope you enjoy your ride!"

"Dennis knows what he's doing!" I rose to the defense, even as I mentally cussed him for pulling a too hot chestnut out of the fire.

Beton called to me. "You're wanted on the phone. Take it in here."

I didn't want to take it in there, but I was glad to get out of Tommy's way.

Vangie was sitting in the chair I'd occupied earlier. She had begun to look defiant.

"I've told them all I know and they won't believe me!" she exclaimed. "I want a lawyer."

"You'll get one—if you need him." I picked up the phone. It was Dennis.

"Mrs. Dellman's lawyer just phoned. He's threatening libel suits."

"Well, what did you expect?" I asked tartly.

"Never mind. Have you anything that will back up what I've already printed on this?"

"Nothing. And the next time you start raving about people who go off half-cocked don't forget to include yourself."

"All right! Maybe I did. But that kid positively identified that car—"

"From a picture?" I asked sarcastically.

"Sure. And that identification will hold. So let 'em sue."

"Maybe it will hold. Maybe not," I said laconically.

"Whadda ya mean?"

"The kid could always cop a plea he'd been mistaken. The camera isn't infallible. If someone makes it worth his while to crawfish on the identification, where will you be? Did you get it in writing?"

Dennis's "No" was surly.

"You should have."

"I will, as soon as I can get hold of him again."

"He was here a couple of minutes ago. Do you want me to tell him to come over there if I see him again?"

"Hell yes! And get me something else on this story that will make what's in the City hold water. I'm in a spot."

"You don't say!" I chortled. "What do you want me to get?"

"Anything."

"Well, well!" I was enjoying this. "There's nothing that will fit the car story. They've questioned the Merceron girls. Ned took them home at midnight. Right now they're putting my kid sister through the paces, but she has nothing new or exciting to offer."

"Why are they questioning your sister?"

"Because she knew him, dope. Same as I did. I'm in the D.A.'s office. I had to take the call in here. They're afraid they might miss something."

"Have they accused your sister of the murders?"

"Of course not!" I retorted indignantly. "How can they?"

"I don't know. They accused you of them, didn't they?"

"Oh shut up!"

"All right. But give me something on this. I've got to have more. What did your sister have to do with it? What did she say?"

"I wouldn't know. They wouldn't let me listen."

"But you just said you were in the office!"

"Only to take this call."

"Oh. Well, what about those sisters. Anything on them?"

"I told you—they left him as the church bells chimed midnight."

"Slone," Dennis sounded worried, "do you suppose Mrs. Dellman was in the hotel?"

"I hope so, for your sake. If not you're in a hell of a mess and old man Phipps will have your hide—unbroiled."

He sighed gustily. "I know. Well, call me if anything at all happens. And let me know what gives with your sister."

"I will." I hung up and leaned back in the chair while silence hung like fog over the room. I made no move to leave, hoping they'd forget I was there.

It didn't work.

Beton walked over and took hold of my shoulder, ungently.

"Rise and shine!" He grinned unpleasantly. "When we need you again you'll be called. Stick around outside."

I shook his hand off. "Don't touch me, you big ape!"

"See!" he appealed to Nelson. "She's calling me names again!"

"You will please mind your language, Miss Slone!" Nelson was really irked. "And you will wait in the outer office until we are through with your sister—then there are some things I wish to check with you."

I stalked to the door without answering. As I opened it Tommy came in, newspaper in his hand. He placed it, front page up, on Nelson's desk. I scooted, fast.

"You wait here," I said to Brett. "I'm going to the pressroom for a few minutes. They can send for me when they need me."

In the pressroom, Morrow and Herrot had their heads together over the same troublesome paper.

"Fine beat!" Morrow said accusingly. "I suppose you think you're smart?"

"I know nothing about that story!" I made a sweeping denial.

"Then what the hell is McCarthy up to?" Johnny questioned.

"Proving himself a proper ass and laying the paper wide open to a sweet libel suit," I answered.

"Now look, I know McCarthy is no intellectual giant, but he's a damn good desk man. He's not fool enough to print this story unless he knew the score and got his dope from you! It says here that the elevator boy—"

"I know what it says," I interrupted wearily. "I read it all, each and every word in each and every line, and Dennis had no business printing it. Now he's in the soup and screaming for me to throw him a life line."

Morrow and Herrot both seemed unimpressed.

"It says the Dellman car was identified as the one Sullivan saw leaving the hotel lot. Where did Dennis get that from?"

"From me, naturally. I told him to put a sneak camera on the cars, but I didn't think he'd spring with a thing like this until he had better proof."

"But he has proof!" Morrow exclaimed. "Sullivan's identification is proof enough."

"You think so? Suppose Mrs. Dellman is the woman and she gets to Bob with enough dough to pay him to back down? Then where will Dennis be?"

"Then you do believe she was the woman?"

"I didn't say that!" I protested. "I said 'suppose she was.' The only facts we have to go on is that a car, like the Dellman's, was driven out of the hotel lot that night. Also a woman, driving a powerful motor, might have been the one who came down to that building the night Lili Cheng was killed. And Lili strongly believed Ned was killed by a woman, preferably Mrs. D."

"How do you know that?"

I turned puzzled eyes on him. "You were right there when she said so!"

"I was not. At least I didn't hear her say anything like that."

"Well, here's what she said then, or close to it."

I gave him a brief outline of Miss Cheng's suspicions and accusations.

Morrow whistled. "Pretty strong words! Well, good thing you came clean. I was fixing to phone in the story of those letters your sister wrote."

I shrugged. "That will have to come out eventually."

Herrot perked up his ears. "What letters?"

"Love letters various women, among them Vangie, wrote McGowan."

"You going to turn in the story?" Johnny asked.

"Not until I have to. Of course if you do, that forces my hand."

He hesitated, then. "Oh, to hell with them. I'll just call in this stuff you gave me."

His desk promptly refused to print anything about Mrs. Dellman until more evidence was brought forward. Morrow held the receiver so I could hear—and the air was blue with Briggs' opinion of McCarthy.

I grinned, but the grin was wiped out by a cop beckoning me to go back upstairs. I waved a wan farewell and followed him.

Vangie was near hysterics. They were going to hold her as a material witness, which meant they could hold her indefinitely.

I dissented violently, claiming she knew no more about it than Sullivan, who wasn't being held.

I might have saved my breath. They took her away

while I held forth about getting a lawyer and seeing how habeas corpus worked.

I sat down and glared at Nelson and Beton.

"Now, Miss Slone, how did you happen to know so much about the Dellman car?"

"If the police force was as competent as it should be, it could add two and two," I said, cuttingly. "That's all I did."

"Oh. Good at arithmetic, are you?"

"Lousy." I yawned. "But even I can do simple problems."

"Well, simple figuring tells *me* you know more about these murders than you are admitting!" he snapped angrily. "I warn you that if you think you'll get a better story by holding out on the police, you're heading for trouble."

"Oh for Pete's sake!" I exclaimed disgustedly. "I simply followed a hunch. I figured the Dellman cabriolet was the only one in town that could fit Sullivan's description. Make what you want of it."

"I shall do—"

The entrance of Terry Grogan, head of traffic files, interrupted. Grogan was excited.

"We traced that car! It answers the description of one of the Gerald Dellman cars. It's imported from the Eyties."

"You're a little late, Grogan." Nelson sounded sarcastic. "Miss Slone has given us that information—in a roundabout sort of way."

"And how would she be knowing?" Grogan wanted to know.

"The way reporters seem to know everything," Nelson said drily. "Or, perhaps I should say, the way reporters *think* they know everything."

"Oh, a smarty, huh?"

"Never mind, Terry. You may go now—and don't bust in here again without knocking. I don't like it."

"Yessir!" Grogan ducked his head and hustled out of the office.

"Well, Miss Slone!" Nelson turned to me. "You see the police department does function at times."

"Takes them plenty of time, too," I said acidly. "They've been almost four hours chasing down something they should have had in ten minutes." I smiled unpleasantly. "And, *Mr.* Nelson, it strikes me you're being damned formal today. When you were up for election it was 'Margaret' this and 'Margaret' that. Humph!"

His smile matched mine. "We weren't investigating a murder then. Now, Miss Slone, would you go over once more what you were doing the night the doctor was killed and also the night of Miss Cheng's murder?"

"Oh nuts! I've told those stories a hundred times! I know them by heart!"

"Oh you do?" Beton broke in. "Got your alibis down pat, have you?"

I reached for the paper weight but Nelson was too quick for me. He moved it and the inkwell to the far side of the desk and gave me an angry look. "I'll have no more scenes in this office!" he warned.

"There won't be any if you'll just get that guy out of my hair!" I retorted. "That means out of my sight," I added.

Nelson waited a second, then. "We want you to repeat your story in order that we may be sure we have all the facts straight."

"Yeah," I muttered. "You want to be sure I tell them the same way."

I settled back in the chair determined to give them a show. They'd asked for it—they'd damn well get it.

I closed my eyes and began to monotonously chant the happenings of the two previous nights. Never changing tempo I sing-songed through the whole story. When I finished, the monotone had almost put me to sleep in the chair.

"Sure got it down pat, haven't you sister?" Beton jeered. "So pat it doesn't even ring true!"

I jumped from the chair and advanced on him.

"Why you dim-witted, low-jawed, son-of-a-sea-going cook who used the offal—"

Nelson leaped from his chair and stepped between us.

"I told you I'd have no more scenes in this office!" he almost screamed. "I meant that! Les, you're asking for trouble. I believe Margaret is telling the truth. As for her sister, I don't know. She may be hedging."

I gave him a surprised and grateful look. "What did Vangie tell you?" I asked.

"What did she tell you?" he countered.

I thought a moment, then reasoning that her story couldn't possibly hurt her and might even help her, I sat back down and gave them the whole narrative, including the scrap I'd had with her and my own feelings in the matter.

When I'd finished I leaned back feeling smug and quite sure they'd let her go home at once. I'd figured wrong again.

Nelson remarked quietly that it was just as well they had Vangie in custody where no harm could come to her. She had heard the woman's voice and should be kept where she'd be safe.

I pointed out that a word to my mother would keep Vangie safe at home and why wasn't the same vigilance being exercised over Sullivan?

Nelson opined that Sullivan could take care of himself but Vangie was a girl and a nice, quiet cell in the women's wing of Parrish Prison with a matron looking after her would be safer than home.

I blew up.

"Damn it to hell!" I yowled. "If you think you can keep my sister in your stinking jail you're nuts! I'll get a lawyer and have her out of here in an hour! Just watch my smoke! Bunch of lousy bas—"

"Margaret! Shut up!" I hadn't seen Tommy come in, but

he had me by the shoulders. "They're only holding your sister for her own good!"

"Her own good, hell!" I howled. "What's good about it? Would you like to be in jail?"

Tommy squirmed. "Look, Margaret, there's been two murders and you were assaulted. Vangie might be next if the killer gets wind she knows something."

I realized he could be right but, dammit, the same thing applied to Bob Sullivan and he was free as air. I shrugged away from Tommy.

"Leave me alone. I'm all right now." I turned to Nelson. "Are you all finished with me?"

"Yes. Unless you're going to be foolish."

I cocked an eyebrow. "What do you mean?"

"Try to get your sister out of protective custody."

I faced him squarely. "See here, if I wanted to get her out I could do it. Make no mistake about that. Nothing but a murder warrant could stop me and you know damn well you can't get that."

"So?"

"So I'm going to let her stay where she is, for the time being. It might teach her a lesson. And now, if you haven't any more surprises to pull out of your bag of tricks, I'll leave."

"There'll be nothing pulled until tomorrow morning," Nelson said. "At 9:30 Mr. and Mrs. Dellman are coming in to explain your paper's accusations."

"Are they now?" I marveled. "Well, I'm going to lunch, then I'm going home—and guess what I'm going to do?"

Beton and Nelson looked blank, but Tommy's eyes held a twinkle.

"I'm going to bed," I announced. "And I'm going to sleep—I hope. And nothing short of a fire or a tornado will get me up before tomorrow morning."

I marched out of the office, then I had another thought and turned back.

"If you think you scare me about the Dellmans being here tomorrow, you're off the track," I said. "It was her car and she's the same size and build as the woman both Sullivan and Vangie saw in the hotel."

I closed the door with gentle finality.

14. *Vangie on Ice*

THERE was only a uniformed man in the anteroom.

"Where's my brother and sister and the Merceron girls?" I demanded.

"They've gone," he answered.

"No?" I glanced around the room. "Would you know where?"

"I think those two sisters went home. Your sister went to the Parrish with a matron and was she hot! She cussed that matron out good!"

"Good, was it? I'm sure it will do *her* a lot of good! Didn't my brother go with her?"

"They all left at the same time."

I headed for the pressroom. Joe Shem was snoring on the reporter's couch. I shook him rudely awake.

"What the hell are you doing in here making sleep tunes? Are you a reporter?"

He raised up and gave me a blank, sleepy look. "Oh, hullo, Maggie. I jest lay me down to rest a minute."

"So I notice," I said drily. "Where's everybody? Have you seen my brother?"

He assumed an injured air. "You needn't get snippy. I only took a short nap. Sure I saw your brother. He went out with Johnny Morrow and Herrot."

I made for the Greek joint across from the building. Vangie would keep on ice until later. I found Brett at a table with Morrow, Herrot, and two photographers, Elliot Sellers and Miles Hansen. Brett was sitting at the end of the booth.

"Where did they put Vangie? Or aren't you interested?" I asked brusquely.

"Of course I'm interested!" he retorted. "She's in the matron's dorm. She's okay."

I'd been having visions of her in a common cell and relief swept over me. Perversely enough, I grew irked. "It's a damn sight more than she deserves!" I retorted. "From what I heard of her behavior with the matron I marvel at the woman's kindness."

"Vangie did cut up," Brett said ruefully. "I didn't know she could cuss like that!"

"She's had a liberal education in profanity, between the two of us," I said sharply.

Brett grinned, so did the others. I walked over to a separate table and sat down. I ordered a combination sandwich and coffee and leaned over toward Brett.

"All jokes aside, I don't know but what we should get that brat out of the can before night. I don't like the idea of leaving her in jail, even in the matron's quarters. I think I'll call Barnett Ansley."

Morrow shoved out of the booth and stopped at my table.

"What's the dope on your sister, why is she in custody?"

"They're holding her as a material witness. Didn't Brett tell you?"

"That guy? He tells nothing!"

I laughed. "Smart lad. He's protecting his sister—Vangie, not me."

"You sticking around?"

"Hell no! I'm going home and McCarthy can fire me if he wants to."

"He won't. There isn't anything cooking until tomorrow morning anyhow."

"What do you mean?" I asked innocently.

"Don't tell me *you* don't know?"

"Uh uh."

Morrow puffed up importantly. "The Dellmans are being brought in."

"Oh! I knew *that!*" I deflated him. "Nelson told me and in a manner that appeared he blamed me for them having to come in."

"Well, you started it! You and McCarthy."

"Maybe. But I don't like the idea of getting her burned with me. After that story she'll probably have it in for everyone on my paper."

"You ought to have thought of that before you told Dennis about the car."

"Would you have thought before you told Jim Briggs?" I asked sweetly.

He smiled. "You got me, kid. Well, I got to beat it. See you tomorrow."

"Wait a minute. Gerry Dellman is supposed to be out of the city. How come he got back so fast?"

"You should know the answer to that! He flies everywhere in his own plane."

"Oh, that's right."

Morrow left, and I moved over to the booth, sitting by Art Herrot.

"Nobody tells me anything," he complained. "Why are they holding your sister?"

"Because she wrote some silly letters and she also happened to be in the hotel that night. She saw the same woman Sullivan saw and later heard her threaten Ned. She can't identify her though; she didn't see her face."

"Maybe she can identify the voice. Are you going to give the story in?"

"Not if I can avoid it. If you do I'll have to."

"I'll let it ride for the present. If I can."

I smiled my thanks. He and the photographers got up to leave. I waited until they were out of the place, then told Brett.

"They're holding her in protective custody. The only way

we can get her out is on a writ. If you want me to, I'll call
Ansley now."

"Why don't we just leave her where she is for tonight?"
he asked.

"Are you kidding?" I gaped at him.

"No. She could be in danger, and if she is, she's safer
in jail than at home. She'll be all right for tonight anyhow."

"But what will we tell Mother?"

"The truth. She can take it."

"Maybe. But you can tell her. I don't want the job."

"Okay. There's nothing to get upset about."

"You don't know your mama very well, do you sonny
boy?" I grinned.

"Oh, I can handle her all right." But he didn't look
enthusiastic about it.

"Well, I'm going to the office and then home." I got up
to leave.

"I'll ride with you. I let Toni take my car."

"Come along then."

In my car I stretched and yawned. "You drive. I'm about
to fall asleep." I handed him the keys.

He parked in front of the newspaper building to wait for
me while I fought it out with Dennis. Riding up, the
elevator girl, Ruth, looked at me as if I were a curiosity.
"I hear you got mixed up in a murder!"

"A couple of murders got mixed up with me," I told her
as I got out and went into the city room.

Dennis looked up in surprise. "What you doing here?"

"I came to give you what I've got before I go home.
Nothing is going to happen until tomorrow morning. The
cops are just going to sit on their fat fannies and think about
it. Tomorrow the Dellmans are being questioned. If you've
got a grain of charity in your system you'll let me go home
now. I'm going anyhow."

"Go home!" he yelled. "At 2:30? Can you imagine that?"

"I *can* and you needn't put on an act for me. I've had no sleep, there's nothing more happening on this case so there's no reason why I shouldn't go home."

He studied me silently for a minute. "Okay, beat it. Scram, screw on out of here, and be in at 7:30 sharp. Get it?"

I got it and hustled out before he could change his mind. I'd half intended to tell him about Vangie, but I wasn't going back to do it.

In the car I let out a gusty sigh. "Home, brother—and don't spare the horsepower. I'm two feet ahead of collapse."

Brett nosed the car out into the traffic and we rolled uptown. At home he drove into the garage and we went in the back way. Bertha popped her head out of the kitchen, looking past us, her eyes searching.

"Whar at ma white chile?"

"In jail," I said bluntly.

A wail went up and she darted for Mother's room.

"Miz Sally! Dey done gone put Miss Vangie in de jail-house!"

Brett gave me a look. "That tore it," he said grimly.

"I leave the shreds with you!" I replied and scuttled upstairs.

I found Ida, my maid, mending some underwear.

"Get me a gown and run me a hot bath, please," I asked her. "I'm going to bed and no one is to come in here or bother me until I wake up. Not if you have to stand guard at the door with a loaded gun! Understand?"

"Does dat includes you maw?"

"It includes everybody! I'll talk to Mama later, if I'm awake before she goes to bed."

I'd just climbed in the tub when I heard Mother's voice raised in argument. "I don't care *what* Miss Margaret said, Ida! I'm going in there. You seem to forget I'm mistress here! Stand aside."

I knew that tone.

"Let her in Ida," I called out. "Tell her to come in the bathroom."

Mother stood in the door, worried and annoyed. "Never dare give a maid in this house such an order!" she said tartly. "I won't stand for it."

"You might remember I pay Ida's salary!" My tartness matched hers. "She's my maid and this is my room. I want to get some rest. Now what do you want?"

"What's this ridiculous story about Evangeline being in custody? I won't stand for it."

"That's two things in two minutes you won't stand for," I said wearily. "But I'm afraid you'll have to bear up under the latter. Vangie will just have to spend the night in jail, and I hope it teaches her not to write silly letters or go chasing after men in their hotels!"

"What letters? When did she chase after a man?"

"Didn't Brett tell you? Didn't Vangie say anything when the police came after her?"

"Brett told me nothing about this. I was out when Evangeline left, and she said nothing about being taken by police. She told Bertha she'd gone out with friends."

"Truthful child, isn't she? She must have thought she'd be home and you'd never be any wiser."

"It doesn't matter what she thought. I want to know what letters you mean."

"Some drivel she wrote McGowan. She even threatened his life in some of them. Crazy little fool!"

Mother whitened to the lips. "Threatened him? How?"

"Wrote him that she'd fix him or get me to fix him. Words to that effect. The police got hold of the letters." I refrained from telling her how they got them.

"But that doesn't seem much of a reason to hold her in jail! Is she under suspicion?"

"Didn't Brett tell you *anything?*"

"Only that she was being held. He said you had the details."

"The welcher!" I exclaimed disgustedly. "He was supposed to tell you all about it. Now he passes me the buck. Nuts!"

"Margaret! Can't you speak decent English?"

"I express my feelings better in slang," I said, and launched into the story of Vangie's visit to the hotel and why the police thought she was safer in jail than at home.

"And you left the child there when you could have had her released?"

This time I passed the buck. "Your *son* thought it best for her to stay there overnight. He's the man of the house, isn't he?"

"Yes, but jail is no place for that child."

"Oh, she'll be all right. She's in the matron's dormitory. She's had four years of boarding school so she shouldn't mind."

"I hope you're right, but I don't like the idea."

"I don't like it too much myself. But she got herself into it."

"That's neither here nor there!"

"I know it, but there's nothing we can do about it now. And I'd like to get to bed, if you don't mind."

She sighed heavily. "Well, if we can't do anything we can't. Will you be down for dinner?"

"If I'm awake. If not, Ida can bring me a tray later or I'll just raid the ice box."

She nodded and left. I got out of the tub, dried off, and went into the bedroom where Ida sat looking anxious.

"Miss Marg'ret, Ah couldn't stop Miz Sally. She wuz sot on comin' in."

"It's all right. Now she'll leave me be and I can get to sleep."

Ida turned down the covers and plumped the pillows. I crawled gratefully in between the sheets and was asleep in one-nothing flat.

I awakened to a dusky room and looked at the bedside

clock. Just 6:00. I felt wonderfully refreshed for having had only about three hours' sleep, and I was as hungry as a wolf on the prowl. I slipped on a robe, thinking I'd go down and filch a hot biscuit and some jelly before dressing for dinner.

The house was strangely quiet and there were no smells of food cooking. I wondered about that for only a brief moment, then I caught a glimpse of the east windows. The sun was just rising. I'd slept the clock around and then some extra.

I giggled and continued on to the kitchen where I foraged for eggs and bacon and made coffee. I was about finished when Bertha came in to start breakfast.

She fastened surprised indignant eyes on me. "Whut you doin' in hyar?"

"Eating," I said, with commendable brevity.

"Eatin' and a sleepin' in yo comfitable home while Miss Vangie sits in de jailhouse. Ought to be 'shame fo youself."

She grunted disgustedly and went about preparing breakfast. I sat over a second cup of coffee and listened to her grumble.

"Settin' in de kitchen lak a suhvant. Got no bizness in dis hyar kitchen, nohow."

I got up. "To hell with you. I'll get out of your damned old kitchen!"

"Sich talk fum a lady! Sounds jes lak a no good fancy woman, dats whut."

"Is that so?" I sneered. "Well, I hear your precious Vangie used some language to burn the ears off the jail matron!"

"Effen she did she sholy larned hit fum you!" she blazed at me. "Now git on out fum ma kitchen! Git!"

I beat a hasty retreat, went out on the porch and brought in the paper and the milk. I went back and put the milk on the kitchen table.

"Why don't you bring these things in?" I asked. "Isn't that what you're being paid to do?"

I didn't wait for an answer but scooted back to the dining room where I found cigarettes and settled down to open, in some fear, the morning paper. I breathed easier as nothing appeared on the front page or elsewhere in the paper about Vangie's being held. I was reading the story of how the police expected to make an arrest at any minute in connection with the two murders when Mother came into the room.

I put down the paper and started for the stairs. I was rested but I still wasn't up to coping with parental arguments about Vangie. I'd just put my foot on the second stair when she called me.

I returned reluctantly to the dining room.

"Yes, ma'am?"

"I hope you're going to get Evangeline out of that place this morning?"

"Of course."

She cast a jaundiced eye at the paper.

"Is there anything about her in that thing?"

"Nothing. The boys promised they'd lay off if they could. There's nothing about her in it at all."

"That's good. Margaret—" hesitantly—"do you suppose Ned McGowan was the sort the papers are making him out to be?"

"Ned McGowan was a heel," I said flatly and with no hesitation. "Had he been older he'd have been a rake. As it was he was just a heel."

Her eyes raised to mine, a mute question in them.

"I don't know," I said gently. "I don't know. I can only hope Vangie had more sense than to let him take her over the full route."

Mother nodded miserably and I went to my room where I dressed in a gray tailored wool. I came back down the stairs ready for work, kissed Mother good-by, and left the house.

When I walked into the city room, Dennis cocked an

eye at the clock and let an exaggeratedly surprised look creep over his face.

"Early, ain't you?"

"Ummm," I murmured. It was just 7:05.

"How come? Afraid you might miss something?"

"Uh huh."

"Ummm and uh huh! Is that all you can say?"

"Huh?" I looked at him.

"All right, smarty! Why didn't you tell me they were holding your sister at Parrish Prison?"

"How did you find that out?"

"Never mind! Why didn't you tell me yesterday?"

"Because I didn't want her name spread all over the papers!" I snapped. "The kid's just been foolish and there's no reason she should be involved in a stink. She's only a material witness anyhow!"

"*Only* a material witness!" Dennis howled. "And you say nothing!"

"None of the other papers said anything about her! She's my kid sister and come hell or high water, job or no job, I'm going to protect her if I can."

He scratched his chin reflectively. "Maybe I better send someone else on this today. You're letting your personal feelings interfere with your work."

"You can do as you damn well please," I retorted. "But if you take me off you can find another reporter. I've suffered too much for this thing to let it go without a fight."

"If I didn't have two men out now I'd call your bluff," he said. "But I want a story on your sister right now."

"Well, you won't get it!" I blazed and waited to be fired.

"Okay, kid. I'll pick it up from the other paper and when I do—" He left the threat unfinished.

"I'll promise you you'll have it before any of the other papers."

"See that we do. Now get these done and then go on to headquarters." He handed me a bunch of rewrite stuff.

For over two hours I pounded out routine rewrites and then handed them in to the desk.

"I'm leaving," I told Dennis. "I'll call you from over there."

"Get me something to pin on that Dellman dame," he instructed. "I'm in a spot over that thing."

"I'll try," I promised and left the office.

My dash clock said 9:15, and what with traffic, I pulled up just as the big shiny town car of the Dellmans came into the parking lot by the court building.

I hesitated, then spoke.

"Good morning!" I said brightly. "This is early for you two, isn't it?"

Gerald Dellman smiled, showing even white teeth in a bronzed clean-shaven face. "Not for me. I'm usually up and out by this time or earlier."

I waited, expecting a freeze from her, but to my surprise she extended a cordial hand.

"Good morning, Miss Slone!" We shook hands. "Dear, you remember Miss Slone? She's Brett's sister."

"Of course." We shook hands too. "I'm pretty keen about your brother. He's a great flier. One of the best. Wish he'd come to work for me, but he likes that old crate of his."

I smiled at the millionaire planter and aviation enthusiast. "Say rather he likes his independence. Flying his own ship he can do as he pleases."

"I suppose so." His face sobered. "I'm going to miss the trips he and Ned and I used to take together. We had some fine times."

"I'm glad you two aren't angry with me," I said quickly. They both looked puzzled.

"About that car story my paper printed," I explained.

"Your paper?" He looked sharply at me. "Did you write that thing?"

"Hell no!" I denied flatly. "My city editor pulled that boner."

"I'd quite forgotten you worked for them," he said. "Although now I do recall seeing your name over stories. Margaret Slone, isn't it?"

"That's right." I grinned. "My paper pays off half in money and half in bylines. Bylines and a quarter will get you pork chops."

"Really?" He smiled dubiously.

A voice spoke at my shoulder. Morrow had come up and must have heard the last few words.

"She means that sheet she works for is not too generous with cash but it never stints on credit in the way of bylines."

Dellman laughed lightly. "Oh! I see! Well, don't worry about that story, Miss Slone. Even if you had written it, you'd only have been doing your job."

"You're very kind, but I don't write such a story unless I've adequate proof to back it up."

"Why, I believe you were worried!" Mrs. Dellman laughed. "Truthfully, I am angry about the story, but not with you. There is a perfectly good explanation and the paper should have called me before they printed the story."

I thought: So she has an explanation all ready! I wondered if that could mean she was going to admit having been in the hotel. That seemed incredible inasmuch as it would mean admitting she'd been doing some sweet cheating on her husband. She must know the woman had been heard to threaten Ned. That story had been printed.

"Shall we go in?" I asked.

"Of course." They turned to follow me and Morrow fell in step by my side.

"What do you think?" he asked in a low voice.

"Nothing," I said sharply, sniffing the air. "We'll just have to wait and see what happens upstairs." I sniffed again.

"What are you smelling the air for?"

"What? Oh, nothing! Just a perfume Mrs. Dellman is wearing. It's very odd."

15. *Listening In*

TOMMY GROSS was standing by the door of the ante office when we stepped off the elevator. He came forward to meet us.

"I'm sorry to have caused you this inconvenience, Mrs. Dellman," he apologized. "Mr. Nelson believes you may be able to help us in this case."

He ushered them into the inner office and closed the door on them.

"Hey!" I yelped. "I thought the press was in on this!"

Tommy silenced me with a look and motioned us into another room on the other side of the ante office. The inter-telephone communication box sat on a small desk.

"Oh! I get it." I sat down close to the desk as Jolly brought in Bob Sullivan, sleepy and annoyed.

"Look here, captain! I've got to get some sleep. I can't work all night and be hauled out of bed every morning like this!"

"Sorry," Tommy soothed him. "We want you to listen to this voice and for God's sake be sure of any identification. Before she leaves we'll place you where you can see her as she goes out."

"All right," Sullivan said ungraciously. "But this is my last trip up here in the morning. My nerves won't stand the gaff!"

"Shhh!" Tommy waved him to silence and flipped the switch on the box. Murmurs began to issue from it. We caught the end of a sentence in Nelson's voice.

165

"—feel sure you can furnish ample evidence the car which was seen back of the hotel was not yours."

"But I can't." Mrs. Dellman spoke softly. "You see, it was my car."

"It was!" Nelson's act was convincing.

"Yes."

"But what was it doing there? Who was driving it?"

She hesitated, murmuring small distressed sounds. "Oh, dear! Must I tell? Gerry, darling, must I?"

"I'm afraid so, Marta," Dellman's voice answered. "It's the only way to clear the whole situation up with the police and the papers."

She sighed. "I suppose you're right. Well, the car was mine but I was not driving it."

To my disgust Tommy closed the switch. He turned to Bob "How about it?"

Sullivan looked uncertain. "I can't be sure. The woman I heard was mad. Her voice wasn't controlled and—and—"

"Cultured?" Morrow suggested.

"Yeah. Turn it on again."

Tommy flipped the switch and again we caught part of a sentence.

"—and you let her take your car?"

"Yes. You see Miss St. Clair is more like one of the family than a nurse. I have bad migraine attacks and both the doctor and my husband felt I should have someone with me at all times. Lucille was not very strong, she'd been ill and was not up to nursing duty, but Ned felt she was quite strong enough to be with me."

I leaned toward Tommy. "She's talking about Lucille St. Clair!"

He nodded and motioned me to be silent. That box works both ways.

"How long has she been with you?" Nelson questioned.

"About six months. I've grown very fond of her."

"Dr. McGowan introduced her to your household?"

"Yes, he did, and she's been a great help and comfort to me, almost like having a younger sister around."

"Is she a large woman?"

Her laughter trilled out. "Lucille! Oh no! She's about my size but perhaps a little thinner. And, as I told you, she's not very strong."

"Is she strong enough to wield a poker and kill a woman?" Nelson shot the question in a staccato voice.

Through the inanimate box I could sense her recoil.

"Oh don't say that! I'm sure Lucille couldn't do such a thing!"

"Forgive me." Nelson was smooth again. "But this is a case of two murders and assault with intent to kill."

"Assault?"

"Miss Slone was struck with the same poker shortly after Miss Cheng was killed. She was trying to play detective. Only luck and her heavy hair saved her from a crushed skull."

"How awful! I didn't dream it was she who found the body. The story said only that a reporter was also injured in an attack."

"Well, it was she. Meddling little fool."

Smirks appeared on three faces while mine got red. I stuck out my tongue at the box.

"Please continue, Mrs. Dellman." Nelson sounded a trifle impatient.

"Ned, Olivette, Antoinette, and Brett Slone dined with me that night. Gerry was called out of town and Charles Craig, his pilot, went with him. Lucille then asked to be excused. She was to dine with us but when the other two men were called away she said she was not feeling well and would prefer a tray in her room.

"She was pale and had seemed rather upset for several days. I didn't dream at the time that it was because of Ned's engagement. Of course I suggested she go to bed and let Ned have a look at her, but she said she didn't need a doctor, she just wanted to be alone.

"Our evening was quite pleasant. Ned was happy and Vette was radiant. When we were having coffee Lucille joined us in the drawing room. She was wearing a soft rose silk hostess gown I'd given her and she looked lovely."

"You gave her clothing?" Nelson interrupted.

"Why, yes. You see when her father lost his money and committed suicide, she had nothing. She took up nursing and was something of a protégée of Ned's. It helped her for me to assist her in filling her wardrobe."

"I see. Please go on."

"Well, Lucille joined us and offered her congratulations— the usual nice things said in the usual nice way. About 10:00 Brett said he must leave. Ned and Vette were in no hurry so I suggested Toni take my car and drive Brett to the field."

"The same car?"

"Why yes."

"You're rather generous with such an expensive motor." Nelson sounded dry. "So Miss Merceron also had your car that night?"

"Yes, but Ned was still with us when she got back. We had another brandy and then started to break up. Toni and Vette went to the powder room off the main hall and Ned got his own coat from the closet. Lucille followed him out. I went back to the drawing room, then started out again to send for the butler to clear away the coffee things. The thick carpets deadened my steps and just as I got to the door I heard Lucille say: 'But I must see you alone tonight. I'll do something desperate if you try to put me off!'

"I was shocked and surprised and stayed in the drawing room until I heard Ned and the girls leave. When Lucille came back I told her I'd heard what she said and asked why she'd never told me she was in love with Ned.

"In a bitter scornful tone she told me I must have been blind and stupid not to have seen how she felt. Then she burst into sobs and rushed out of the room. Such things upset me and my head began to ache badly. I tried to find some of the tablets Ned prescribed for me but the box was empty. I finally called Lucille and asked her to give me something for my head. She came in, her eyes red from weeping, and apologized for being ugly to me. Then she said the powders were out, but she gave me a hypodermic.

"From then on everything is rather vague. I recall, as in a dream, seeing her leave my room dressed for the street."

"What time was that?"

"I have no idea, except it was well after midnight. When I awakened I looked for Lucille, but she was out. My maid said she'd gone for a walk. I called Ned's office, then the hotel, and heard of his death by poison. A horrid suspicion formed in my mind, and when Lucille came in I flung the news of his death at her."

"You say you 'flung the news at her'?"

"Yes. I said, 'Ned's been murdered! Poisoned!'"

"What did she do?"

She just stared at me for a moment then she said, 'But that's impossible! He was alive when I left—' Then she broke off and clapped her hand to her mouth.

"I demanded she tell me the truth. I told her I believed she had seen him that night after he left here. She admitted it, admitted she'd given me a strong opiate, and when I was asleep she had taken my car and gone to the hotel where she had pled with him and even threatened him. He'd told her to stop the dramatics and finally she had realized the hopelessness of it and left him. But she assured me on oath she had never killed him. I believed her. I still do."

There was a short silence and I thought Tommy had turned off the switch. Then Gerry Dellman's voice came through.

"I'd like to take my wife home now," he said. "She's highly nervous and should be in bed."

"In just a few minutes," Nelson answered. "Mrs. Dellman, why didn't you bring Miss St. Clair with you this morning?"

"Because she is in a state of near collapse and I wasn't going to cause her more worry unless I had to." Her reply was spirited.

"What did you think about the second murder? Was this girl home when that took place?"

"She certainly was!" she retorted confidently. "Home in bed in the room right next to mine."

"You're sure of that?"

"Quite sure."

"When did Mr. Dellman arrive home?"

"I called him in Cleveland early Thursday, as soon as I heard of Ned's death and learned for sure Lucille had been to his room. He got home late Friday morning."

"Must be nice to fly like that," Nelson commented. Then, "Do you realize you should have come to the police with this story as soon as you knew it?"

"I suppose I should have, but I thought no one had seen her or my car, and I was convinced in my own mind she hadn't killed Ned."

"And you're sure she didn't leave the house Thursday evening?"

"Certainly!"

"That is not to your knowledge?" Nelson baited the trap.

"That's right."

"But to your positive knowledge neither were you sure she left the house the night before. You only saw, as in a dream, that she appeared to be dressed for the street."

"I told you all about that!" Her voice rose angrily and I saw Bob lean forward attentively. "I told you Lucille had told me the whole story of her going to the hotel. You can't bully me, Mr. Nelson. I won't stand for it!"

Bob's eyes brightened and he snapped his fingers. "Now she sounds like that woman!" he exclaimed.

Tommy signaled him to be quiet as Nelson's voice came through again.

"I don't mean to bully you, Mrs. Dellman. But we must question that girl. Is she at home now?"

"She is and she's not well. You'll have to send someone there to see her. She couldn't come down."

"Very well, that will be all. Thanks for coming in."

Tommy flipped the switch and we hurried into the outer office where Bob sprawled in a chair, his hat over his eyes. I stood near the door, Morrow beside me.

Beton showed the couple out of the inner office. They both looked worried and annoyed, but she spoke pleasantly to me and cast an incurious glance at Bob.

"I heard about your experience," she said. "I suppose you're fortunate not to have been badly hurt or killed. It's all so horrible."

Her eyes filled and she groped for a handkerchief, found a tiny lace-edged square and dabbed at her eyes. The handkerchief was torn and soiled and something pinged in my memory. Then I got a whiff of that scent again. Without doubt it was the same perfume I'd smelled in that apartment. A nameless sensation crept over me, not fear exactly, but a strong feeling that something was clicking the pieces of a puzzle together and that the answer lay in a small piece which should be right to hand.

Mr. and Mrs. Dellman were facing me, their backs to the room. Bob Sullivan had his hat pushed back and was studying her, his brows knit with uncertainty. Tommy was murmuring sounds into the phone. He looked at me and his eyes held the force of a blow. He was trying to tell me something with that look. I followed a hunch it was to keep the Dellmans talking.

I caught Dellman's hand and looked at an unusual ring he was wearing.

"What an odd piece!" I babbled. "I've never seen one like it before."

"It's a museum piece," he said. "I found it in Egypt when Marta and I were on our honeymoon." He glanced affectionately at his wife. "I guess I'd better get you home, dear, you look—"

"I crave odd jewelry!" I interrupted hastily. "I have some rather interesting pieces. This ring, for instance," I extended my hand. "It's old Moroccan and has married five generations in my family. Someday it will be my wedding ring. It came to this country with an ancestor who sailed a privateer for the king of Spain."

He made polite sounds and studied my outstretched finger.

"An unusual piece. You should be proud of it."

"Oh! I am!" I at once launched into the history of the ring. Partly legend, partly fact, it takes about five or ten minutes to tell. I knew Dellman was bored stiff and wanted out, but he couldn't very well walk off and leave me in mid-sentence without being obviously rude. I was just about to wind up the narrative when Tommy strolled over.

He smiled easily at the three of us. "I'm glad your jewelry interests kept you here a few minutes," he said. "Mr. Nelson wants to ask you another question or two. He told me to ask you."

Dellman's irritation was plainly apparent.

"Yes?" The word was a curt question mark.

Tommy turned to his wife. "Do you know how Dr. McGowan died, Mrs. Dellman?"

"Why he was poisoned!"

"Yes, but do you know how the poison was administered? The question is asked because you seemed so sure of Miss St. Clair's innocence, simply because she told you he was alive when she left him."

"Why, there was something—" Her voice faltered. "There

was something about a toothbrush. I didn't read the account very closely."

"Yes, there *was* something about a toothbrush. The poison was applied to the toothbrush by someone who knew he'd had a tooth pulled recently. That would account for his being alive when his murderess left his room. He was alive because he didn't brush his teeth until his visitor had left the room and he'd locked the door. If Miss St. Clair was that visitor then she must have been the one who applied that poison!"

She stared at him. Then, without warning, she crumpled to the floor all of a heap.

Dellman turned on Tommy furious. "You fool!" he shouted. "Why did you have to spring a thing like that on her? I could—" He bent over his wife, mouth working with anger.

"Get some water, you idiot!" he snarled. "Get some brandy! Get a doctor! Don't stand there like a jackass!"

I giggled nervously and he turned on me, including me in his rage.

"You and your damned ring! If you hadn't detained us with that thing we'd have been home by now! Well! Do something! Don't stand there gawking!"

I recovered my dignity. "That wasn't what made her faint!"

He recovered his balance. "I'm sorry I lost my temper." He sought to smooth mine and Tommy's ruffled one. "She's subject to these fainting spells and they always frighten me."

Tommy grunted and went over to the water cooler, running ice water over his handkerchief.

"Please help me with her," Dellman appealed to me.

I bent over her, loosened her collar, and bathed her face with the wet cloth. "Does she carry smelling salts?" I asked him. "Some women who are given to fainting do that."

"I don't know," he said helplessly.

"I'll look in her bag." I reached for it but as I was about to open it she shuddered and opened her eyes. She didn't ask where she was; she knew that and apparently didn't like it. A sob caught in her throat and she burrowed her head into her husband's side.

"Take me home, Gerry! I want to go home right away! Take me there!" The last word mounted a note of hysteria.

Nelson's voice spoke at my shoulder. "I'm terribly sorry about this. You may go whenever you wish."

Dellman assisted her to her feet and she gave Nelson a glance—a very unpleasant one. When she spoke though her voice was pleasant enough.

"I think there is one other thing I'd better explain to you, Mr. Nelson. I loaned Ned some money, quite a large sum— almost seventy thousand dollars. He was to give me notes for it but he simply overlooked it, he was like that. They may be in his office and of course his estate is liable for the loan. Isn't it, dear?" She turned to her husband. He nodded.

"I just thought you'd better know before your office or the papers got hold of it and made it something scandalous."

With this parting shot and no indication from Nelson that the notes were in his safe, the couple left the room.

"Thank God that's over!" I sank limply into a chair.

Nelson turned to Sullivan. "Well? Was that the woman you saw? Did you recognize her voice?"

"I can't be sure," he answered. "Twice she sounded like the same woman. Once when she told you not to bully her she used the same words, said she wouldn't 'stand for it.' Then when she hollered for her husband to take her home, she sounded pretty much the same, but I wouldn't swear to it."

"So much for the voice." Nelson shrugged. "What about her looks?"

"She seems taller than the woman I took up. Her husband

is about my height and she hit him at the cheekbone. That woman in the elevator would have hit me about the chin." He gestured to illustrate.

Nelson studied him. "That would make her about five feet. Mrs. Dellman is around five-two. Well, I've sent Jolly for the nurse. We called but there were orders not to disturb her. So I had to send a man. She'll be disturbed, all right," he ended grimly.

I looked at my watch: again it was five minutes to a deadline! I got up and tore out of the door, Morrow on my heels. We pounded down the stairs and into the pressroom. I caught forty different kinds of hell from Dennis, which was what I expected to catch, but he quieted down as I went along with the meat of the story. When I finished he was almost human.

"Get back up to Nelson's office," he instructed. "I'll send a camera over to get pictures of that nurse as soon as they bring her in. Call me as soon as you have any follow throughs on this."

I assented hurriedly and went back upstairs with Morrow. Nelson, Beton, and Tommy were standing in a huddle. Sullivan was sound asleep in the chair.

Suddenly I thought of something else.

"Hey! How about my sister? Why wasn't she listening in?"

"She was," Nelson told me. "She was on a dictaphone in the matron's quarters. She is as uncertain as Bob here." He indicated the sleeping boy.

"That's a big help. Can she go home now?"

Nelson hesitated. "As soon as Jolly gets here with that girl she can. We want to see if she can identify her. We'll wake him up too." He nodded, smiling at Sullivan.

As if the words had summoned him, Sullivan opened weary eyes. "Can't I go now? I'm pooped and if I work tonight I got to get some shuteye. This makes two days now I've had practically none at all."

"I want you to have a look at this woman we're bringing in," Nelson said. "And I want you to hear her voice. If you're too tried to work tonight I'll call the hotel and get you the night off."

"No thanks." He shook his head. "The hotel docks you for all time off and you can't make tips not working. I need the dough. I'm fixing to get married this summer."

I looked at him and on an impulse suggested he come down to the pressroom and stretch out on the couch. When Jolly got back they could send for him. He hopped up eagerly.

"How about letting my kid sister wait there too?" I asked Nelson. "I'll bring them both up when you send for them."

Nelson agreed, and Bob and I sped downstairs. "I would like a drink," I said as we hiked down the steps. "And I want to take it before my precious sister gets there. She might tell Mama on me."

In the pressroom I took a bottle from under a pile of old copy sheets in my desk drawer and we took a quick drink of warm bathtub gin and warm coca-cola. Then Bob flopped on the couch.

"You know, you're a good sport," he told me sleepily. "I'm glad your sister is okay. I hated like hell to give her away, but she brought it on herself."

"It's all right," I assured him. "Vangie isn't too bright at times."

16. *Disappearing Act*

A FURIOUS voice spoke from the doorway. I turned to see Vangie tugging to get free from the matron.

"Just you wait, Margaret Slone! You can't talk about me and treat me as if I were an incorrigible and incompetent child! I'm going straight home and tell Mama! She'll fix you all right!"

"Hold it!" I warned her. "That's the very expression that got you in trouble. You damned little fool!" I yanked her away from the matron and gave her a hard shake. "You're going no place until you're allowed to leave! Right now you've been released in my custody. *Mine*—get it? And you'll stay right here until they send for you, get that? If you weren't an incorrigible and wholly incompetent brat you wouldn't be in this mess! You just give me any trouble and I'll pin your ears back!"

The matron left hurriedly. She'd had enough of Vangie and I didn't blame her. Bob sat up, admiration in his eyes.

She squirmed in my grasp but I had a tight hold.

"Margaret, you let me go! Let go of me, you nasty old thing. You damned old bitch! You—"

I let go then, on the heels of a wallop that sent her spinning.

She recovered balance and lit for the door. She ran right into the blue and brass wall of Joe Shem's uniform. Vangie recoiled in panic, wilting into the nearest chair. She began to bawl and my anger wilted with her tears. I surveyed her and resisted the impulse to comfort her.

"Regular hell cat, ain't she?" Shem asked.

177

I shrugged. "She may outgrow it—I hope."

He chuckled. "You sure took care of her tantrum. I was watching. Kids that age are funny. They think they know it all and they'll fight folks who want to help them, but they always wind up by bawling and trying to get out of a jam with their tears. My kids do it too."

Vangie lifted an angry, tear-stained face. "I'll thank you not to talk about me as if I wasn't here!" she snapped. "I hate you, Margaret Slone! And you too, whoever you are! I hate you! Do you hear?"

"I hear," I said acidly. "And whoever-you-are happens to be Officer Shem, a friend of mine. Now you shut up."

She opened her mouth to give me what for, but the entrance of Brett interrupted. He took one look at her tear-smudged face and turned on me.

"Now what have you done to her? Why can't you leave the kid alone?" He started toward her but I grabbed his arm.

"You leave her alone," I said sternly. "Nasty little hellion, let her bawl."

He fell back a step and glared at me. "What's eating you?"

"She's been exhibiting some more of her temper and I slapped her. And you're not to baby her. She's had too much of that all of her life."

Brett stuck his jaw out. "I'm going to take her home."

"Oh no, you're not! She hasn't been released yet. What's more, she's in parole to me at the moment and I'm responsible for her. She has to go back to the D.A.'s office in a little while."

"What for?"

"To see if she can identify someone." I turned to Bob, who'd been too entertained to worry about sleep. "Sullivan, will you go up and find out what gives with that nurse they're bringing in?"

He rose immediately. "Sure."

Brett stood and glowered at me over Vangie's sobbing figure.

"I think you're—" he began, but Morrow burst into the room shutting off what he thought.

"Slone! Where you been while things were happening?"

"What things? What's happened?"

"Go on up and find out! Did you give me a break on that car angle?"

I wheeled, but as I started out a wild-eyed Bob Sullivan blew into the room. I grabbed him. "What is it?"

"That girl!" he gasped. "The nurse! She's done a disappearing act! Gone, skipped, vanished, taken the air! The D.A. and Captain Gross are frothing at the mouth!"

I just gaped at him.

"That office upstairs is a madhouse!" he exclaimed. "They sent a dick after the girl and the maid told him she was asleep. He pulled a badge and ordered them to rout her out. In a minute or so the maid came running down yelling that the girl was gone. No one saw her leave—she just disappeared."

"Were the Dellmans home when this happened?" I found my voice.

"No, but they came in while this copper was yelling his head off. Then Mrs. Dellman threw another fit and had to be put to bed."

I called Dennis and gave him the story on this development, then I looked at Vangie—wondering how this would affect her freedom. I got to thinking of Lucille St. Clair and the picture of her banging anyone over the head wouldn't come clear. It just didn't fit. She was an insipid little thing, one who might use poison but hardly a poker. Then this disappearing act, right after that pat story of Mrs. Dellman's. It was all too damn pat. I had a brainstorm and beckoned Bob out into the hall.

"I want you to find out something for me," I told him.

"What?"

"Go back to the hotel and talk to all the boys who worked the shift ahead of you. Find out if Dr. McGowan was alone when he got in from the office that afternoon. If not, get a description of whoever was with him. Get descriptions of anyone who called for him at the desk Wednesday. Then check the register for anyone, man or woman, who was roomed on the tenth floor Tuesday or Wednesday and who checked out either late Thursday or early Friday."

He looked dubious.

"I'm going on the theory that Ned may have been killed by a person we don't know anything about or don't remotely suspect. Someone who may have had a key to his room and who checked into the hotel and put that poison on his brush while he was still in his office."

"Say! You could be right! You oughta be a dick yourself."

I glowed. "Will you do it?"

"Sure."

I gave him detailed instructions and told him to be sure and make notes on what he found out so he wouldn't forget anything.

"Okay. What do I do when I get the dope all together?"

I gave him my home number. "Call me here. If I'm not in call the paper. I'll be one place or the other or I'll leave a message where you can get me. We'll meet sometime to-night and see what we can figure out."

"Swell. I'll go ask Nelson if I can leave and I'll see you later." He highballed out of the door.

I put both hands on my hips and surveyed Vangie.

"Well, Miss! Are you through squalling?"

She edged closer to Brett. "You better leave me alone!" she said. "If you touch me once more I'll—"

"I'm not going to touch you," I assured her. "I just wanted to tell you that the girl they suspect of these murders has done a disappearing act and Nelson may feel it safer for you to stay here until they catch her."

"Who is she?"

"F'Pete's sake! Where are your ears? The whole room has been talking about her!"

"I wasn't listening," she said sullenly.

"Well, it's Lucille St. Clair."

"*Lucille!* That namby-pamby thing!" Her voice was scornful. "She couldn't kill anyone, she wouldn't have the guts. She's a sissy bitch."

"That's fine language!" I snapped.

"Never mind *my* language! Better mind your own—I learned mine from you!"

I took an angry step forward and she huddled against Brett. I took a deep breath and counted to ten.

"I didn't ask for your personal opinion of Lucille. What I do want to know is did that woman in the hotel have about the same build as she has?"

"We-e-ll, Lucille is little and ash blonde—very colorless." I hid a smile at that last. "But her hat and coat collar hid her hair so I don't know if it was blonde or what."

"Never mind that. Was she the same general size?"

"About the same height, but Lucille was skinny as a rail and looked like she was going into T. B. The woman I saw was plump and that coat was a real expensive one. Lucille couldn't afford one like it."

"She'd been living with the Dellmans and Mrs. Dellman gave her clothes. That might account easily for both the coat and the plumpness. The Dellmans eat well."

Vangie was quiet for a moment, thinking seriously. "No. I don't think that was Lucille," she said at last. "There was something about her walk, it wasn't light and sort of tiptoey. Lucille always went along like she was in a hospital corridor."

"Neat bit of figuring," I applauded. "Notice anything else?"

"Yes. She wore low-heeled, real flat-heeled shoes. Catch Lucille doing that!"

"Why not?"

"She wouldn't have owned such shoes except maybe for work! Why, she always got the highest heels she could buy to make her look at least an inch taller than a midget!"

"I take it you were very fond of her."

"You needn't be so sarcastic!" she blazed at me. "I couldn't stand her!"

"In that case you surely wouldn't try to protect her," I mused.

"Protect her?" She screamed the question. "If I thought she killed Ned I'd tear her to pieces!"

"The police think she did. You don't. I'm undecided, but I still think he got what was coming to him."

"If you feel that way why are you bothering about finding out who did it?" she sneered at me.

"I'd like to get even for that clout I got on the head. Also I'd like to find Miss Cheng's killer. I don't care about Ned. He was killed cleverly, Miss Cheng brutally. The more I think of that the more riled I get and the more certain I am that the person who did that job would kill again and again. Such a person should be put away. But as for Ned, I wouldn't trouble if the killer had stopped with his murder."

"That's what you say. Are you sure it isn't a blind to cover up being in love with him yourself?"

"They didn't find any letters from me in his things, did they?"

She turned white but slashed back at me, "You could have got rid of them! You were in that apartment!"

"Oh nuts!" I turned on my heel and went upstairs to the D.A.'s office. It was bedlam with Nelson blaming everyone for the nurse getting away. Even Tommy, usually self-controlled, was yelling about inefficiency.

"That girl should have been sent for as soon as her name came up!" he shouted.

"She probably wasn't there then," I consoled him.

"That makes no difference! This case is full of blunders!"

"I agree with you there!" I pounced at the opening. "My

sister being held, for instance. She ought to be home in bed, she's in foul shape."

"I don't know about that." Nelson frowned thoughtfully. "With that woman at large she may be safer here."

"That's silly," I said flatly. "She doesn't need protective custody any more than Sullivan and I do. Besides," I dropped the bombshell calmly, "Vangie says that woman she saw was not Lucille St. Clair."

"What?" Nelson shouted the question. "Of course it was!"

"I'm just telling you what Vangie said and she knows the girl," I said placidly. "The woman Vangie saw was heavier than Lucille and wore low-heeled shoes, something she never did, and she walked differently. Anyhow, I want Vangie sent home. There's nothing to link her with any knowledge of the killer, nothing has been mentioned in the papers about her seeing the woman or hearing her voice. If it wasn't Lucille then it shouldn't be necessary to hold Vangie here."

"Nonsense!" Nelson was impatient. "It has to be that girl. She had the car, she told Mrs. Dellman she'd been to his room and now she's skipped. And what makes you think the papers haven't mentioned your sister?"

I looked at him. "What do you mean?"

"Have you seen your 1:30 edition?"

I shook my head. He reached for it on a desk and silently handed it to me.

The whole story was there, complete with pictures. I read it, getting angrier by the line. Damn Dennis McCarthy for a heel and a louse! I blinked back furious tears and Nelson patted my shoulder.

"Don't cry, it had to come out sooner or later."

I took advantage of my tears. "I want my sister released!" I wailed.

Nelson hesitated but, intimidated by a threatened deluge, agreed to let her go if I would promise to see she didn't leave the house until they had the St. Clair girl in custody. I promised blithely, never dreaming how nearly impossible it would be to keep my word.

I went back to the pressroom to get Vangie and Brett, and found her reading the paper.

"Pretty, isn't it?" I asked.

She raised angry eyes. "Who wrote it? You?"

"You know better than that!" I snapped. "When did they take that shot of you?" The picture showed her struggling with a matron in the hall.

"I don't know. I was too mad to notice a cameraman."

"Well, it can't be helped now. It's a dirty trick for Dennis to play on me and I'll make sure to tell him, but I guess he thought it was news."

"I hate newspaper people!" she said viciously. "They're the scum of the earth!"

Several pairs of eyes turned on her, angry glints in them. "One more crack like that out of you and I'll slam you!" I told her. "That's a smart remark to make in a pressroom!"

"I don't care," she said sulkily, her lower lip jutting like a Ubangi belle's. "I'm entitled to my own opinion—you screamed enough about being entitled to yours about Ned."

I glared at her. "I'd like to tell you this story could have been much worse and it could have been in print yesterday and this morning, complete with photostats of your letters. But the boys made me a promise and they kept it. That's more than McGowan ever did for anyone. This double cross didn't come from any of these guys but from my own editor. So shut up and get up. You're going home where you can bellow all you want."

She jumped to her feet. "They're going to let me go?"

"They're letting you go home."

She gave herself a little shake. "That's where you're wrong. I'm not going home. I'm going other places."

"Oh, no, you're not! Either you go home or stay here. Take your choice."

She looked appealingly at Brett but this time she got no help there.

"You heard Margaret. I guess she knows what she's talking about. Let's go home."

"Have you your car?" I asked Brett. He nodded, and I told him what Nelson had said about seeing Vangie was kept safely inside the house.

"You tell Mother that's orders and if she gets out they'll pick her up and put her back in the coop. Take her on home. I'll see you later."

He left and Morrow walked over to me.

"I'll have to let go with the story now," he said. "Briggs will give me unshirted hell as it is. I can add that she's been released for a new lead. You don't mind, do you?"

"Why should I? You heard what she had to say about us, didn't you?"

"Yeah. I heard."

"So okay. Go ahead and print anything you want. I'm leaving now."

"Where you going?"

"To tell a certain Irish pot-washer what I think of him!" I went out and got in my car, rehearsing the words I meant to pour in Dennis's ear.

The hum of Saturday's activity filled the city room. I stalked over to the city desk and planted myself, hands on hips and legs spread apart. I stood so until Dennis looked up.

"What's eating you?"

"This is eating me!" I flung the paper at him. "I think you're a heel!"

"All right. I'm a heel. But I'm a newspaper editor. You're only supposed to be a reporter. I told you this morning I wanted a story on your sister and you wouldn't give it to me. So I got it another way."

"Where did that picture come from? You didn't have a camera there when that scene occurred."

"I got it from Sellers. He didn't want to use it."

"I get a decent break from the morning paper and a kick in the pants from my own!" I raged.

"Keep those pants on," he said. "Now, look here. You'd have done the same thing if you were on this desk. If the other papers had beat me with that story—and you on the staff here—I'd never live it down. All it does is make your sister out a crazy kid with a bad temper and a crush on a wrong guy. She's not accused of murder and the story says nothing that will hurt her rep. Where is she? Still in jail?"

"In the first place she wasn't in jail. She spent the night in the matron's dormitory in protective custody. Right now she's on her way home."

"They let her go?"

"They did. Nelson didn't want to—he's a regular old woman. The one who needs protection is Bob Sullivan."

"How about you?"

"No one will molest me. The killer knows I didn't see who hit me."

"I hope you're right. Well, give me a new lead on your sister's release, then I've got some other stuff for you to do."

"I'm going to lunch after I do a new lead," I told him. "I haven't had anything since breakfast and I'm hungry."

I wrote a couple of paragraphs on a new lead, handed it in, and went back downstairs. But I didn't go to lunch. I went home. Vangie and Brett must have stopped somewhere along the way because Brett was just parking his car in the garage as I drove in. We entered the rear door together.

Mother, Marian, and Bertha rushed out into the hall and three pairs of troubled eyes took in our group. Vangie started for Mother, but Bertha reached for her and folded her against her bony breast, glaring over the bright curly head.

"Whut dey bin doin' to ma baby!" she crooned. "Dar now, honey chile, you is safe to home. Miss Marg'ret, you oughta be shame yo'self lettin' dem keep dis chile in a jailhouse all night!"

"Oh shut up, you lanky, slat-bottomed wench," I retorted listlessly.

"Miz Sally! You heahs huh callin' me names? Ise shet, awright! Ise plumb shet of you! You is no good!"

"I thought I told you to shut up. Take your precious brat to her room and put her to bed. Give her some lunch on a tray."

"I'm not going to bed," Vangie protested. "I'm not sleepy and I'm staying right here."

"Well, stay then. I don't give a hoot. I'm done with you, damned little fool!"

"Margaret!" Mother looked shocked.

"I mean it. I've been through six shades of purple hell and she hasn't helped any."

"But she's only a child!" Mother remonstrated.

"Child, me eye! She's a hateful, spoiled little hell cat! And I want no part of her from now on! She can get out of her messes alone. I'm done."

"That's no way to speak of your sister!" Mother was sternly reproving.

"Oh damn my sister!" I exclaimed.

"Margaret, you may go to your room!" Mother said severely.

I just looked at her. "I'm too old for that sort of thing. I'm an adult if that one isn't. Besides I have to get back to work, I'm on my lunch hour. I just came home to tell you Nelson, the district attorney, said she is not to be allowed out of the house until they pick up a woman suspect who's disappeared. And I wanted to show you this, so you'd know what to expect." I thrust the paper at her.

Vangie recoiled from the sight of it and started up the stairs.

"Hah!" I said. "That sent you running, didn't it?"

Mother looked at the picture and read a few lines of the story.

"You told me there wouldn't be anything in the papers!"

"I tried to keep it out, but you can't fight fate and Dennis both."

"This is deplorable!"

"Nasty too," I said. "Well, I've got to go." I turned toward the door.

"Just a moment, Margaret. I suppose you realize this story is grounds for a libel suit?"

I gaped at her in slack-jawed amazement.

"Are you nuts?" I asked inelegantly. "How do you figure that?"

She was as calm as a pond. "Libel, I believe, is a printed or written lie defaming or undermining a person's character and reputation. Isn't it?"

"Certainly, but there's nothing libelous about that story. Every word can be proved by the police."

"It's a pack of lies," she said tersely.

"It isn't! It's the same story I told you last night! For God's sake don't go making a fool of yourself by starting a libel suit. They can get those letters and make the story much worse than it is!"

"I'll use my own judgment about what to do." She stalked from the room.

"Well!" I gasped and turned to Brett and Marian.

"You're a cold-blooded wench," Brett accused me out of a clear sky. "I wouldn't be surprised but what you did write that stinking story."

Fury possessed me and I hurled the first thing my hand touched. It happened to be a valuable Bohemian glass vase. I rushed out of the house, the tinkle of shattering glass still sounding in my ears, got in the car, and drove recklessly back to the office. I took the city desk phones and a few minutes' work on them quieted me down. The six o'clock Final was just ready to roll when Bob Sullivan called me.

"I called your home and they said you were still working," he told me. "When can I see you?"

I told him Dennis had me working until late, checking the Sunday paper, but that I'd be going to dinner in an hour and would drop by the hotel.

"I'm not working tonight," he said. "I want to get some sleep. But how about meeting me for dinner? I'll take you to the best one-arm joint in town."

"I'll go if you let me stand the check," I said. "It will go on the swindle sheet. And no one-arm joints. I want some good food."

"Okay," he agreed and added, "I think I've got something."

"Good!" I applauded and hung up. I worked another hour then got up and went over to Dennis.

"I'm for food. Back in an hour."

"Make it half-hour," he directed. "I need you here."

I didn't bother answering, just left and drove over to the hotel. Bob was waiting out front and he looked excited. I opened the car door and he got in. We drove over to a good Italian place on Prytania Street and when we were comfortably settled in a booth I asked, "What's up?"

He handed me Morrow's paper of the day before and pointed to a shot of Vette and Toni walking down the courthouse steps.

"See that?"

"Sure. What about it?"

"The boy who runs the other elevator on my shift says this dame, this one," he pointed to Toni, "came in the hotel about 11:00 Wednesday night and got off at the tenth floor."

I stared at him.

"He said he took her back down in the elevator about fifteen minutes later and she was shaking all over. Reason he noticed her was because he'd seen her earlier—she was with the doctor and her sister before they went out to dinner. Another man and Doc's brother and the two sisters. The Doc's brother left before the others."

"Which probably means nothing," I said. "The other man must have been Brett. If he was with Toni that explains that part nicely."

"Yeah, but it doesn't explain that late trip she made alone."

"No, it doesn't. I can't understand how Vangie missed seeing her. She was parked right on the exit stairs from about 9:30 until Ned came in."

"Your sister was?"

I nodded. "What else have you got? Anything on registrations?"

He consulted a notebook. "Two guests were roomed on the tenth Wednesday and one the day before, Tuesday."

"Get any descriptions?"

"Yeah. A Morgan Leeds of New York was put in 1010 and a G. W. Danton was in 1014. He checked in from Chicago. They both came Wednesday. One left Thursday. Leeds checked out early in the morning and Danton late Friday morning. The Tuesday guest was a dame, Alice Marvin from Houston, Texas. She left early Thursday too. Leeds was tall and skinny and wore thick glasses. The other guy was short and very dark, with a heavy black mustache, bushy eyebrows and nose glasses. The dame was tall and slim and red-haired." He looked at me. "Sounds like you." He laughed.

"Well it wasn't," I said curtly.

"For baggage Leeds had a gladstone and a flat bag. The dame had a small suitcase and the other guy carried only a briefcase."

"All the way from Chicago?"

"Yep, paid for his room three days in advance. Leeds had a limp and was roomed on seven first, but he complained of paint smells and they moved him during the night to ten."

"That about eliminates him. His being on ten was an accident."

"Yeah, but both the dame and the Danton guy asked for rooms above nine. Not that it means anything, lots of people like to be high."

"You said Ned's brother was with him Wednesday evening?"

"Sure. Nothing wrong with that, is there?"

"Nothing, except that when they tried to reach him Thursday the police were told he was out of the city."

"You aren't suspecting a guy of doing in his own brother, are you?"

"Why not? It's been done. Didn't Cain kill Abel?"

"Yeah, but a woman did these jobs."

"That's what the cops think. But they've been wrong before."

"Don't you think so?"

"In a way, yes—in another, no. The more I think of it the less possible it seems for a woman to have handled that poker. It's out of character."

"They've used hammers and axes!" he exclaimed. "Why not a poker?"

"I was thinking, mainly, of Lucille St. Clair. She was a gentle sort of girl, what I know of her. It could be she hit one person with a poker if she was in a panic but I can't see her ambushing and deliberately slamming another one."

"I see what you mean. What about this Toni?"

"That has me puzzled. She could have gone to the hotel, she had time after she left Brett and she knew Ned and Vette were at the Dellmans. But how did she get in his room, if she did go in there? Of course she could have had a key and let herself in to plant the poison."

"Where would she get a key? The hotel wouldn't give her one without a note from the doctor."

"Keys can be lost—or stolen." I winced slightly at the last word.

"That's true!" He snapped his fingers. "And Doc lost his or left it in his room a couple of times. I remember letting him in with a pass key."

I sighed and finished my coffee. "This case gets clearer all the time. Just like a stirred mud puddle. Suspects grow as thick as blackberries on a vine. Or do they grow on a vine? No matter. I think I'll go back to work and let the cops solve this."

"But you ain't going to drop it, are you?" He sounded disappointed.

"I don't know." I shrugged. "What I do know is that a city editor is asking where the hell I am. Being a reporter is slavery and no money worth mentioning. Nor do you get thanks or recognition for a job well done. All you get is a lot of abuse, and if you don't believe me, see the movies."

"Gee!" His eyes shone. "You sure must have the most interesting life!"

17. *Check and Double Check*
~~~~~~

I TOOK Bob home and went back to the office. It was 8:10 when I got in. I checked the police pressroom and learned nothing new. Then I checked Tommy, who told me a picture of the St. Clair girl had been sent to all the papers in the state, and city outlets were all guarded. The police were quite confident she would be "apprehended within twenty-four hours." He added that her picture and description was being wired all over the country and she couldn't get far.

As a matter of fact she didn't get far—but it was over a month before they found Lucille St. Clair.

I wrote up what Tommy had told me, adding an idea or two of my own, but putting them in quotes as having come from Gross. I said, in effect, that while Miss St. Clair was the logical suspect, anyone, man or woman, who'd been in McGowan's room that day could have been the poisoner. I finished the story and handed it in at 8:45. Then I sat back to mull over what Bob had told me at dinner.

Toni's reported visit to the hotel worried me plenty. After all, my brother meant to marry that girl, and damned if I relished the idea of a possible killer in the family. If she had been fifteen minutes between her elevator trips she certainly couldn't have been walking the hotel halls all that time. I decided to call her and see if I could get her to meet me.

When she answered the phone I asked if Brett was there.

"Why no. He's flying tonight," she answered. "Didn't he tell you?"

I said he hadn't but didn't mention the glass vase.

"Look, I want to talk to you, alone," I said. "Can I come out there and pick you up? We'll go have a drink somewhere."

"I'm pretty tired," she said. "Can't you tell me over the phone?"

"I can't," I said bluntly.

"All right then, come on out." She didn't sound enthusiastic.

I checked out with Dennis, saying I'd be back later—maybe. He told me not to bother, things were working okay without me. When I got to Toni's she was waiting on the front porch and came out to join me at once. We drove to a speak I knew on Esplanade Avenue and ordered highballs. When we'd been served and the waiter had gone away I leaned toward her.

"What were you doing in the Bienvenu, on Ned's floor, after you took Brett to the airfield that night?"

The color drained from her face. "How did you know that?" she whispered.

I leaned back in my chair, watching her narrowly. "Never mind how I knew it. Just tell me what you were up to. You knew Ned wasn't home."

"Do, do the police know this?"

"Not yet," I said laconically.

"Have you told Brett?"

"No. I wanted to hear what you had to say first."

She toyed with her glass, then drained the contents. "I suppose I'd better tell you. I think you'll understand."

"Wait a minute." I finished my drink, ordered two more, and when they came settled back to listen.

"When Brett was away Ned gave me a rush and I thought I was in love with him," she said. "Then he fell for Vette and I was wild with jealousy. I wrote him letters, foolish letters filled with wild protestations of love and finally all kinds of threats."

I groaned. "You too!"

"Me too, but mine were worse than Vangie's, I'm sure. Anyone reading them would have thought—well, you know what!"

"And that wasn't so?"

"No—and to give Ned credit it wasn't my fault it didn't happen. I'd have done anything he asked me. I even offered myself to him, body and soul. He turned me down flat. I began to hate him and I thought he was just fooling Vette the way he had me."

"Oh, so you hated him?"

"Violently."

"Enough to poison him?"

"Nothing so mild. I'd lie awake and dream up real tortures for him. Then Brett came home. He was pretty mad for a while about my having gone out with Ned, but he got over it and I got over Ned. Completely. But I began to worry about those letters, and when I asked Ned about them, he teased and said he was keeping them among his souvenirs. They were souvenirs I'd never want Vette to get hold of, and when they got engaged I was frantic. About a week ago I swiped his hotel key, and the night we went to the Dellmans gave me a perfect chance to look around his room."

"And did you find the letters?" I expected a negative, but her face lit up and she giggled.

"I sure did! They were in a dresser drawer all tied with a string."

"What! No blue ribbon?" I asked derisively.

She made a face. "No, just a plain old drug store string. Green."

"What did you do with them?"

"I took them home and burned them with my own little white hands."

"You were lucky he had them at the hotel instead of with the ones the cops got hold of. Maybe he had brought them over meaning to return them. I should think he'd have felt like you did about Vette seeing them."

"Maybe. Anyhow I got them and scooted out of there. Boy! Was I nervous!"

"You're lucky Vangie didn't see you. She was parked on the stairway waiting for him. She'd have sworn to high heaven you were the poisoner."

"I know. Poor Vangie. But she'll get over it."

"She certainly shows no signs of it now! Next thing I know she'll be wanting him canonized as a saint and a martyr!"

I beckoned the waiter again and we had refills.

"Vette's terribly broken up too," she said. "Like Vangie, she thinks he was an angel and could do no wrong."

"He was a heel. A first-class heel." I stated flatly.

"Oh, I don't know." She smiled mischievously. "He could have taken me up on my offer."

"That's right, he could. I hope he was as restrained with Vangie."

"Oh I'm sure he was! I know just what he told her."

"How come?"

She giggled. "From experience. He looked tenderly into her eyes and said, 'My darling, much as I want you I cannot take you like this. But I shall always treasure this moment. Ah, if you were not so young and innocent!' Then he kissed her and rushed her straight home!"

"Migawd! And you fell for that crap!"

"Among others. What a sap I was!"

"Among others!" I laughed.

"Not you too?"

"Good God no!" I denied explosively. "I wasn't so young and innocent, so he had a different line with me. Our affair was 'going to be an experience to remember forever.' I'd heard that story before—so I declined with thanks."

"Wasn't he a mess?" She giggled again. The drinks were taking hold.

I put my hands together piously. " 'Tain't fitten to speak ill of the dead!" I said.

"Thass right." She nodded solemnly. "But he was a mess."

I figured it was time to take her home so I got her out and drove her to her house. She was as gay as a Christmas tree and I was feeling no pain. I went home and went to bed. I had checked and double checked Toni and I felt in my heart she was telling the truth. For the first time I also felt that she and I could be friends. She had a damn good sense of humor.

Monday was a routine day. Fred McGowan came back to town and had a perfectly straightforward story to account for his absence. He'd been in the strawberry section shooting rabbits that had been pestering the planters. He'd gone hunting with Joe Warner, a big planter, and had been in the woods when the police tried to reach him. As soon as the Negro messenger found the camp, he had left and come home.

Tuesday we had another murder, but it didn't seem to be connected in any way with the other two. The only reason for it appeared to be petty robbery.

Early Wednesday morning the body of a cab driver had been found huddled over the wheel of his taxi on a lonely stretch of the river road, back of Audubon park. He'd been shot under the left ear with a small caliber gun and his pockets contained only small change. His wife, who identified the body, said a heavy gold signet ring and a watch were missing. He'd been shot about 11:30 Tuesday night and a roving patrol car squad had found the body about 5:00 on Wednesday morning.

Morgan was still sick and Dennis sent me to cover police, so I went into the morgue to have a look at the dead hackie. Beton was there with the man's widow.

"Plainly a case of robbery and murder," he said to me.

"Looks like it," I agreed, a little surprised at his speaking to me.

"Nothing clever like poisoning a guy's toothbrush here, is there?"

"Naturally not," I said sweetly. "A woman did that, remember? They haven't caught her yet either."

The usual order for a roundup of the city's two-bit gangsters went out and the cops gave them the usual unpleasant going over. The gangsters got the usual mouthpieces with the usual writs and were out, as usual, within twenty-four hours. A check into the driver's life disclosed he'd peddled booze in a small way so the cops concluded it was either a small-time gang killing or a small-time holdup shooting. And that was the end of it.

Meanwhile I was having trouble at home and in the office.

Mother gave me the ice treatment and Vangie was openly hostile. Brett and Marian treated me like an ill-favored stepsister and I was getting sick of it. I seriously considered moving into a place of my own.

At work Dennis regarded me with a jaundiced eye. The entire blame for the Dellman libel suit was shoved off on me, and the atmosphere around the city room, even though Dennis well knew whose fault it was, was not pleasant. When newspeople feel a head is about to fall they take care to avoid the vicinity of the basket. Things didn't improve a lot when Mrs. Dellman agreed to drop the suit if the paper printed an apology. Papers hate to apologize—but they also hate libel suits. So they apologized.

After two weeks passed, the McGowan and Cheng murders were retired to the limbo of inactive stories. They would lay in the morgue of clippings until something happened to bring them to life again. Ned had been buried in Texas, Miss Cheng in California. Lucille St. Clair remained a fugitive, one who'd simply disappeared into thin air. So the papers went to sleep on the story. Not so the police.

Bit by bit Tommy, the Homicide department, the D.A.'s men, and the lab experts worked and built up a background about the personal lives of the two murdered people. Little stories gathered here and there, small items studied under microscopes. It didn't seem a lot and they didn't appear to make much headway, but little by little it all began to add up. And I was in on it, because I hadn't given up the story and I still had my hunches. So I spent a lot of time with Tommy, and we went over and over the myriad small details of the two murders and the vanished nurse.

"Sooner or later we'll strike something definite," Tommy said to me one day. "We know that girl took a small luggage case when she left, but how she got out of the house without being seen is a mystery. We know that Dellman was in Cleveland when McGowan was killed—but we also know he has a fast plane and a private field here and in Cleveland."

"You don't suspect him?" I asked, astonished.

"I suspect everyone in a murder and there was talk about McGowan and Mrs. Dellman. A lot of that has been reported since the papers dropped the case. Gossip in back pantries and hotels. A man as well as a woman could have planted that poison if he had the chance. You have to figure all angles."

I grinned at him.

"What are you smirking about?" he asked.

"Oh nothing! I just remembered I put those words in quotes when you hadn't said them at all!" I laughed.

"Humph! Well, I'd have said so anyhow sooner or later."

We let the case drop in favor of a drink and the next day I was taken off police when Morgan came back to work.

Midway through the third week a woman called me one morning about 11:00. At first she would give no name and that annoyed me.

"If you won't tell me who you are I'll have to hang up," I said tartly. "I've no time to waste in nonsense like guessing games."

"Please don't hang up!" she begged. "My name in Harmon and I have something important to tell you. I can't go to the police about it."

"If it's something for police you'd better call Tim Morgan," I told her. "He's our man at headquarters."

"I don't want to talk to him," she said. "You're a woman, you may understand my story."

I looked at the clock, sure I had a crank on my hands.

"I go to lunch in half an hour. I'll be at Nancy's lunchroom across the street from the paper. If you want to see me I'll meet you there."

"Oh thank you," she whispered and hung up.

When I walked in Nancy's a woman was seated at a rear table. She was drab and worn looking and the woman who'd called me had a young voice. I started to take another table but Nancy beckoned me.

"That woman is waiting for you," she said. "Leastwise that's what she told me. Don't you know her?"

"No, but she must be the one who called me. I told her to meet me here." I walked back to her table.

"I'm Margaret Slone. Did you call me?"

She looked up from her coffee. "Oh yes! I didn't see you come in!" She smiled and dropped ten years. Then picked them up again.

"Why did you want to talk to me?"

"Because you're the girl I saw in the morgue the day my Joe was killed."

I stared at her. "Morgue? Your Joe?"

"You've forgot." She sounded defeated. "I thought you'd remember."

I thought a second, then light dawned.

"Of course! You're the cab driver's widow!"

"Yes, Joe Harmon's widow."

"What did you want to tell me?" I asked gently.

"I'm not much good at talking to men, and I don't like to talk to police anyhow. I thought maybe you could help me. The cops haven't done a thing about finding his murderer. Maybe you could catch him."

I thought: My God! She is a crank!

"Look, I'd love to help you if I could, but I'm in trouble now for sticking my neck into police business," I told her. "The police know their business and I'm sure they'll catch the man who robbed and killed your husband. They've picked up a lot of men and questioned them."

"Oh questioned!" Her voice was wearily bitter. "Sure they did, but they didn't get the man who killed my Joe."

"I'm sure the police are doing all they can," I said a little stiffly. "They have a pawnshop checkup watching for the stolen jewelry he was wearing. I think the only thing you can do is wait and let them handle it. I can't see how I could possibly help you."

"Don't get angry with me!" she pled, pitifully. "I only wanted to tell you—and show you—something."

I felt sorry for her. "I'm not angry." I smiled reassuringly. "What did you want to show me?"

She handed me a piece of writing paper. "Read it," she urged.

18. *Blackmail, Bootlegging and Bait*

~~~~~~

"PICK me up at the corner of St. Charles and Audubon Place," the typed lines read. "We will then reach an agreement which will suit both of us. I will wait for you from 11:00 to 11:15 Tuesday night and at the same time Wednesday if you cannot be there Tuesday. But this will be the one and only payoff. I'm not afraid of you and you have nothing on me. I only wish to avoid a scandal." There was no signature.

I studied the note. Obviously the writer was an educated person and also obviously there was a threat contained in the lines. More obviously, the cabbie had been out to collect blackmail in some form.

I looked at the woman. "Well?"

"I found that note in Joe's pants. He'd changed before going out to work that night."

"Yes?"

She looked embarrassed. "I just thought maybe Joe had something on somebody and the person may have been trying to buy him off. Cab drivers see and hear a lot of things people wouldn't expect them to notice."

"There's more to it than that," I said, beginning to get interested. "What's the rest of it?"

"We-e-ll, Joe told me to stop worrying about bills. He said he'd found a way to get a lot of money. I begged him not to get in trouble with the police, but he just laughed. He said he couldn't get in any trouble on this deal because of what the papers would do."

"Even so, I don't see how I fit the picture. He's dead, the

202

papers or police can't hurt him now. Or anyone else he had
a deal on with."

"You're a reporter, aren't you?"

I nodded. "Yes, but I—"

"Well, then why can't you find out who might be mixed
up in a big swindle or a robbery or murder? Then we could
find out who wrote that note and who it was Joe went to
meet that night he got killed."

I stared in amazement.

"What do you take me for? A miracle worker or a fortune-
teller? I'm only a reporter, not a detective or a crystal
gazer!"

Her shoulders drooped. "I suppose it does sound crazy.
But I was afraid to take this to the police."

"Look here, don't be afraid of the police," I said earnestly.
"You take that note straight to Tommy Gross, he's chief of
detectives. Tell him your story. Tell him I sent you. He's a
grand guy and I know he'll do all he can to help you. Will
you do that?"

She nodded unconvincingly and stood up, her whole bear-
ing one of utter defeat. I knew she'd never go to Tommy.

"Wait a minute," I stopped her. "Where did your husband
drive from and what were his hours?"

"He drove extra shifts for the Yellow Cab company and
most of the time he hauled from the Bienvenu hotel. But
he often just rolled in behind the next cab at the nearest
station to one of his trips."

A feeling of excitement stirred in me.

"The Bienvenu! Then he could have been working the
hotel the day they found Dr. McGowan's body! Was he?
Did he mention it to you?"

"Dr. McGowan? Oh, him. But a woman killed him. No
woman killed my Joe."

"I'm not so sure of that! A woman possibly killed that
Chinese nurse and smacked me on the head with a poker.
Suppose she had been in your husband's cab and somehow

he knew what she'd done? Do you think she'd stop at killing him? She could have taken the jewelry to make it look like robbery."

She shook her head uncertainly.

"You come with me while I go talk to my boss," I decided. "If he'll let me off I'll take you to see Tommy. Okay?"

She nodded and followed me out of the lunchroom.

I took her up and introduced her to Dennis, telling him I wanted to take her to headquarters to see Tommy.

"Go ahead," he growled. "You're no salve to my eyes anyhow. Go on and stir up another hornet's nest for yourself. You're the one to get stung."

I grabbed the woman's arm and beat it.

We found Tommy in his office. I told him the story and gave him the note. He read it and told her she should have turned it in right away.

"I was afraid it would make Joe look like a blackmailer," she said in a low voice. "He wasn't *really* one."

Tommy bit back a smile and tucked the note in his vest pocket.

"I'll keep this and get in touch with you later," he told her.

"Tommy, her husband hauled fares from Ned's hotel. Do you suppose he might have got hold of something that gave him a lead on those murders? Cab drivers get to know a lot of people by sight, you know."

He shrugged. "It's an angle to consider," he said. "I'll let you know if it leads to anything." His nod was a dismissal and I led the woman out of his office.

"You see?" she asked bitterly. "He didn't care. He wasn't even interested."

"You don't know Gross the way I do," I assured her. "He's interested."

We got in my car and I asked where I could take her. She gave me an address in a shabby down-at-the-heel section uptown near the river. I drove to a small, ashamed-looking house.

"Won't you come in?" She didn't expect me to accept, but impelled by curiosity and something else deeper, I got out and followed her.

Inside the house was painfully neat and the furniture surprisingly good.

"I had most of these things when I got married." She seemed to read my thoughts. "I've had to sell some pieces but I haven't brought myself to let these go yet."

"That chair is very good," I said awkwardly, indicating a rosewood arm chair.

"Yes." She pushed it toward me. "Won't you sit down a moment?"

"I should be getting back to work," I said, but I sat down.

There was a picture of a couple standing on the mantel, a handsome man and a pretty girl. It was hard to accept the fact that the girl was the drab woman sitting opposite me. A large snap of a man in riding breeches was tucked in the corner of the picture frame. I got up and studied the snap.

I thought: I've seen him before—but where?

Again she read my mind. "That's Joe. Did you know him?"

"I'm not sure," I said uncertainly. "I've a feeling I've seen him somewhere."

"You saw him in the morgue," she reminded me.

"I didn't mean that time. I may have ridden with him. I've seen him like he was in this snap, smiling and dressed just like that."

"He worked in breeches and boots," she said, then asked, "Won't you have a drink?"

"Drink?" I repeated stupidly. "No. No thanks. I better get back to work."

"I mean a good drink," she said quietly. "Not bathtub gin

or corn. This is good Scotch. Joe had connections and he sold it to the boys in the hotels. There are still a few bottles around. I'm afraid to try and sell them."

I hesitated then accepted. She went to the kitchen and came out with two glasses filled with Scotch and water.

"I hope you don't mind if I join you," she said. "I feel like a drink might help me. I haven't had one since Joe died."

"Why should I mind?" I asked in surprise. "It's your home and your liquor, isn't it?"

"I know. But I'm only a murdered taxi driver's wife."

I felt uncomfortable. "Don't get to feeling inferior!" I said somewhat tartly. "What difference does it make what he was? You're the one who counts now. By the way, what did you do before you were married?"

She brightened. "I had a good job as a supervisor for the telephone company. I was the youngest full super working there." There was pride in her tone. "Then I met Joe and three months later we got married. He didn't drive a cab then and he made good money—plenty to live and keep a nice home and save some too."

"What did he do?"

"He was a trouble shooter for the company. You know, repairing broken lines and such."

"What happened? He didn't quit that to drive a cab, did he?"

"Oh no. He got hurt in an accident out at the airport and it left him slightly crippled."

"Fall from a pole?"

"No. It was during that big storm a couple of years ago. Lines were blown down at the airfield and Joe got the job to go fix them. He'd started across the field when a plane tore loose from its moorings and struck him. It broke both of his legs and one hip. The doctors had to take bone from his left leg and it made it shorter than the right one. It wasn't very noticeable but he couldn't climb any more and they gave him a desk job. He'd always worked with his hands, so he didn't last long on a desk. After he left the company he took a job driving a cab."

"Cab drivers don't make much in this town now that they put on the city limit rates," I said thoughtfully. "I suppose it took all your savings to pay his sick bills?"

"No. The man who owned the runaway plane paid them and the company paid his wages all the time he was laid up. It wasn't bad even after he first went on the cabs. Then they made that city rate limit and he took to bootlegging. Then he got killed."

She sat staring at the wall, dry-eyed and tense.

"He didn't tell you anything about who he might be getting that dough from? Not even a hint as to whether it was a woman or a man?"

She shook her head. "Joe changed a lot after the accident —it made him bitter and surly. He stopped telling me anything. I wouldn't have known he was selling whisky if he hadn't stored the stuff here."

"In that case it's a wonder he said anything about expecting the money."

"He wouldn't have if I hadn't been almost frantic about bills we owed. I was crying and Joe told me to shut up and stop worrying, he was going to get enough dough to pay all the bills and have plenty left over."

"So he got killed instead."

She nodded. "I had a feeling he'd get in trouble, but he just laughed at me and told me to stop nagging at him. When I kept after him he got mean and finally he hit me. He'd never done that before. Never."

"Of course you realize that he must have been planning on blackmail," I said. "I know it isn't a nice thing to say but it's the only answer."

"I suppose so," she said miserably.

I stood up and got ready to leave. She went to the door ahead of me and I slipped a folded twenty-dollar bill on the small table near the door.

She held out her hand. "Well, thanks for helping me."

"I'm afraid I haven't been much help," I said wryly. "All I did was listen to you talk."

"That often helps more than people imagine." She smiled and again I was struck by the change it made in her looks.

"Listen to me," I told her. "You've plenty of living to do. Get yourself fixed up in a beauty parlor and buy a decent dress, then go get a job. Will you do that?"

"On what? Of course I can sell something—"

"Maybe Santa will send you a present in advance!" I drove off feeling like Santa and rosy with the sense of having done my good deed for the day.

When I got back to the city room Dennis was one jump ahead of a fit.

"You've been gone three hours!" he exploded at me. "Where in hell were you?"

"You told me to get out of your sight," I said frigidly. "I've been listening to another woman's troubles."

"You'll have troubles, financial ones, if your salary stops," he snorted. "Get over to the Roosevelt hotel and interview Rudyard Kipling. He just got in from Brazil."

I departed in haste to interview the man whose poetry and prose I'd loved all my life. We had a grand talk and I pleased him by reciting some of his poems. He rewarded me with two double strength highballs of Irish whisky and a signed copy of *Barrack Room Ballads*.

I went back to the office walking on air, with all thoughts of violence and murder temporarily erased from my mind. I handed in my story and relaxed in my chair until Dennis found something for me to do. My thoughts drifted back to murder and violence and the feeling that I'd missed something, some small thing that might be the piece that opened the key to the puzzle, came back to plague me and wipe out the glow induced by whisky and Kipling.

A bellow from Dennis brought me back to the present and I looked up to see Fred McGowan standing by the city desk. I went over to them.

"Mr. McGowan wants to put up some dough to catch his brother's killer," he said. "You get the dope for the story from him."

I took Fred over to my desk, his resemblance to Ned giving me a slightly weird feeling. I thought: No one should ever kill a twin and leave the other one walking around to haunt people!

"Go ahead," I invited. "What have you in mind?"

"I want to offer a reward, but you'll have to help me word it. I've no experience with this sort of thing." His mouth was set grimly.

"Okay. How much do you want to offer and for what information?"

"Five thousand dollars for any clue or information that will lead to the murderer."

"Whew!" I whistled. "Nice bait."

"Word it so it will be understood that anyone who turns up this clue will get the money. If it takes several different informants, they will all share in the reward. All we want is the guy who did it."

"Don't you mean girl?"

"Guy or girl. It doesn't matter what sex."

"I suppose you know you're letting yourself in for a lot of crank calls," I told him.

"I don't care about that. Maybe one of the cranks will have the key to the whole thing."

"Key? Oh, of course. I was thinking about the other keys that figured in this case."

"What keys?"

"Oh the maid's key that wouldn't unlock the door and the

master key that did, and the keys to the drug cabinet and the one to that apartment in the Quarter."

"I see. Who has that apartment key, by the way?"

"The police, I imagine." I hastily stuck a piece of paper in my machine.

I wrote along, asking questions as I needed information. He wanted the notice to say that anyone having anything to report was to call either him or the paper. I told him he'd have to settle that with Dennis first.

"I have settled it," he told me. "He said it was okay to run it that way. I'll pay all expenses such as out-of-town calls."

"Advertising in a newspaper for a murderer," I muttered. "A new wrinkle."

"I beg your pardon?"

"Nothing," I answered. "How long is this to run?"

"Until we catch whoever killed Ned."

I refrained from expressing the opinion that it was more money than Ned was worth, dead or alive, and thought of Miss Cheng. If it helped avenge her killing it was well worth the five grand.

I gave him the finished copy, he read it and took it over to Dennis. Then I checked out.

19. *Home Sweet Home*

~~~~~~

WHEN I let myself in, Brett was in the phone nook and I overheard him say, "Compartment A, Car 302, Southern Pacific Chieftain, Union Station—and be sure they're delivered before 11:00 Thursday morning."

"Someone leaving town?" I asked when he had hung up.

"Toni and Vette. They're going to California."

"Oh. Are you seeing Toni tonight?"

"Sure, and tomorrow night too."

"I have a feeling you go for that gal." I grinned at him.

For the first time in weeks he grinned back. "You don't say!"

"Ummm. You should marry her and make the trip a honeymoon jaunt."

"Not with Vette along!"

"Guess not," I agreed and started upstairs to clean up.

"Any trace of Lucille yet?" he asked as I turned away.

"Only the usual reports placing her in every state in the Union. I imagine the police have given some small, blonde nurses several unhappy moments. Things should really start popping now. Fred McGowan has offered a five-thousand-buck reward for Ned's killer."

"Fred did that? When?"

"Today. It ought to catch something or somebody."

"I should imagine," he agreed and I turned away again Then back again.

"Will you promise not to fly in my face if I ask you a question?"

"Why should I fly in your face?"

"You might not like the question. Everyone around here seems to blame me for everything that happened and I'm almost afraid to open my mouth."

"You'll have to admit you did cook up a fine stew and mostly it was your fault."

"I'll admit no such thing! It was not my fault!" I denied indignantly.

"Okay, okay, let's skip it. What was the question?"

"Well, you said a lot of things that day at the hotel. At times you sounded like you hated Ned's guts. Did you?"

He stared at me for a long moment. "Is that the question?"

I nodded.

"There was a time when I hated Ned. But we got things all straight with each other."

"What did he do to you?" I knew what he'd done.

"He dated Toni knowing she was my girl. I quit that job in Chicago and came home. I asked him if he was in love with her or just playing his usual game. He made some crack about having told me all women could be had and I hit him. I had it out with Toni and she told me it was Vette Ned loved. One night we got together at her house and after that we were good friends again."

"As good as you'd ever been?" I asked searchingly.

"No. It was never quite the same," he admitted honestly. "But I didn't hate him at the time he was killed. I really rather liked Ned. He was a fool but a pleasant sort to be around."

"Well, someone hated him enough to poison him."

"I know. You don't suspect your brother, do you?" His smile was teasing.

"I've suspected everyone else at one time or another, even Vangie. It's a wonder I don't suspect myself. Heaven knows I couldn't abide Ned."

His smile died. "That's a very unfunny joke."

"Maybe." I shrugged. "If I'd known what he was doing

to Vangie I would have been mad enough to kill him. How about you?"

"I don't know what he did to Vangie but," his hands clenched, "if I had found out there was anything to be ashamed of I'd have throttled him with my bare hands."

"Don't let it worry you. I found out that Ned never went the route with jail-bait girls. So Vangie is as good as new."

"Who told you that?" He eyed me keenly.

"None of your business. But Vangie was nuts about him. I hope she gets over it soon. I'm pretty tired of her growling and glaring at me and I'm fed up with her dramatics and yelling to go out."

"She has been hard to handle," he admitted. "But don't forget you spoke cruelly of the man she loved!" He placed his hand over his heart.

I giggled. "One more question before I go wash city room grime off me. Did you ever hear anything scandalous about Ned's *friendship* with Marta Dellman?"

"I wouldn't go so far as to call it scandalous. There was some talk, but Gerry Dellman is insanely jealous of Marta and if there had been anything to get suspicious about he'd have blown his top. Of course he goes out of the city a lot and Ned hung around while he was away. I know she lent him a wad of dough."

"To furnish his offices," I reminded him.

"Oh sure. It was all perfectly businesslike. No, I don't think they were intimate. Nothing more than a middle-aged woman being flattered by the attentions of a younger man who knew she could help him get ahead."

"It sounds slightly disgusting, put that way." I turned up my nose. "However, I guess that's about the size of it. Well, I'm going to wash."

I had just finished cleaning up when the silver tinkle announced dinner and I'd hardly put my foot in the dining room when Vangie jumped on me.

"Just how much longer do you think you're going to keep me imprisoned in this house?" she demanded.

"Until the police tell me it's safe for you to go out all by your little self," I said calmly.

"Well, I'm not going to put up with it. I'm going out—tonight!" She glared at me. "What's more, I'd like to see you try and stop me, you nasty old—"

"Evangeline! That will do," Mother said sternly. Vangie subsided sullenly.

We finished dinner, but the glow of the Irish whisky was still with me. I got up from the table and walked over to Vangie's chair.

"You're a nasty-tempered spoiled hellion," I whispered in her ear. "But you're my sister and you're probably still a virgin and I love you anyhow."

She stared at me, wall-eyed. "Whoever said I wasn't a-a—" She looked at Mother and stopped abruptly.

"No one. It was just an idea I got. Skip it."

Mother's cool eyes were faintly inquiring, and following the habit of weeks in the doghouse, I excused myself and went up to my room. I'd barely got comfortable with a book in my hand—not a murder mystery—when Vangie came in without knocking first to see if she was welcome. I surveyed her calmly.

"Just what did you mean by that crack you made downstairs?" she demanded.

It may have been the afterglow of the highballs. But I sat up straight and intoned in a deep, moving voice, "My darling, much as I want you I cannot take you like this. But I shall always treasure this moment. Ah! If you were—"

Shock held her speechless until I got that far. Then she interrupted, eyes blazing. "You spied on us! Or Ned told you! Oh! He couldn't have done anything so low, so awful!"

"Take it easy!" I warned, moving to the far side of the

bed. "Ned told me nothing and I never spied on you. I just happen to know that was his stock line with girls of jail-bait age."

"Stock line! Who told you that?"

"Never mind who told me. It was someone who knew what she was talking about. He told her the same thing."

"I don't believe it! Ned wouldn't do such a thing!"

"Oh he wouldn't!" I raised up angrily. "Well he did. You don't really think you were his one and only, do you? What of Vette? He was going to marry her, remember?"

"But he said he loved only me! He said he was marrying her because—well, just because," she finished lamely and red-faced.

I thought with sudden unhappy suspicion of Vette's sudden decision to go to California. Vette was past the age of consent.

"Marrying her because he'd got her in trouble, I suppose? And he told you that?"

"Well, he said—" She stopped again.

I threw the book at her.

"And that didn't show you what kind of a louse he was? Oh, get out of here! I'm disgusted with you! Go on, scram!"

She wilted completely. "Please, Margaret. Who told you he said those things to her?"

"You think I'm crazy? Why should I give her away? Now go on, get out."

"But I want to know. Truly I do."

I sighed. "I daresay. Well, it was a girl I know, and he told her the same slush. Who she is happens to be my business. But it isn't my business that you happen to be a gullible little fool. That's your own headache."

"I have been a fool," she said bitterly, her shame and surrender complete. "I wouldn't have believed it if you hadn't known all the words."

"And the music," I added. "Yes, you've certainly been an ass, but you had company. Lots of it. Now don't cry!"

Tears were beginning to flow. "Just forget it. He wasn't so smart after all. No smart guy would have handed all his girls stock lines. He might have known they'd meet and compare notes sooner or later." Hysterical merriment seized me. "Just suppose," I choked out between spasms, "just suppose they'd have done so while he was alive! He'd have been better off dead!"

"Oh, Margaret!"

"I'm sorry." I tried to stop the near hysterical laughter. "Excuse me, baby, but it just struck me as being funny. It's bad taste, I know."

"Margaret—" she hesitated. "Margaret, if he told all the girls the same thing he must have been a louse, mustn't he?"

I went off again. "To think I'd ever hear you say that about the man you loved!" I hooted. "Baby, I think you're cured!"

"Well, isn't it the truth? He was just a—just a big mess!"

"Sounds familiar." I was suddenly very sleepy. "Somewhere I've heard those words before and you know 'tain't fitten to speak ill—" I fell asleep.

I awakened in the morning to find Vangie in bed alongside of me. She hadn't done that in a long time. As I watched her she opened her bright blue eyes and smiled at me.

"Hi, hussy," I said.

"Hi, hussy yourself. Tell Bertha I'm in here and not to wake me up until 11:00. If I have to stay home I might as well sleep most of the time, and your bed is the best in the house."

"It should be. I paid a fortune for that spring and mattress. Before you go back to sleep, you lucky wench, I want to tell you there's a reward out for Ned's killer. Why don't you try to collect the dough?"

She opened one eye. "Why should I bother?" she asked and turned over.

I went down to breakfast feeling better than I had in

weeks. Brett was my pal again, Vangie had been cured and had slept with me, a token of utter forgiveness, I knew Mother and Marian would come around in a day or two at the most. The only fly in the salve was the thought of what poor Vette must be going through if Ned had told Vangie the truth. I didn't want to believe he had and felt so good I decided not to believe it. I spoke blithely to Bertha and asked for coffee.

I got a frigid silence and coffee.

I grinned. "Miss Vangie is sleeping in my room," I told her blandly. "She said to tell you not to wake her up until 11:00."

"Miss Vangie in yo room?" She sounded incredulous. "Whut she doin' dar?"

"Sleeping, I told you. Why not? She's done it before."

"But not lately she ain't!"

"Well, she's in there now."

She beamed on me. "Now, Miss Mar'gret, you jest go sot in de brekfuss room 'n Ah brings you yo vittles right fast!"

I went in, knowing I'd get breakfast served with a smile. I sighed deeply. Home was home sweet home again. I felt at peace with the world and I was sure something nice was going to happen almost any minute.

It was Saturday before anything happened and it wasn't nice.

On Saturday they found Lucille St. Clair.

Dennis had stuck me on the phones to answer the calls coming in about that reward. Not less than a thousand people had seen Lucille or a reasonable facsimile of same. They'd seen her in cities, towns, villages, and hamlets. We accepted all calls, collect every time. By 2:00 P.M. Saturday I was beat taking them and relaying them to the police to chase them down.

Lucille had been seen on a train, a bus, a steamer, and a plane. She'd even been detected hitching a ride on the highways, and she'd been positively identified as a passenger in no less than fifty cars bound for Texas, Georgia, Alabama, and points east, north, and west. By 2:00 P.M. of that same Saturday the paper owed the telephone company a shocking sum and Fred McGowan owed it to the paper.

When the real call came I wasn't ready for it.

It came from New Iberia, a town in the Bayou section, and was actually phoned in from a Bayou crossroads station a few miles from the town.

The caller was a French Cajun, a trapper and pirogue fisherman who lived near New Iberia.

I accepted the call, bored and annoyed with the whole show and most particularly with Dennis.

"I 'ave information!" the voice said excitedly. "Me, zis is Jean Pierre Rebault, an' I 'ave zis girl who is want for ze murder of *le docteur!*"

"You and ten thousand others," I said wearily. "Okay, let it go. Where did you find her? Hiding in a Tabasco bottle?"

"Eh? You do not make to understan' what I say! Me, Jean Pierre Rebault, I feesh in ze bayou an' today I fin' zis girl for who ze gendarmes look. I fin' her, I tal you!"

"Did you really?" I marveled. "And what did she say to you?"

"Say? She say nossing. She can say nossing. She is ver' dead!"

20. *Bayou Butchers*

"WHAT! What did you say? Hey, wait a minute! Hold the phone!" I yelled for Dennis to cut in on my wire, then I went back to Jean Pierre.

"Now, just a minute, Mister! Take it easy, don't get excited. What were you saying?"

"Excite? Me? I am not excite. Mebbe it is you who are excite. Me, I am ver' calm. I jus' to tal you zat girl she is dead. I fin' her today but she has been dead long tam. Two, t'ree week, mebbe. Ze gar feesh, ze bayou butchers, 'ave mos' eat her up. All but ze face is mos' gone, mebbe ze butcher he don' lak ze powder she use." He chuckled.

I shuddered. "You're sure it's the girl we're looking for?"

"*Mais certainement!* Is ze face, lak I tal you."

"What time today did you find her?"

"Two, t'ree, mebbe four hour ago. Her body, she has float to ze top and is caught in ze rush weed by ze bank. She has been dead long tam, ver' long tam."

"Ugh! Where do you live?"

"Me? I live by here and I feesh ze bayous and trap ze woods. Everywan knows Jean Pierre! Everywan!"

"Everyone but me. Now exactly *where* do you live?"

"Sairteen mile from New Iberia, nort' by ze wes' road. Is easy to fin'."

"How do I get there?"

"Listen by me. You tak' wes' road from New Iberia and turn nort' on fork which goes nort' and sout' and zen you find Jean Pierre. *Comprez-vous?*"

"I don't know. Where are you now?"

"By ze fork wiz ma fren Sheriff Beaudron. He is in charge of whole Parrish and by him you fin' me. You come now, no?"

"And how! Where do I find this sheriff?"

"By his office in New Iberia. How soon you come?"

"Soon as I can get there. Just hold onto that girl!"

"Hol' on? She can go no where. She is dead!"

"I know that! You wait for me. I'll be there as soon as possible."

"Is long trip to here. You come tomorrow?"

"Today, brother! Just wait for me.

I grabbed my hat, shoved it on the back of my head and went over to Dennis.

"Where do you think you're going?" he asked.

"Why, to New Iberia of course!"

"Morgan's going. This is no job for a woman."

I blew up! "Why you louse! I am so going! Right now too!"

"You're not!" he shouted. "You've stirred enough trouble with this case. Sit down, dammit!"

"Don't shout at me!" I yelled. "Shouting is the defense of a limited mind and I am going, dammit!"

"Not on any order from me, you're not."

"Now look, Dennis, be reasonable," I pled. "You know these have been my murders right from the first one. If you send Morgan he'll take hours getting there by train or car. I think I can get Brett to fly me down and I can phone in the story in time to make the Sunday paper, maybe even make the Saturday Final! Please, Dennis!"

He looked at me. "If you can get your brother to fly you for free you can go. Otherwise Morgan goes. I'll give you ten minutes to see about it."

I flew to my desk and started phoning. Brett wasn't home! I frantically called the field and after waiting for what seemed hours, he came to the phone. At first he flatly refused to fly up there unless the paper paid for the gas.

I wept, begged, screamed, and howled, and at last he agreed to take me.

"You're lucky," he said. "I still have gas left from that last charter I took out. Enough to get us there and back several times. It's only about an hour's flight. But hurry up. I want to be back by dark."

"I'll be there as soon as my car will bring me." I hung up and yelled to Dennis it was all right, Brett was going to fly me. Then I called Tommy Gross.

"Talk fast," he warned. "I'm leaving town right away."

"To New Iberia?"

"How in hell did you—oh, those reward calls, of course! You got the news before I did."

"How are you going?"

"I'm driving—and no, you can't go with us. I've got a full load."

"Wait until I ask to go!" I snapped. "I thought maybe you'd like to fly, that's why I called you."

"Fly? With who?"

"Brett and me. He's taking me up and we'll make it in an hour."

"That would be swell! Got room for Beton?"

"If he must come along, yes. But no one else."

"What about these reporters and camermen?"

"Let them get there the best way they can. I'll pick you up in a few minutes. Be outside waiting."

I slammed down the receiver, grabbed my purse, and galloped out. Tommy and Les were waiting for me. We made it to the field in less than forty minutes and piled into the plane which was all ready to take off. It seemed I'd barely got settled in my seat after the takeoff before we banked and came in for a landing on a field that looked like a cow pasture. It was just 3:45 and I'd taken that call at 2:00. Ten minutes after we landed we were in the sheriff's office.

Sheriff Beaudron was a large and typical Cajun and his

car was a large and typical Lincoln capable of doing a hundred miles an hour. With no regard for life and limb, he did it—piloting that sixteen-cylinder juggernaut as fast as it would go over the worst roads in the country. We turned on one wheel into the narrow oak-lined road that led to the fishing settlement and from then we stayed on one wheel—first on one, then the other. By some miracle of gravitation the car stayed upright and we reached the settlement at 4:00—a record which must still stand.

We paused to pick up Jean Pierre and then went to the spot where the body lay on the banks of the bayou. It was about three miles from the fishing docks. We made it in one minute. Or so it seemed.

I got shakily out of the car as Beaudron said, "Me, I 'ave not move ze body wan inch. Jean Pierre, he pull her from ze bayou and, pouf! Ze arm she come off!"

I gulped and walked over to the bank of the waterway. I'd thought after seeing Ned McGowan no dead body could ever affect me again, but the sight of the water-logged and mutilated corpse of Lucille St. Clair was almost too much for me. The stench was awful, even in the open air, and flies and other insects hovered around the spot where the body lay. I moved hastily into the lee of the wind, gritted my teeth, and looked at her.

The butchers of the bayou and other scavenger fish had done a good job. In another three weeks it would have been a thorough one. Only a few shreds of mortifying flesh hung on the leg and arm bones and a pair of stilt-heeled black leather tie shoes hung from the feet bones. The clothing was in tatters, torn by the needle-sharp teeth of the gars. Miraculously her face and neck had barely been touched. Part of an ear was gone and a piece was out of the right side of her neck and the right eye was only an empty socket.

There was a small round hole just behind her left ear, a shot from a small caliber weapon. A small caliber bullet hole under the left ear? Memory stirred lazily—that combination seemed familiar.

Case-hardened Tommy and Beton stared and both were pale pea green. Brett gasped, "My God in Heaven! What a sight!" and staggered to the side of the road, out of range of stench and view. I stood quietly, trying to pin down whatever was stirring in my mind about that wound.

Tommy recovered his self-control and spoke rapid patois French to the settlement people who had gathered around. I caught enough to know he had asked for a conveyance to take the body into the town morgue and for a smudge fire to keep insects away. Then he started questioning the pirogue fisherman-trapper who'd found her.

He told a straight, clear, highly accented story.

"Firs' I pole down bayou from ma house and catch wan, two small feesh. I see feesh seem to go up bayou so I pole up and catch t'ree feesh. Zen I catch zis!" He indicated the body, which was now covered with sacking. "I pull her from bayou and pole fas' for home where I get ma Ford and go fin' Sheriff Beaudron who is ma fren. I tal heem what I fin' and he shows to me ze picture. It is same girl. So he show me ze *papier* and I call heem and tal girl what I fin'. It is all."

It wasn't quite all. A boy of about twelve ran up, carrying a leaf-stained bundle.

"*M'sieu Gendarme!* Jacques and me, we fin' dese tings back by a tree, half bury under leaves! Look!"

The bundle was wrapped with a black fur-collared coat. It contained a wide-brimmed, soft felt hat, a small overnight kit, and a black leather pouch purse. Tommy opened the purse and explored its contents. I watched.

Besides the usual women's trappings there was a thermometer in a black case and a bank book showing a balance of over six hundred dollars. The book was in Lucille's name and her nurse's registration card was pasted inside the cover. The overnight kit held what an overnight kit usually does.

Tommy sighed. "Well, that seems to be that." He turned to Beton. "I'm going to leave you here to attend the inquest Monday. I'll go back with Margaret."

"Okay, Captain. This was a tough one to crack all right, wasn't it?"

I looked at him in surprise.

"You mean you think the case is cracked? Now?"

"Sure. It's murder and suicide."

"You're crazy! It's three murders, that's what it is!"

"You're the one who's crazy! Why it's as plain as the nose on your face!"

"That's because you never look beyond your nose," I said disgustedly. "How you ever made a grade as detective is beyond me! I suppose she came to this out-of-the-way place, shot herself under the left ear, and then walked into the bayou! You don't make sense!"

The arrival of a covered truck interrupted our argument and Brett took advantage of the pause to tell Tommy he wanted to leave.

"I want to get away from—that," he said.

Tommy nodded and walked over to give instructions as to the handling of the pitiful body. Beton took up where we'd left off.

"To my mind the picture is perfectly clear. She got a ride and was let off somewhere along here. She waded out into the water and shot herself. It's simple."

"And so are you!" I retorted. "But it's not reasonable and neither are you. How could she shoot herself under the left ear? Unless she was left-handed—and I don't think she was."

Tommy came back as Les lifted his right hand and pointed the forefinger at his left ear.

"That would be easy to do, particularly with a small gun."

I snorted. "You're nuts! Why should she come way out

here to kill herself when she could have done it in New Orleans?"

"She may have meant to skip, but gave up the idea in favor of suicide. She probably thought her body would never be found here."

"Baloney! Why did she leave her purse and all her identification? Why not sink that in the bayou?"

"Aw! You got murder on the brain," he said disgustedly. "But this is suicide."

"Yeah!" I derided. "That's what you said about McGowan, then when I proved it murder you tried to pin it on me. If you would stop to figure out things with that dim-witted half of brain you own you'd see this is murder too!"

Tommy sighed deeply. "Migawd! Are you two going to start that name-calling again? Break it up! And shut up, both of you."

"All right. I'll shut up," I said. "We'll leave it to the coroner. Even a Cajun coroner should be able to tell that wound was never self-inflicted."

Tommy took his gun out of the holster and pointed it toward his left ear, using his right hand.

"Let's see. The bullet hole was about here." He placed the muzzle in the approximate spot, under and somewhat back of the ear. "She was shot with a smaller bore, probably a .25 automatic." His hand was twisted trying to match the proper location. "It would be awkward, almost impossible." He shifted the .38 to his left hand and tried again. That time it looked much easier. "She could have done it with her left hand."

His fooling with that revolver was making me nervous.

"Be careful with that damn thing!" I begged. "If it went off and killed you Beton would swear it was my fault!"

He grinned and replaced the weapon. "The safety was on," he said and herded us all back into the sheriff's car.

We rode for about five minutes without speaking. Finally I broke the silence.

"I still think it's murder," I said stubbornly. "And it's all part of a pattern somehow. Ned poisoned, Miss Cheng brained with a poker, Lucille killed with a pistol. Poison, poker, and a pistol. All weapons starting with the same letter; strange coincidence that. Strange too the way Lucille was brought into the story and promptly disappeared. And the woman Vangie saw in the hotel and said wasn't Lucille because she wore low heels. The corpse wore stilt-high ones. Then this coat and hat find, just like the ones both Bob and Vangie described. It's too damned pat."

"Who do you suspect of the murders?" Brett asked.

"Mrs. Dellman. She's the only one left to suspect."

"Oh, come off that, Margaret!" Brett protested. "I know Marta Dellman very well. She couldn't have done anything like that Cheng killing."

"Do you think Lucille could have done it?"

"N-no. I can't. She was always so gentle and soft-spoken."

"The thing I can't get away from is how it all ties up with Mrs. Dellman. Everything."

"What do you mean, Margaret?" Tommy asked.

"You may think I'm batty. Bob said the woman in the elevator nervously tore a handkerchief to pieces. When Mrs. Dellman was in Nelson's office she pulled out a torn linen handkerchief from her purse. There's the car angle, even though she said Lucille was driving it. And the plumpness, you could see by her body that Lucille was very thin. Mrs. Dellman is plump. The height too. Lucille never wore low heels but I've seen Mrs. Dellman wear them and they do make her look shorter. And then there's that scent I smelled in the apartment that night. I've smelled it since —on Marta Dellman."

"You mean that odd sort of odor Marta uses?" Brett asked.

"Yes. It's distinctive, not something you'd confuse with Shalimar or Christmas Night."

"It's distinctive all right, but the whole Dellman house and everyone who lives in it smells of the stuff. It's oil of Patchouli and Marta sticks pieces of cotton saturated with it everywhere. In drawers, closets, under sofa cushions, and even back of picture frames. I can detect it on my clothing after only spending the evening there."

"Oh," I said flatly. "Well, I still don't think this is the end of the story. The final scene is going to be played in New Orleans. I'd bet on that."

We had reached the sheriff's office. It was just 5:45 and I was talking to Dennis by 6:00. Tommy instructed me to say that there was a definite possibility of it being suicide and I reluctantly complied. Dennis seemed pleased at getting the story from the spot in time for the Final, but he had to growl about something so he growled that he'd had to hold the front page after deadline waiting for the call to come in.

Beaudron gave us a fast ride back to the field and we landed in New Orleans a few minutes after 7:00. Tommy and I got in my car and drove leisurely back to town. I'd had enough fast driving to last me for some time.

"Did you ever meet anyone who drives a car like that maniac?" I asked.

"Huh?" he asked absently.

"That Beaudron. I said he drives like a maniac."

He laughed. "He does. Even I tore the upholstery going around some of the turns."

"Me too. You know something, Tommy—" My voice trailed off.

"What?"

"Oh, nothing. I was just thinking."

"About what, Margaret? What are you cooking up in that red head of yours?"

"I'm not cooking up anything!" I protested, all innocence.

"Oh yes, you are. I know you, baby. You've got a brain wave and when you get one you usually ride it to shore. So tell papa."

"There's nothing to tell," I insisted.

"Don't give me that wide-eyed innocent look. You're fixing to do something you shouldn't. Now what is it?"

"I'm fixing to go home and eat. I'm starved."

"It won't go over. What are you really planning?"

"Nothing."

"Very well. You stay with me until you come clean."

I gave up. "Oh, all right! I thought I'd go out and see Mrs. Dellman," I said sulkily.

"That's what I figured. You believe she's a triple murderess, but you were going right out to her house and tell her you knew she'd done it and she might as well tell the police all about it! Are you nuts?"

I slowed the car to a walk and looked at him.

"Oh ho! So you don't believe Lucille was a suicide!"

"Of course not. Look, Margaret, you're a bright child and a good reporter, but I'm a detective. I didn't make chief by letting people get away with murder. Crime is my business and I make a fair living at it. If you could see it was murder, give me credit for having the intelligence to do the same."

"Well, Beton hadn't!"

"Oh, murder makes Les work too hard."

"But you even demonstrated how she could have held the gun! And you made me tell Dennis it could be suicide!"

"That was what I wanted Dennis to print," he said smugly. "I didn't want the quarry to become alarmed. I wasn't going to say anything to you until I got the hunch you meant to go barging in on Mrs. Dellman."

"Aren't you a smarty pants!"

"Sure," he said blandly. "Now I want your word you won't go there tonight or any time alone. If you won't promise I'll either have to keep you with me or send a man to see you stay at home. I don't want you to get hurt. I have too much fun with you when you're alive. Airplane rides and fights with Beton; things like that. So promise you'll be good."

I hesitated. I hate to make promises unless I'm sure to keep them. But I knew Tommy meant what he said and I didn't want any tail put on me.

"Okay. I'll be good. But I want the first break on this story. It's mine from start to finish. If you cross me I'll hex you!"

"I won't cross you up. You'll get the first break. I give you my word."

"You do believe she's the killer?"

"Everything points to her. McGowan was killed out of jealously, Miss Cheng was either a surprise witness or she was deliberately playing detective—as you were. But this last is the worst of the lot. This girl was killed because she found out something and was going to tell the police or," his voice hardened, "she was killed to provide an alibi for the real killer."

"That's horrible!" I shivered. Then added, "But that's just about how I had it figured!"

"I said you were a bright child." He smiled, then grew serious. "This girl was done away with sometime between Ned's death and Saturday morning. If it was murder for an alibi she could easily have persuaded the unsuspecting girl to go riding with her, killed her, and thrown her body in the bayou. The body had been in the water a long time, there's no way of telling just how far up the stream it floated before it was found."

"Not far," I said. "Remember her things were right there on the bank."

"That's right, too. Those things were planted so that if the body was found it would look like suicide from remorse. My God!" he exploded. "It seems incredible a delicate, gentle woman could do such things!"

"That's about what a jury will think, too," I said drily. "Unless you can get her to make a confession. That might prove tough. She's not so gentle as she appears to be—not if she handled that poker!"

"We'll take care of that angle," he promised grimly.

I looked at his set jaw and felt sorry for anyone who tried to best him. I knew too that once the law nailed you to the cross, money meant nothing and social position even less. Suddenly I began to shake. I pulled to the curb and stopped.

"You drive," I said, my teeth chattering. "I've got a sudden attack of the jitters."

"Reaction from your nerves," he said calmly. "What you need is a drink and I could use one myself. Let's go find us a joint where they break the law and sell that nasty stuff."

21. *Alliterative Deduction*

I MOVED over and he took the wheel. About eight blocks away he made a right turn and pulled up in front of a large private home.

"Here's where we get that drink," he said. "Come on."

I followed him into anything but a private home. It was a rather elaborate private speakeasy. Tommy and I went to a room marked "Private Drinking Room."

I giggled at the sign. "This is a new one on me. How did I manage to miss this joint?"

"It hasn't been open long. I only found it two weeks ago."

We ordered highballs and after the second one I began to feel better.

"Tommy, what about Mr. Dellman? He must have known that girl was not in the house Saturday morning!"

"I thought of that. Either he's protecting his wife or else the girl was gone when he got back from Cleveland and Mrs. Dellman told him she had skipped, but gave him to believe she was protecting Lucille. He's the kind who'd ride along with her story if he liked Lucille."

"I suppose so. It must be pretty awful to live in the house with a murderess, though."

"If you know she's one, yes. But Dellman is mad about that woman and would probably swallow anything she told him."

We finished our fourth drink, Tommy paid the bill, and we left.

"You take me down, then take yourself home. And stay there," he ordered.

"Okay, but I want to stop by the office first. I forgot to get my pay check and Dennis must have it for me."

I drove to headquarters and let him out. He stood for a moment with his foot on the running board.

"Now remember. No visiting the Dellmans tonight."

"You don't have to keep harping on that!" I said irritably.

"And you needn't snap at me either." He smiled. "It's just that I want you to keep your health. I have—"

"Yeah. I know. You have too much fun with me when I'm alive. G'by."

I let out the clutch and drove down to the paper. It was 8:15 and Dennis was out to dinner. Carter gave me my check and I left for home.

Driving up St. Charles I passed the lighted marquee of the Bienvenu hotel. I glanced over as two cab drivers began scuffling together. Memory made a loud chime in my cranium.

"Of course!" I spoke out loud. "That's where I'd seen that guy who got killed! He was in front of the hotel that Thursday morning!"

I realized I was talking to myself and shut up. Then I began wondering if his murder was any part of the same pattern that had started with Ned McGowan. It could be. He had been going to blackmail someone. Why couldn't that someone be our criminal? And he too had been shot under the left ear with a small caliber gun! It fitted almost too snugly into the puzzle.

I drove home slowly with my brain spinning like mad, turned in the drive and sat in the garage for several minutes, just thinking. Then I got out of the car and went inside of the house.

I started for the kitchen to raid the ice box when Mother called to me.

"Is that you, Margaret?"

"Yes'm. I'm going to make a sandwich. I've had no dinner."

She came to the door. "I don't wonder they call stomach ulcers the occupational disease of newspaper people! The way you eat and drink with no regard for regularity is bad for you."

"Yes'm," I said meekly. "But I had to go out of town and just got back a little while ago."

"I know, Brett called me from the field. It must have been a shocking experience, seeing that poor girl's body in such a condition."

"It wasn't particularly appetizing," I admitted, munching cheerfully on a beautifully sloppy sandwich. "Our paper had the only eyewitness story to the grisly details, thanks to me—and Brett."

"I saw it. They think it's suicide."

"Don't believe everything you read in the papers," I advised her.

"What do you mean?"

"It's a secret. I can't tell you now. Anybody call me tonight?"

"Yes. Mrs. Dellman called twice."

"Mrs. Dellman! What did she want?" I thought: She's seen that story and wants to hand me a lot of oil about how shocked and upset she is!

"She didn't say."

"Humph. Well, I'll call her in a minute."

"She said she didn't want you to call her, that she'd call you later if she had a chance."

"Had a chance? What's to stop her? There's phones all over the place."

"Perhaps she was going out."

"Perhaps. Well, if she calls again I want to talk to her. If I'm asleep wake me up."

I made another sandwich and took it with a glass of milk upstairs and into the bathroom. I filled the tub, poured

half a bottle of bath oil in, undressed, and climbed gratefully into the warm water, sandwich in hand. I ate the
sandwich, drank the milk, then lay soaping luxuriously
and reviewing the three—possibly four—murders.

Again the combination of weapons teased my mind.
Poison, poker, and pistol. Alliterative choice of weapons;
a peculiar coincidence. Idly I began to play a game of
linking combinations of three words starting with the
same letters. I chanted them out loud as I applied the
soapy sponge.

"Chasing, cheating, chiseling; crime, confidence, cabs;
blackmail, bludgeon, bayous; discreet, deceit, disguise; fear,
fury, fate; home, husband, hussy; innocent, indecent, in-
discreet; man, motive, murder; poison, poker, pistol; perfidy,
perfume, patchouli—"

Suddenly it was as though someone was whispering those
words in my ear, telling me how to group them. I dropped
the sponge and sat gazing open-mouthed into space, re-
peating the words in my mind. I sat so for some seconds,
then I scrambled out of the tub and dried off hurriedly. I
had work to do and my promise to Tommy could go to
hell!

I thought: My God, have I been stupid! The key to
the murders lay in the words of that alliteration game and
I was pretty sure I'd found it!

I pulled on my clothes and raced into Brett's room
where I searched through his snapshot album until I
found two clear enough to suit my purpose. I ripped them
out, went to my room, and did a little job of crude retouching on one of them with a pen and ink. That finished,
I clattered downstairs to the phone and called Brett, hoping he was still at the field. I got him, held a brief conversation, with me doing most of the talking, which mainly
consisted of asking him questions.

I hung up and called Bob at the hotel, gave him some
rapid instructions, and then tried to reach Tommy, both

at home and in his office. He wasn't either place and I had no time to waste looking for him. I put up the phone, figuring I'd try to get him from the hotel, but if he should call me I didn't want him to know I was out. I wondered how to fix that.

Mother heard me and came to the door. Her eyes widened as she saw I was dressed for the street.

"I thought you were home for the night!"

"So did I, but urgent unfinished business calls me and I've got to go."

"You'll wear yourself out racing around all hours," she protested. "I wish you'd give up that job and get something ladylike."

I chortled. "Ladylike! Me? I wouldn't last a week!"

"Well, you were raised a lady and acted one until you went on that paper," she said stiffly.

"I know, darling. But I like my work, really I do. Hey, where's Vangie?"

A smile quirked her lips. "Out. As soon as she saw the paper she got dressed and went out of the house like she was escaping prison!"

I laughed. "I have to go fast myself. If Mrs. Dellman calls me, just tell her I said I'd see her soon."

"Margaret, what are you up to?"

"Don't be so inquisitive."

"I wish you'd stay home. Please don't get into any more trouble. We've had enough of that. I know I have."

"I won't," I promised and added silently: I hope.

"Look, if Tommy calls me will you tell him I'm asleep and you can't disturb me?"

She went stiff on me again.

"Now, Margaret, you know I've always refused to lie for you children."

"Fiddlesticks! This is vitally important and you can confess it next week. I'm going to call him later. In fact, I'll need him later."

I got out before she could give me any more argument, flopped in the car, and backed out of the drive. As fast as lights and the speed limit would allow I kited for the hotel and parked near the cab stand in front of it.

Bob was standing by the desk in the lobby talking to a sandy-haired, weak-chinned fellow who wore his pale blue eyes protected by bifocals. I went straight over to them.

"This is Craig," Bob said. "He's the guy you want to talk to."

I said, "Hello," and he said, "Pleasedtameetchamsure," and I handed him the two snapshots.

He studied them side by side for almost a moment. Then he said, nodding his head, "Mmmmm, yep."

I waited for him to elaborate on that, but apparently he'd had his say. He went back to talk monosyllables to the operator.

Bob brought over a boy in uniform. I handed him the pictures.

He looked at them closely, emitted a succinct "Yeah," handed them back and walked off.

I gazed at his retreating back.

"Migawd! How do you stand these talkative people you work with?" I asked.

Bob grinned. "I guess they were struck dumb by your art work."

I laughed and went to the phone booth, Bob on my heels. I called Tommy and was relieved when he answered his office phone. I told him where I was and he let out a howl.

"Dammit! Didn't I tell you to stay home and didn't you promise me you would?"

"Shut up and listen," I snapped. "Meet me here in ten minutes. I'll wait just that long for you. If you're not here by then I'll go by myself or take Bob with me."

I hung up before he could answer and turned to face a staring Sullivan.

"Jeepers! Have you got nerve, sister! I wouldn't dare talk to a plain harness copper that way, let alone the boss detective! Do you suppose he'll come?"

"Sure he will. In ten minutes too."

He made it in five. I started toward him as soon as he stalked through the door.

"Let's go." I grabbed his arm. "I'll tell you the story on the way out."

"Now just a minute! I want the story before I start any place!"

I dropped his arm. "If you're going to fiddle around I'll go on my own. I only called you for protection." I was out of the door and in my car before he caught up to me. He climbed in.

"Okay, you win this trick. But you better take the pot or you'll be in the soup. With me, a promise is a promise."

I was three blocks from the hotel before he stopped griping. Then I opened up and told him the whole story, including the weird feeling that someone was giving me the right grouping of words.

He whistled, a long, low whistle.

"You may have had the blind luck to strike something," he said. "I hope so, because you're in a sorry spot if you're wrong."

"If I am you can crucify me."

"I won't have to. The D.A. and Beton will do that with pleasure!"

I grinned mirthlessly and thought: How right you are!

It was just 10:00 when we pulled into the side street by the Dellman mansion and parked. We made our way to the front door across an expanse of lawn where shrubbery and trees etched wavering, ghostly shadows in the moon-silvered night. We went up the wide marble steps and Tommy leaned on the bell button.

"Very pretty," I said, hearing the silvery chimes echo through the house.

A white-coated butler opened the door. Tommy beckoned him out and showed him a badge, then gave him rapid, tersely phrased instructions. The frightened servant was speechless, but he agreed to everything by the simple method of nodding his woolly head. We went in the house and Tommy took up a stand behind the heavy drapes which hung at the drawing room door. The butler entered with me close behind him. His voice barely faltered as he announced: "Miss Slone, ma'am."

I barged right in. The couple was seated in chairs near the ornate fireplace. They both stared at me in surprise.

"I'm a late caller, I know," I said apologetically. "But I was passing this way and I wanted to see you. I hope you don't mind?"

"Not at all!" she said with great cordiality. "Won't you have a drink?"

"Just a short one," I accepted.

She poured the drink and handed me the glass.

Dellman remembered his manners then. "Won't you sit down?

"Thank you." I moved in on his chair. It gave me a view of the door. He sat on the love seat facing us.

"Have the police called you?" I asked.

"Why no. Why should they call us?" Dellman asked.

I looked at her. She shook her head negatively.

"But you've seen the papers, of course?"

"We don't take your paper any more," Dellman said curtly. "And the newsboy failed to deliver the other afternoon paper. We've seen nothing. Just what are you driving at?"

"Oh. Then you don't know they found Lucille St. Clair?"

"They did!" Mrs. Dellman's face was expressive of a strong emotion. "Is—is she all right?"

I let her have it bluntly. "In the words of the fisherman, Jean Pierre, who found her, she is 'ver dead.'"

She half rose from her chair. Then she sat back down, hard. "Dead!"

"Dead. Suicide, no doubt. That's what the police think."

"But it can't be!" She looked at her husband, a query in her eyes.

"Oh sure," I shrugged. "Guilty conscience. It often happens." I watched her narrowly.

"But she had no reason to have—"

Dellman interrupted. "Miss Slone, it's really too bad you had to make your visit one of being the bearer of such unhappy tidings! I'm sure you must have more important things to do on a Saturday night!" He watched his wife anxiously, as if fearing she'd have another fainting spell.

"It is too bad," I murmured. "But I don't mind if you don't. You know," I went on hastily before he could tell me how much he minded, "this is really a lovely home. One you must be proud of—or is it one of which you should be proud? Words are my business but I seem to mix up the parts of speech."

He laughed shortly. "In either case you're correct. I am proud of it."

"You must also be proud of being such a philanthropist," I said.

"Philanthropist?" he echoed, staring at me in puzzled amazement. "What in the world are you talking about? I'm no philanthropist! Of course I give my share to various charities but that's about all."

"Oh, come now! Don't be so modest. I know all about how you paid the bills when Joe Harmon's leg was broken by your plane during that bad storm."

"Joe Harmon? Oh, that! That wasn't philanthropy. It was my plane which injured him and I felt responsible so I paid the bills. That's all. How did you ever learn about that? It happened a long time ago."

"Two years ago," I said. "Newspapers work during storms, you know."

"Oh, you covered the story? I didn't see anything about it."

"The accident was reported," I hedged. "By the way, have you heard from Joe recently?"

"No. Should I?"

"You couldn't. He's dead. Murdered in his cab on the river road." I watched them both for reactions. She breathed faster and leaned forward. He seemed shocked.

"Murdered! But why?"

"The police think it was a gangster killing—he'd been bootlegging in a small way. I think he was blackmailing someone and got killed to be shut up. In either case it's bad, isn't it?"

"It's horrible!" he exclaimed. "Do you always bring such bad and lurid news when you go visiting?"

"Not always, only when necessary." I pawed through my bag and brought out the snapshots. I handed them to him.

"I think you will find these interesting," I said.

He looked at them. "You're very clever, Miss Slone. I wasn't aware you were an artist as well as a reporter."

"I'm not. It's a bad job of retouching and faking, but it served the purpose beautifully."

He sighed. "I suppose so. This complicates things." He tucked the snaps in his pocket.

I reached out a hand. "I'll just keep those, if you don't mind."

"But I do mind. This development necessitates you and I going some place for a chat."

"Oh, no, it doesn't," I said, chills crawling on my spine. "Besides, I have the negatives."

Marta Dellman was leaning forward in her chair, her breath coming in short gasps.

"Well, we'll deal here," he said. "What do you want for those negatives and this bit of artistry—and your silence?"

"None of the three are for sale," I told him.

"Then you force me to insure your silence."

"You can't scare me," I retorted. "The police know all about it and if I don't show up in a few minutes you're in for it. You're in for it anyhow! You can put that thing away." He'd taken a small automatic from his pocket. "It might go off and hurt somebody—meaning me."

He kept the gun trained on me and I said mental prayers that Tommy would be quicker with the trigger than Dellman—if shooting began.

"It won't do you any good, Mr. Dellman. You're caught. You're a filthy murderer and you're hooked."

Marta Dellman leaned toward him and in a low, tense voice spat words: "Filthy murderer! You're a fiend, Gerry! Why did you have to kill that child? She'd never harmed you?"

"I did it to protect your reputation, my dear, and to provide an alibi for both of us if such were needed."

He spoke blandly and indifferently.

"You don't think I believe you've informed the police, do you?" He turned to me. "Oh, no. Your type of ego is well known to me and it was proved by that car identification which appeared in your paper. You denied writing the story, but I know the tip came from you. You didn't share your knowledge with the police then. You haven't done it now. If so they would have been here by this time."

I thought: They are here—only you don't know it. And I also thought how close I'd come to making this visit on my own. That thought gave me a shiver.

"You think you're smart," I sneered. "But you must know you can't get away with murdering me. You can't shoot me here, the shot would be heard and you'd spoil your rug."

"I have no such intention," he said calmly. "I knew I should have to disappear eventually and my plans are completed for that disappearance. I own property in a place which has no extradition laws and my plane is ready to take me there. You and Marta will go with me, but only she will make the full journey. You see I love her and I shan't let her go. As for you, at some point over the water I shall put you out and make you swim home." He smiled at his grim joke.

"You *are* murder drunk!" I said appalled.

"No. I don't think I am." He shook his head judiciously. "I meant to kill only one person. The others were forced on me by circumstances."

"I could have forgiven you McGowan's murder," I said. "I suppose you thought you had good reason for that and it was clever, done with amazing finesse. But Lili and Lucille, they were bestial, brutal killings."

"Both of which I deeply regretted having to commit."

"How about Joe Harmon? I suppose you deeply regretted that too?"

"Not particularly. You know, that was really clever of you, pinning that one on me. I find it hard to reconcile your clever deduction with your stupid actions, such as coming here alone."

I smiled smugly, secure in the knowledge that Tommy was at hand.

"That was just what you called my type of ego working," I said.

"That snap trick was well thought out," he said conversationally. "How did you hit on that?"

"Through the process of alliteration," I said, smiling faintly at the paraphrase. "It struck me that the weapons used all had titles starting with the same letter. I began to link other words together in groups of threes. One group had deceit and disguise in it. Suddenly I saw the whole picture and knew you were the murderer. At least I was pretty sure of it. I knew Brett had snaps of you in his album. I got a couple, inked in the disguise you wore when you checked into the hotel, and took them down to be identified. You know how well it worked. The hotel employees identified the one I'd retouched as a George Danton who'd been a guest there when Ned and Miss Cheng were murdered."

He nodded. "It was very clever. You mean you got your clue just through linking alliterative words together?"

"Exactly. Not just the words I mentioned, of course. There were several groups and then there were other things too. Mrs. Dellman's perfume for one. I'd smelled it in that apartment and several times after that. I knew about those notes and I had a hunch she had been playing around with Ned. As I linked words like cheating, chiseling, husband, hussy, fear, fury, I began to form a picture of a cheating wife, a chiseling lover, a furious husband—a man disguised to commit what he hoped was the perfect murder. It might have been, if you'd stopped with the one. But you couldn't stop and finally all these killings began to tie in together. They pointed straight to you."

"I SEE. I daresay the initials being the same gave you a lead?"

"One, among others. It was more than just initials that pointed to you."

"Really? Have you figured out just how everything happened?"

"Not entirely," I admitted. "I'd like to hear it though, before we go."

"I'm glad you're willing to go quietly. I'd hate to have to use force. I'm a very sensitive man and the use of force disturbs me."

"I can imagine," I said sarcastically.

"Truly! Well, I shall satisfy your curiosity, knowing you cannot use your knowledge to harm me. Too bad you shan't be able to write the story for your paper. It should make good reading."

"It should make good hearing, too," I said drily, glancing toward the heavy drapes.

"I'd known for sometime that Marta was having an affair with Ned and I knew it was getting out of hand on her part. It wasn't the first time she'd let a younger man make a fool of her."

"That's not true!" she burst out. "Ned was the only man I was—"

"Intimate with? Perhaps. It doesn't matter. Please don't interrupt again, my dear. To get on—I'd planned for some months to do away with Ned but I hadn't perfected the means or method until he had that tooth taken out. I'd worked with him on poisons and knew the chemistry of curare. I also knew he had it in the hotel cabinet.

"I told Marta I was called to Cleveland on the Tuesday after the tooth had been pulled. I did go and stayed overnight. I then told my co-pilot that I was going away for a few days and that I didn't want anyone to know I was not in Cleveland. If anyone called he was to say I was out and take the message. He thought, naturally, there was a girl involved.

"I packed my large briefcase, got my ship, and flew back, landing on my private field near my rice plant across the river. I took the car I keep there, drove it some distance up the road, then turned off into a quiet lane. I've done a lot of Little Theater work and also Carnival pageants, and I know a good bit about makeup. I disguised myself with a black mustache, heavy eyebrows, pince-nez glasses, and dark makeup. Then I drove across the Napoleon Avenue ferry, parked the car on a residential street, walked over to a drug store, and called a cab. Then I went to the hotel.

"My case had my initials on it, so I had to make the alias fit them. I asked for a room up high, around ten or eleven, and was put on ten."

"Conveniently next door to Ned!" I interjected.

"Yes, that was a bit of luck. I'd secured a key to his room months before and I had keys to the drug cabinet padlocks. I knew where he would be for the evening, and as soon as I was sure he had left, I went to the room, applied the poison to the toothbrush, and took the bottle back to my room with me. The only chance I took was that he might miss the poison and become suspicious. But that was very slight.

"I'd planned on going to the St. Ann Street place that night also. I had keys to it and had known of it right along. I'd followed Marta there when she had assignations with her lover." His lip curled scornfully. "I wanted to look for letters she might have been fool enough to write. But I

considered the possibility Ned might go there before re-
turning to the hotel, so I decided to go the next evening.
I ordered dinner in the room, ate, and went to bed.

"I remained in my room all day Thursday, having my
meals sent up. I heard the excitement when the body was
found and later the breakfast waiter gave me a graphic
account of the mysterious death of the tenant next door!
At that time I knew nothing of Marta having been to the
hotel the night before."

"You must have slept soundly," I said wryly. "Else you'd
have heard her voice when she sailed into him."

He looked at Marta and shook his head reprovingly.
"That visit ruined all my plans. If it hadn't been for that, I
believe I'd have been the man to commit the perfect crime.

"Thursday evening I went to the apartment. I'd just
begun to search when I heard someone come up the stairs
and stop at the door. I picked up the poker and when the
woman stepped in I warned her not to turn on a light and
to stay with her back to me. Unfortunately she recognized
my voice. I must say she showed pluck. She said, quietly,
'What are you looking for here, Mr. Dellman?' My answer
was a blow with the poker and she dropped without a
sound. Seconds later I heard someone else on the stairs. I
waited near the door."

"And bashed me on the head as I bent over Miss Cheng."

"Yes. I became nervous and left the place without further
search. I went to a phone booth and called Cleveland.
Charlie told me Marta had been trying to reach me, so I
hung up and called home—pretending I was still in
Cleveland. She told me of Ned's death and asked me to
return at once. I told her I'd be in the next day. Then I
called Charlie back and told him I'd have to return to New
Orleans without seeing him but that he was to carry on
with the business attached to the air races. I returned to the
hotel and spent the night, checking out Friday morning.

"I took a cab to the Union Station, went to the men's

room, and waited until it was empty, then removed my
disguise. I went back out, got in a cab, and was driven to
where I'd parked the car. I got in and drove to my home.
I'd made a mistake, however. I hadn't noticed the cab
driver. It was Joe Harmon. He'd driven me to the station
and picked me back up to take me to my car. He recognized
me without the disguise. He also recognized me as the
passenger he'd taken from the hotel. That briefcase is unfortunately a distinctive one. That was bad."

"For him," I said curtly.

"Ummm, yes. When I got home Marta was near hysteria.
She showed me your paper with the car pictures in it and
told me she had been in the hotel. My plan to avert an
open scandal began to form as I watched Lucille trying
to comfort and quiet her."

Marta Dellman began to sob brokenly.

"I talked to Lucille and asked her if she would allow
herself to be under temporary suspicion of having been the
woman in the hotel that night. I pointed out that she and
Marta were nearly the same size and that she would not be
placed in the bad position Marta would. I suggested she go
to my lodge in South Louisiana, disappear for a few weeks,
and when the murder was cleared up she could return. I said
I'd drive her down at once.

"She agreed instantly, but Marta stubbornly refused to
accept the plan, saying she was not going to be a party to
ruining Lucille's name. We both insisted it was the only
thing to do to save a scandal and finally she gave in. I told
Lucille to pack a small case and one large one and to wear
the hat and coat which had been described in the paper,
so they would be missing in the event of any search. I got
the servants out of the way and got her out of the house,
telling her I'd pick her up on Broad Street.

"I took the Packard and drove to Broad Street. Unfortunately, there is a cab stand there and, also unfortunately,
the one cab at the stand was driven by Joe Harmon. He

saw me pick her up, recognized me, and got a good look at her.

"We drove south until I reached the road that forks off toward a small fishing settlement. When we'd passed the settlement and reached desolate country, I stopped the car. She knew at once what my intention was and she began to scream and struggle. I was forced to knock her out, then I shot her. removed the hat and coat, and disposed of •the body in the bayou, hoping the bayou butchers would finish the disposal. I threw both bags in the water and the large one sank but the small lighter case floated. I fished it out, wrapped it and her purse in the coat, and buried them under leaf mold by a tree. If her body was found I meant it to look like suicide."

"What about the shot? Weren't you afraid someone would hear it?"

"In that country shots are common!" He laughed. "One or one hundred wouldn't excite any interest."

"I hadn't thought of that," I murmured.

"I had," he assured me. "When I was finished I drove back to the city, arriving home in time for dinner."

"And feeling perfectly safe, no doubt," I said. "Then Joe Harmon got in touch with you and upset your peace of mind."

I stole a glance at the drapes, wondering what Tommy was thinking of the Dellman debacle.

"That's right. He read the story of Lucille's disappearance and saw the picture in the paper. He recognized her as the girl I'd picked up and his having seen me in disguise excited his suspicions. He wasn't sure just what I'd done but he knew it was something I would prefer the police not knowing. He thought he saw a chance to pick up some easy money so he called me. I wrote him a note, to the address he gave me, telling him to meet me. Then I went to the bank and drew out five thousand dollars, intending to pay him off if he'd leave town. But after thinking it over, I realized few blackmailers operate that way and he was a menace to my safety for the rest of my life."

"So you decided to kill him too?"

He nodded. "When he picked me up I told him to drive out the river road, beyond the park. When he reached a deserted spot I told him to stop. He did, but he turned on me with a revolver in his hand.

" 'I don't know what you may try to pull, Dellman,' he said. 'But I'm taking no chances. Now we'll talk.'

"This was a development I had figured on. I told him he had nothing on me but I wanted no scandal and was willing to pay to avoid one. I asked how much he thought his silence was worth. Unlike you, he placed a figure on it. Ten thousand dollars. I handed him a sheaf of bills.

" 'There's five thousand there.' I told him. 'I'll have to get the rest tomorrow. Count it to make sure it's all there.'

"He bent down to the dashlight and began to count. I shot him in the head and he slumped forward. I took the money from him, removed his watch and ring and what money he had, threw the jewelry in the river along with his gun, cut across the park, and got a cab home."

"Thus making the number of your murders an even four," I said.

"I meant only one murder," he said, somewhat wearily. "The others were incidental and committed in self-protection."

"Self-protection!" I snorted. "Lucille St. Clair was killed to provide an alibi for your own worthless hide! To save your carcass from the hangman to whom it actually belongs!"

I turned to Marta Dellman, who had stopped sobbing and sat stony-eyed.

"Were you the woman who came to that apartment the night your husband murdered Miss Cheng?"

She nodded. "Yes. I went there for the same purpose Gerry went—to find my letters and look for the notes. Ned told me once they were there. When I got almost to the apartment I thought I heard someone, so I turned and ran."

"And I ran after you but you got away. You were wearing a certain odor. It was what got me off the track and had me suspecting you of the killings. Then, strangely enough, it put me on the right scent."

"That's rather oblique," Dellman said. "What do you mean?"

"Today Brett told me about how Mrs. Dellman used oil of patchouli all over the house. Tonight I began playing that game of alliterative words. Those words gave me the key, and remembering what Brett had said, I realized that the same odor of patchouli would be on anyone living in this house. Joe Harmon's wife had told me how you paid his bills when your plane crippled him, only she didn't know it was you. I called Brett and found out it was your plane. That tied you up to Joe's murder as well as the others."

"How really clever of you! And how too bad you must make this trip with me."

I reached up and took my hat off, the signal Tommy and I had agreed on when it was time for him to move in.

"I don't feel like going anywhere with you," I said, leaning back in the chair and watching Tommy move across the room, his steps deadened by the thick carpet. Marta Dellman watched too, her eyes wide and frightened. "No. I don't want to go any place but home. I don't relish the company of a cold-blooded murderer."

"That's too bad, but I'm afraid you have no alternative. I shall shoot if you force me."

"You'd get shot first," I said. "Take him, Tommy. I want to get out of here."

Dellman didn't blink a lash. "That old dodge won't work with me," he said. "It was well acted, however, and you, my dear," he looked at his wife, "played up beautifully."

"It's no dodge, Dellman!" Tommy's voice was crisp. "Drop that gun. My revolver is aimed at the back of your head and I wouldn't need much excuse to put a bullet right through it."

The gun dropped from Dellman's nerveless hand and he stared at me. "So you didn't come alone! I counted too much on your ego!"

"You sure did," I answered, and just then Marta Dellman's nerves let go and she gave out with one piercing shriek after another.

The servants who'd been huddled in the hall, wondering what was happening, added their shrieks to hers, and Dellman, taking advantage of the confusion, moved quickly to retrieve his weapon. But Tommy moved more quickly. He brought down the butt of his revolver on Dellman's head and the killer lost interest in everything.

I jumped up and strode over to the screaming woman. "Stop that yelling!" I gave her a good, hefty slap across the face and she stopped howling.

Tommy snapped handcuffs on Dellman and ordered the terrified butler to send for the police car. In a few minutes a siren howled into the drive and four cops rushed in, guns in hand.

Tommy motioned to Dellman. "This guy killed four people last month. Take him down and book him for murder."

One officer gaped at Dellman, then at Tommy.

"But that's Mr. Dellman! He ain't murdered no one!"

"He murdered four someones!" Tommy snapped. "Book him for the murder of Dr. Edward McGowan, Lili Cheng, and—what did you say that driver's name was, Margaret?"

I told him.

"And for the murder of Joe Harmon on the river road. New Iberia will have to worry about his killing of Lucille St. Clair. He can only hang once." He smiled grimly.

"Well! I'm damned!" The cop exploded. "You mean this guy done all them killings?"

"I mean he done 'em all," Tommy said drily. "Now get him out of here before I put the slug on him."

The cop grinned. "Looks like you already put the slug on him."

Tommy nodded. "Take this automatic with you too." He picked up the small weapon. "Have ballistics check it with the bullet taken from that cab driver. I guess we'll have to send it to New Iberia for them to check."

"Okay." The man walked over and hauled Dellman to his feet. He was *not* handling him with the deference his wealth and position called for. "C'mon, you. Get going!"

Conscious, but still groggy, Dellman staggered out between two cops. He went with never a backward glance or a word to any of us.

Marta Dellman was sobbing again, quiet body-shaking sobs.

Tommy walked over and looked down at her bowed head.

"I guess you'll more than pay for your cheating which cost the lives of four people, two of them innocent girls," he said.

She sobbed wildly.

"I guess we ought to call a doctor," I said. "She's in foul shape. Try and get one with a size fifty waistline, a bald head, and a calm, middle-aged bedside manner. If she'd have left Ned alone four people would be alive today. I'd hate to have it on my conscience that I caused the death of four human beings. And when I think of the act she put on in Nelson's office, that long string of lies about Lucille, I lose what sympathy I might have managed to stir up for her."

She stopped crying and looked at me. "You heard him say I refused to do that at first! Besides, you weren't in Mr. Nelson's office. You didn't hear me tell that story."

"Yes, I did. I heard it over the inter-office communication system. The act was good. Tell me, why did you call me tonight?"

"I began to get suspicious. Gerry acted so strange and he wouldn't let me move out of the house at all. I got fright-

ened and today I accused him of having killed Ned and
Miss Cheng. When he didn't deny it I was really terrified,
so I called you."

"I see." I walked away and joined Tommy. "Better have
her put to bed."

"But she's a material witness."

"Have a guard put on her. Not that she'll run away."

He nodded and phoned for a guard to be sent out. As
soon as the man arrived we left. In my car we drove several
blocks without speaking, then Tommy laughed shortly and
said,"I don't think the district attorney should be allowed
to go to sleep without hearing how Beton's pet suspect
solved the poison, poker, and pistol murders with a snapshot, some ink, and a lot of damn fool luck! Turn left at
the next corner and we'll dump this in his lap for an Easter
present."

"Easter present? Oh! Tomorrow is Easter, isn't it?" I
looked at my dash clock—11:45; the final Sunday edition
rolled at 1:00 with a 12:30 deadline. I turned left and
pulled up in front of Nelson's house. There was a light in
the front room.

Nelson admitted us, and when he heard the news almost
kissed us at the door. Tommy and I sat down in the living
room and he gave Nelson a brief outline of Dellman's
capture, giving me all the credit for having solved the
murders.

Nelson gazed at me admiringly. "It's a splendid piece of
work! How did you hit on a man as the killer?"

I smiled smugly. "Oh, that was easy! A woman was obviously meant to be suspected. Too obviously. I couldn't
believe a woman would kill wantonly."

Tommy looked at me, an amused gleam in his eyes. I
blushed.

"Tell me all about it," Nelson urged.

One eye on the clock I reeled off a hasty account of the
story.

"That's all." I rose to leave.

Nelson patted me on the shoulder. "Margaret, you've done a fine job for us on this. I wish I had a few men on my staff like you. I could use them."

"Thanks." My voice was slightly dry, remembering the different song he'd sung a little over four weeks ago. "Come on, Thomas, let's travel."

Back in my car, with the clock saying 12:15, I asked Tommy where to take him.

"Back to the hotel to get my car. Then I suggest you go home and get some sleep. You look beat."

I stared at him. "Sleep? Are you nuts? Me go to sleep with this story to write and deadline coming up in fifteen minutes! Sleep hell! Remember me, dear? I'm a reporter—not a detective!"